Green
Bananas

Michael
Drinkard

GREEN
BANANAS

 ALFRED A. KNOPF

NEW YORK 1989

THIS IS A BORZOI BOOK
PUBLISHED BY ALFRED A. KNOPF, INC.

Copyright © 1989 by Michael Drinkard

All rights reserved under International and Pan-American Copyright
Conventions. Published in the United States by Alfred A. Knopf, Inc.,
New York, and simultaneously in Canada by Random House of Canada
Limited, Toronto. Distributed by Random House, Inc., New York.

Library of Congress Cataloging-in-Publication Data

Drinkard, Michael.
    Green bananas/Michael Drinkard.—1st ed.
        p. cm.
    ISBN 0-394-57401-X
    I. Title.
PS3554.R495G7   1989   88-45775
813'.54—dc19   CIP

This is a work of fiction. All names, characters, and events, except for
certain incidental references, are products of the author's imagination
and do not refer to or portray any actual persons or events.

Manufactured in the United States of America
First Edition

FOR JILL

CONTENTS

1   *Where You Go When You Die*   3

2   *Sperm Daddy*   21

3   *Shit Happens*   41

4   *Sylvan Loses Control of His Face*   62

5   *Good for Goodness' Sake*   88

6   *Parents as a State of Mind*   114

7   *This Means War*   136

8   *Trapped Animals*   154

9   *Homestretch*   169

10   *True Suchness*   214

Green
Bananas

1 *Where You Go When You Die*

Imagine naming a kid Adonis, Heaven, or Solomon, Misha, Jethro, Huatlán, Wolfgang, Chamunda, Gaia, singling the kid out like that in a world of Jims, Johns, and Jennifers. Here they are, though, along with Teodoro, Astrid, and Humberto, five-year-olds now, all sitting with their bag lunches at a picnic table just outside the back door of Tres Ojos School. It's registration day and their parents are inside signing them up for the new school year. When Sylvan says hi they start clapping.

"And why are you so tan?" Teodoro Wilcox asks, as he separates the potato chips with green edges from the regular ones, making two piles.

"Spent the summer in the White Mountains," Sylvan says, happy to be back in Santa Cruz, but a little anxious about starting his senior year at the university. He's wearing cutoffs, and a button-down shirt for decency, since he's here on business. "Some of the highest peaks in California, in the whole country." The sun almost rings your ears at thirteen thousand feet, that bright. Burns through fifteen block. "You've got quite a tan yourself. Did your mom take you to the beach a lot?"

Teo's mom is Samantha Wilcox, the ex-"Billboard Stewardess" who lives with Phyllis Mentone, Tres Ojos's director; they're rumored to be lovers. Teo nods, causing Adonis to nod, then Astrid, then Heaven.

"Copycats," Teo says.

"Copycat yourself," Adonis says.

"Copycat yourself," Astrid says, and so on around the table, except for Wolfgang, who has turned his eyelids inside out and is making muscle. "I'm He-Man, Master of the Universe!"

"Stop!" Teo says to Adonis, who is eating a knee scab. Then Teo pushes him the pile of regular potato chips, reserving the green-edged ones for himself. He likes his food brightly colored, the main feature of his lunch today being a royal blue tuna fish sandwich. "Are we gonna be an ecosystem again?" he asks, looking up at Sylvan with chromy blue eyes set in sleepy lids. Seems like he never blinks.

"Depends. If I get my job back."

Last year, besides helping the kids build clay volcanoes and make tornadoes in a box, and taking them on Nature Walks to find things for his collection, Sylvan had them be an ecosystem. All it took was a ball of string. Adonis was bull kelp, Heaven an otter, Humberto plankton, Astrid a garibaldi, Teo insisted on being a great white shark, and on like that, passing the ball of string around until everybody was a sea life form. When they were all interconnected, Sylvan introduced a problem. "Plankton population explosion. Go, Humberto!" Humberto became a population explosion by flailing his limbs, speaking gibberish, and tickling himself until he tangled up the garibaldi and pulled down the sea otter. "Mess with one Sea Life Form and you mess with the whole Ecosystem."

"If we be an ecosystem again, I'm the great white shark," says Teo, hushing every kid at the table, even Wolfgang, who drops his arms and blinks his eyelids back to normal.

Two years ago Teo's father, Salty Wilcox, was killed by a great white while surfing in Carmel. Wildlife biologists weren't surprised by the attack; they happen. Especially off California's central coast, especially at that time of year, during the winter, when the elephant seals are rutting. But what surprised even the scientists was the size of the bite taken out of the surfboard —evidence of a twenty-eight-inch jaw span. Later Salty Wilcox's body washed up missing an arm and most of the torso. Four-inch tooth fragments confirmed that the shark was huge, probably twenty-five feet long and weighing several tons. Despite worldwide media coverage, millions of zoom lenses, and fleets of vengeful surfers-turned-fishermen, the shark was never sighted again.

That explains Teo's obsession. May also explain why the other kids look up to him, and the adults think of him as "exceptional," either gifted or disturbed. Something cosmically humiliating about a human becoming prey, Sylvan thinks, especially if he's your father.

"Well, are we gonna be?" Teo asks. He runs a pudgy finger through a yellow curl—his hair, he pointed out last year, is the *same exact* as Sylvan's.

"Maybe." Sylvan squints his stinging eyes and wipes the sweat from his forehead. So hot out. Heaven is kissing trees and talking to pigeons. Adonis is pinching his dick and saying he doesn't have to pee. Sylvan remembers why he's here in the first place. "Where's Phyllis?" His former boss, who also invented Tres Ojos's philosophy of Process Listening.

"Inside," Teo says. "I'll show you." Grasping the blue tuna sandwich with both hands, smushing it, he uses his elbows to climb out of the picnic table. When he walks, he pushes out his tummy.

Last year Teo had put his hands in everything. Macaroni and cheese, for instance, refusing to use silverware. He also never painted with a brush, but stuck his fingers in the cups of tempera, smeared designs on the paper, then tasted every color. Midway through the school year he did something that sparked the interest of the District Psychologist, who offered, requested, then recommended observation: with a crayon in each hand, he wrote his name twice, simultaneously, the left the mirror image of the right.

"What did you do in the Great White Mountains?" he asks.

"Made maps, tried to keep cool, drank two gallons of water a day. And studied bristlecone pines, the oldest trees known to man," Sylvan says, knowing Teo will consider each activity carefully. "Got tan."

Indoors the air conditioner is going, but it doesn't make things any cooler, just clammier. The classroom is a wide open space, bare redwood and skylights, and a half-dozen or so adults are sitting in kid-size chairs at kid-size tables, banging their knees, trying to fill out forms. Everything is remarkably clean, no paint spatters yet, or pinecone collages. The room is hugely silent, like an empty ballpark.

"Phyllis!" Teo yells, almost making an echo. *"Look!* Sylvan's back!"

She is standing with another woman, and she's got a baby in her arms. Phyllis is nearly as tall as Sylvan. She has the straight, good posture you have to practice to get, and a prominent collarbone that shows through a flower-print shirt. She likes sports, and her eyes—athletic, clear and green—show it. She's wearing car-fuse earrings and baggy shorts. Her legs are hairier than his.

"Syl, I'd give you a hug, but I have the baby—"

"Yours?"

"Ha! I wish. She's Sally's. Do you know each other?" Phyllis introduces him to Sally Jones, Heaven and Solomon's mother, a pretty, pale woman who is flushed from the heat. The newborn is hers. Faith. Another biblical name that's more like a chapter title. At least she's not God. What if your little sister was God?

"Phyllis!" Teo is screaming again, the silence a dare. "I'm

taking out Youngster!" He opens a cage containing a single white rat.

"Are you finished eating?"

Teo pushes the rest of the blue tuna into his mouth. "Now I am."

Phyllis ogles the baby, who pops her lips. Sally Jones looks on and beams. Both women are actually gazing into Faith's slightly lopsided face. Phyllis makes a remark about her own maternal instincts, which makes Sylvan feel left out. He imagines maternal instincts being something like feeling hungry on a full stomach. Still, when he puts his finger into the tiny pink hand, and the miniature fingers close around it, he feels—well, the same kind of immediate love you'd give to any cute puppy in a park. But definitely not an instinct.

"I want one," Phyllis says.

"Too bad you need a man," Sally says. An echo of those lesbian rumors?

"What about artificial insemination?" Sylvan asks. You don't actually *need* a man these days, and Sylvan kind of wishes his sister, Emma, who's just discovered she's pregnant, had done it some other way. Pete, her husband, is a jerk. "I read somewhere about a Nobel Prizewinner's sperm bank in Orange County."

"Just last week the Red Cross held a semen drive," Sally Jones says.

"What on earth for?"

"Disaster preparation," she says. "That's what they announced, anyway."

They both look at Sylvan as if he can explain. People do that, count on him to have the answers. In groups of adults (not kids) he's almost always the one expected to have ready facts. Authority he never asked for and doesn't seem to have any control over, and hasn't yet learned how to abuse.

Teo comes toward him with the rat. It's got pink eyes, white fur, and a tail that sticks out like an exposed nerve. "Youngster," Teo says, proudly showing him off to Sylvan.

"Take him outside," says Phyllis. Then she squinches up her face and rolls out a kink in her neck. Her blondish hair is pulled back in a loose bun, and the skin on her cheeks and neck is pink from the heat. "Hot, hot, hot."

"I forgot how hot it got."

"Every September a heat wave."

"Will you scratch my back?" she asks Sally. "A little higher . . . yeah, there . . . harder."

She could have asked *him* to scratch her back. Maybe she doesn't like men touching her. Maybe she's a man hater. Samantha Wilcox is, even if she used to be married to one. Besides having been the Billboard Stewardess, Teo's mother is a notorious radical feminist, always getting arrested. Phyllis is different, she—

"What can I do for you, Sylvan?"

Not a good sign. He hoped it was obvious. Though it's true he's not in good standing. Last year some of the parents complained that the clay volcano he had caused to erupt with bright orange ammonium dichromate crystals was too dangerous for four-year-olds. And then Solomon Jones jammed his thumb the day they made the tornado in a box. "These things happen, I know," Phyllis had told him. "But parents have a sixth sense about their children's safety. Plus they feel guilty in the first place for dropping them off at day care."

"Um," Sylvan says. "I'd like to teach Outdoors again."

Sally Jones says, "That will make Heaven and Solomon happy."

There's a vote in his favor. Two, in fact. And Phyllis knows how important Outdoors is for the kids. She's a sports freak herself. Last year, Sylvan remembers, she was always talking about scuba diving and skiing and running 10Ks and training for the summertime professional triathlon circuit. But now she looks cross, overheated, as if she wants to sweat but can't. And the baby in her arms has just woken up choking, the tiny pink hand tugging on the collar of her shirt.

"Let me finish up here with Sally," Phyllis says in a voice that makes him want to tiptoe. Why is she hesitating? He's not *that* irresponsible. "Give us half an hour."

"Sylvan!" Teo, now wearing a red cape, runs screaming across the room. "I wanna show you!" He's holding Youngster in both hands. The rat is wearing a tiny version of the same cape.

The baby cries out, every breath a jerk and gasp, shredding her voice box by the sound of it, rubbery arms shaking, little fists pounding air. Sally looks concerned. Phyllis shushes and rocks, rising onto the balls of her feet, swiveling her hips in tight figure eights.

Her voice has music in it. That's why she's a good teacher, Sylvan thinks. Facts and knowledge have nothing to do with it. It's all voice. The kids, in a group, always pay attention to her the way they do to Sylvan only when he reads from books.

Phyllis looks up from the infant, now gurgling quietly, and says, "Half an hour. Take Teodoro outdoors with you." She winks. Just when he thought he had blown it, she winks. And when she said "outdoors," Sylvan heard Outdoors.

Outdoors is so hot you can hear the trees ticking. The other kids have finished their lunches and gone home. Sylvan takes off his shirt, wipes the sweat from his forehead with it. He can see the slow creep of Monterey Bay from here, blue and big and cool, the skyline showing off the curve of the earth. Just looking refreshes.

"It's boiling," says Teo. He puts Youngster on his round, child's potbelly, and fans him. "I wanna show you a secret."

"So show me." Sylvan's impatient to kill the half hour. He's also a little curious.

"I have to take you there." Youngster climbs up Teo's shirt, whiskers twitching, eraser-pink nose sniffing.

"What do you feed him?"

"Rat food," Teo says, as if it's obviously the only things rats eat. He's crossing his eyes to focus on Youngster, now almost up to his neck.

"What do you want to show me? Is it far?"

"No."

"Did your mom sew both of your capes?" They're cranberry red with gold trim. Teo nods, smoothes a wrinkle in Youngster's. "What is it you want me to see?"

"It's secret."

The heat is too much. Lethargy has overtaken him, limbs like sandbags with slow leaks. Even smiling is physical exertion. "Just tell me."

Teo shakes his head no, making Sylvan more curious.

"Can we be back in a half an hour?"

"Prolly."

Sylvan considers. The sun weighs on the back of his neck.

"Something for your klexion," Teo says, eyes still on Youngster. Last year when Sylvan showed the kids his collection—feathers and fossils and personal relics—Teo was fascinated by the shark's teeth, and Sylvan's old baby teeth. "And something even weirder."

Sylvan shakes off the torpor, squints at the sun to determine about what time it is. "So let's go take a look."

Teo leads the way across a winding, rural highway, into the university, and toward the sculpture garden, before Sylvan stops him. "I thought you said 'not far.' "

Teo, like most five-year-olds, has little sense of time or space, but, ironically, a good sense of direction. He shrugs, keeps walking.

Torsos (mostly women's) and abstracts (including the red squiggle people call the flying IUD) are mounted on slabs of concrete just behind student housing. Music blares from some of the buildings. More students are arriving, carrying boxes and suitcases. Sylvan can see from here the apartment he moved into yesterday. His new roommate may even be there by now. He wonders who it will be this time. Last year was Jacques, a marathon runner who kept running shoes in his files and jockstraps in his desk drawers. Sylvan hopes this year will be better. On the form he requested "studious," "nonsmoker," and "sciences." His ideal roommate would be a quiet, serious, neat, nohassle kind of person who also backpacks and takes lots of three-day weekends away. If he and Teo weren't in such a hurry, they could swing by now and take a look. But Sylvan doesn't want to be late for the job interview.

"What do you mean 'weirder'?"

Teo doesn't answer, and shows no sign of slowing down. He cuts through the grass toward a barbed-wire fence that sets off the cow pasture, then stops suddenly to squat next to a spring. One of Los Tres Ojos de Agua—the Three Eyes of Water. The landmark the school is named after. It's bubbling into a pool at the base of a few tufa knobs. Drinkable and cold. He and Teo put their mouths to it and guzzle like animals. Then Teo lets Youngster drink. The other two Eyes of Water are rather distant, one of them back behind the playground, a smallish spring that dries up in summer and becomes mostly a thatch of algae. The third Sylvan has never seen. Supposedly they all connect up in an underground lake.

Something flashes on the ground.

"You ever look in a mirror?" Teo's chin is all wet. Youngster is still drinking. Thirsty rat.

"Sure. Sometimes. Do you?"

"Sometimes. I like to put the mirror down there." Teo points to a pocket mirror at his feet. Sylvan wonders if Teo dropped it, or somebody else. "That way up is down and I'm bigger than you." Teo holds Youngster's face to the glass, but the uninterested rat may as well be looking at a Picasso. Teo makes a series of expressions into the mirror, as if testing to see whether his face could change faster than its reflection. Then he covers his eyes with his hands. "Now I'm not there."

"Yes you are."

"I know," he says, offended. "I'm just joking. But Heaven, she thinks she can make things disappear just by shutting her eyes."

"I know lots of people like that." The Heaven phenomenon.

"Know how old I am?" Teo asks, slipping the mirror into his back pocket.

"Sure. You're five."

He holds up five fingers and the thumb from his other hand.

"Your mom said five," Sylvan insists, remembering the birthday party last June just before Tres Ojos closed for the summer.

"Five and a half," Teo says. "Mom said."

Sylvan's sweat-drenched, tired of this conversation. Kids are always in such a hurry to grow up. He's in no hurry, already feels old at twenty-two, and was probably getting drunk at a high school graduation party the day Teo was born. Depressing. "Let's go, Teo."

"Youngster's not even one."

They climb over the stile into the big meadow, though they could just as easily have slipped through the fence, which consists of three strands of rusty barbed wire stapled to flimsy wooden posts. Used to be a ranch; now university property. More than two thousand acres of forests and pastures for just six thousand students. One of the admissions requirements is a tetanus shot, all the rusty barbed wire.

The grass here is chewed down and every now and then Sylvan sees a large black ant crawl into one of the cracks caused by mud drying fast. Teo points to a pile of limestone jutting out of a slope. "There!"

But Sylvan stops. Ten or so range cattle huddle under a nearby oak. Longhorns, brown with white patches. They stand in their own shit, chewing, eyeballing the humans.

"They don't hurt people," Teo says. "Mom tole me."

"How can an animal that eats grass get so big?" One sidles out from under the tree, blinks, another joins it, this one more raggedy, tufts torn here and there from its hide. Sylvan remembers how he once saw an enraged cow trample to death a dog yipping at the flanks of her calf.

"Wait up, Teo." Sylvan is starting to feel more like the kid in this situation. He catches up and puts an arm around Teodoro. When they reach the limestone, he feels much safer. Cows can't rock climb.

"See?" Teo says, pointing and holding Youngster's face close to the ground. "Seashells."

A band of seashells runs across the face of limestone where a chunk of cliff has slid right off, possibly during a recent earthquake. Very strange, considering that they're standing six hundred feet above sea level. Either the ocean used to cover this spot or the tidal shelf got pushed up over millions of years. Or, more likely, a combination of both. California is, after all, the seam between two continents, each moving about two inches a year, one north, the other south, along the San Andreas Fault.

Sylvan passes a hand along the fossil vein. Bivalves mostly, clams, and a chiton or two, all gone slightly chalky from exposure to air and light, but still remarkably intact. And here some crystal amber inside a shell, the creature itself petrified. And a fish skeleton with what looks like a parrot's beak.

"But wanna see what's really weirder?" Teo jumps into a shallow fissure. "This."

The layer of seashells breaks off, turns vertical, then disappears into darkness where the air smells cloistered. A cave. Sylvan sticks his hand down as far as he can, but doesn't reach anything. Then he bends the whole of his upper body into the cave. "Hello, hello!"

"My daddy's in there."

Sylvan pulls out. "What?"

"It's where you go when you die."

Not knowing if Teo is serious or joking or sad or what, since his voice is so matter-of-fact, Sylvan decides to use Phyllis's Process Listening technique. At Tres Ojos you're never allowed to say "No." Instead of saying "No fighting," you say "Stop fighting." "Don't lean in your chair" becomes "Keep the chair on the ground." And when a kid can't, or won't, say how he feels, you're supposed to repeat his sentence back, or ask the same question again, let him try out a number of answers until one satisfies him.

"Your father went here when he died?" The trick is to keep the incredulity out of your voice without letting the tone go flat. Just keep the kid talking.

"That's where fishes go. See?"

Sylvan nods. Lots of nodding involved in Process Listening. "The fishes?"

"All those clams and fishes lived down there." Teo points to the bay. "And anything that dies down there comes up here after." He explains it, impersonal as the truth. "It's their heaven. See what I mean?"

"I see what you're saying."

"How I know is 'cause that's my daddy's elbow." Teo toes a V of bones embedded in the rock. Then he looks up, blue eyes wide, to make sure Sylvan is getting it. "Proof."

"Your daddy's elbow?"

"Uh huh. More of him's down there." He gestures with the rat toward the cave's mouth. "Can we go down?"

"Does your mom know?"

He shakes his head no. "I don't want her to get hurt feelings. Sometimes she still gets hurt feelings."

"Tell her, Teodoro. Tell your mom."

"If I do, can we go down?"

The idea makes Sylvan claustrophobic, but less so than this conversation about marine heaven. "Sure. Sure we can. But later."

"Promise?"

"Promise."

"Yay!" In his excitement, Teo squeezes Youngster so hard his legs start thrashing and his eyes bug out.

"Careful with that rat."

"He's got a name, you know."

"Sorry, Youngster."

A shadow passes along the ground, then another. Sylvan looks up. Two golden eagles circle the sun, which has moved at least a half hour's worth across the sky. Time to go. Sylvan turns and sees a thick-headed cow standing near the rocks, snout lifted, sniffing for a scent on the breezeless air. It's giant, with eyes like eight balls pushed into matted curls, and—oh shit, no cow at all—testicles hanging like a pair of boxing gloves. The whole pasture to roam and it chooses here. The bull stamps the ground and snorts, as bulls do.

No problem if he were alone. But Teo is slower, with·that round-bellied shuffle-run, and even though the fence is only a hundred or so yards away, he might not make it.

"Don't worry about him. That's El Toro," Teo says. "I fed him before." He tells Sylvan how he once helped the university gardener empty a lawn-mower bag over the fence, the sweet green clippings bringing over a stampede of cows that moved out of the way for El Toro. "If you be gentle, he'll be gentle back."

"Is that what the gardener told you?"

"Yeah."

An easy thing to say when you're standing on the other side of the barbed wire. Sylvan takes a breath, tries to make himself bigger in the chest. "Okay, just walk normal."

They get only a few steps from the rock before El Toro rushes at them, an instant gallop.

Back up on the limestone, Teo's giggle turns into a laugh like slaps. Does he think this is fun? Or is he just out of breath?

The bull backs up, not off, for more running room. Its horns curl inward like a buffalo's, nonstabbing, but potentially rib-cracking. When it raises its nose, its eyes roll back and it screams. Actually screams, high-pitched.

Sylvan remembers having read somewhere that cattle in-stincts were being bred out of cattle. Any remaining wariness, territoriality, roaming urges, maternal instincts, all going,

going. In fact, a friend of Sylvan's has a cousin who lives in Iowa and runs a business inseminating cows. With a pair of rubber gloves and access to gallons of sperm guaranteed to make big, dumb, superproductive dairy cows, this friend's cousin impregnates something like fifty a day, ten thousand a year. It isn't right, meddling with the species like that.

"Now what?" Teo asks.

Instincts or no instincts, a screaming bull like this is a pain in the ass. Sylvan's job-to-be is at stake. Not only that, somebody may get hurt, and Sylvan has the uncomfortable feeling it won't be him.

The cows, indifferent, stand there, chewing, watching or not watching. Nobody would hear if Sylvan yelled for help. Except Teo, who would think him a coward.

"Don't just doooo something, stand there!" He throws a rock at the cows but they don't even seem to notice. Teo laughs, perhaps recognizing the *Alice in Wonderland* line. Sylvan tells himself it's important to keep a sense of humor, and tries to believe it.

"Give me your cape."

"Why?"

"'Cause it's red."

"You know how to bullfight?" Teo's voice is subdued with new respect.

"I took a class." Actually, he's never seen a bullfight. But he's got a plan. He tells Teo to run to the fence. "And don't look back. Think you can make it, kiddo?"

"Cinchy."

Why isn't this child terrified? Most kids would be.

"Think you can make it, Ratto?" Teo asks Youngster, using the same upbeat tone Sylvan has just used.

To give Teo a clear run to safety, Sylvan must walk between the herd and the bull. But putting himself in danger for Teo's sake has a feel to it, a feel he likes, one that gives him an edge over the bull, grimacing now, purple tongue flicking into its nostrils.

He runs out, flapping the cape. A rope of saliva hangs from El Toro's mouth and a whiny growl, like an engine at danger- ously high RPMs, issues from the bull's throat. When it comes after Sylvan in a slow, lumbering run, Teo takes off for the fence. Sylvan jogs backward, waving the cape so hard it pops. "Toro!" His foot lands in a pile of cowshit and he slips. Piss and straw. Hoofsteps approaching fast.

But when he gets back to his feet, the bull is standing still, turning its head back for a look at Teo, who is running, run- ning, much too slowly, head bobbing above a patch of tall brown grass, both arms holding up Youngster. Sylvan beats the air with the cape, whoops, makes exploding sounds with his mouth. The bull goes after Teo anyway.

Hatred means only one thing: you want to kill. With your bare hands, if necessary. And Sylvan will. He roars and, vaguely aware of the clumpety-clump of hooves behind him, flies at the bull running after Teo running for the fence.

El Toro stops, turns round just as Sylvan flings himself on the bull's back. Sylvan scratches, kicks, and yells. The bull bel- lows and bucks and Sylvan flops off. The duel is over. El Toro gallops away, literally scared shitless, leaving behind a trail of runny green excrement.

From the other side of the barbed wire, Sylvan, and Teo and Youngster, watch El Toro swagger and stamp, frustrated, hu- miliated in front of the cows, which all stand facing the oppo- site direction in a show of herd ostracism. Sylvan is so intoxicated with the bullfight that he has a foolish desire to challenge the bull again.

"Doesn't El Toro know he could go through this fence like pasghetti?" Teo asks. He pushes a loose post, causing the low- est wire, which is resting slack on the ground, to snap tight. It occurs to Sylvan that only the very smart and the very stupid don't respect invented borders. Cows are somewhere in be- tween humans and insects.

"The fence is an idea he's comfortable with."

"Bulls have ideas?"

Sylvan can feel a smile coming on, like a pimple, as he and Teo climb the front steps of Tres Ojos. The school seems to be deserted except for Phyllis standing at the door, arms crossed. They're at least an hour late.

"El Toro attacked us!" Teo runs to Phyllis, and she lifts him up, sets him on a hip. Him and Youngster. "But we excaped!"

Only now does she look worried.

Teo jumps down to act out the story, planting his thumbs on his forehead and wagging his pinkies, running at an imaginary cape. Sylvan watches Phyllis listen. She unconsciously makes sympathetic expressions, mouth open in surprise, eyes wide in fear, as Teo tells it, smiling along with him when the bull is defeated. But, unlike Teo, she does not end by looking admiringly at Sylvan. It cures him of his smile.

Her eyes run up and down his body. He realizes he's wearing only cutoffs. Smears of cowshit have dried on his calves. A toenail has somehow gotten ripped off and it's starting to scabcrust and turn purple. Tomorrow he will wake up with bruises. "I guess I'm kinda messed up." Wrong thing to say. "Physically, I mean."

"I guess." Her arms are crossed again, but her hands open in a guarded gesture. "What were you doing there in the first place?"

Sylvan starts to tell about the limestone but stops before revealing anything about the cave, or Teo's dad's elbow. He doesn't want to lie to Phyllis, but he can feel Teodoro's eyes tugging on him. It's secret. "Killing time."

Indoors is hers. Hers by the way she makes him feel at home, therefore really a visitor, offering him an overfluffy towel that smells like flour (he has just hosed himself off) and sitting him down on the couch while she sorts through a first-aid kit. It consists of two Star Wars lunch pails packed with scissors and gauze, sunscreen, children's aspirin and Midol, see-through skin tape, a thermometer, tweezers, an unopened snakebite kit, Band-Aids, and grape suckers. She hands him a sucker and begins working on the toe.

"Snakebite kit?"

"Had a child bitten the first year we opened," she says. "Turned out to be a gopher snake, but you never know. This may sting."

Tres Ojos first opened seven years ago. Sylvan knows most of its history because proud Phyllis talks about it as if it were her only child, precious. Armed with grant proposals and feasibility studies, she had gone to Sacramento and convinced the governor that the school system needed to serve the needs of the kids whose parents were single or pursuing careers or both—non-nuclear, pre-professional families, a growing, and voting, population. The governor said yes immediately—it helped that Phyllis had a doctorate from Berkeley and had just written a textbook on Process Listening, and that the legislature had officially declared the 1980s the Decade of the Child—and he gave the project "pilot program" status, which meant a generous budget for the school and tax credits for the parents.

Phyllis went to work immediately, scouting locations. She loved Santa Cruz (had spent a couple of summers here), and decided on the Tres Ojos de Agua region, a rural neighborhood of wooden houses and open fields, a site convenient both to working families living in town and to graduate students and faculty members whose kids were being turned away from the university's popular but overcrowded day-care centers. She helped the architect design the building—all natural lighting except for the electric lamps in the reading area, miniature toilets and waterfountains, and low doorknobs. And she supervised the construction of a giant rubber jungle gym (also the school's logo) on the playground.

"Stick out your toe." As Phyllis applies the Band-Aid Sylvan notices how bushy her eyebrows are, a full quarter-inch loft.

Even if he doesn't get his job back, very likely now, she's still a nice person. "Finished."

Teo has fallen asleep on a pile of pillows and the sky is starting to change colors. Phyllis snaps shut the lunch pails. "So you want your job back?"

Sylvan takes the sucker out of his mouth. "Look, I couldn't help—"

"Yes or no."

Suddenly, for the first time, his toe starts stinging. He grimaces. "That's why I'm here."

"Fridays from noon to five. Hundred twenty-five a month." She stands up, flexing legs that are well muscled, but so pale they're almost blue, and kind of thick in the ankles.

"But—" It's twenty-five less than he got last year. She raises her big eyebrows and Sylvan looks away. There's a paper spaceship stuck in a roofbeam; the one Wolfgang tossed up there last year. Funny that Phyllis would leave it, her idea of interior decorating. Youngster and Teo are cuddled together, napping. The children's books are neatly stacked for the onslaught next week. Still—

"Okay, a hundred fifty."

"Great," he says, getting up. His back feels like a dented fender. "I'll make it up, I promise." Then he realizes that this is the second promise he's made today. He's not in the habit of making promises. Like tossing that ball of string around, binding everyone in an imaginary system of interdependence. Tres Ojos is not the real world in thousands of ways, but perhaps in this way most: If you give your word, you must not break it.

2 *Sperm Daddy*

Would you be a sperm daddy?" Phyllis can't believe what she's just asked.

Sylvan bends and groans, stretching out his back muscles. His banged-up legs are skinny, and you can see every rib. Phyllis noticed this earlier, when he and Teo first burst indoors— the image linked with the feel of the newborn in her arms, and then that single drop of sweat trembling between her shoulder blades. She had to get Sally to scratch it.

"You mean like make a deposit at some bank?" He tests his weight on the freshly bandaged toe.

"No banks," she says. "Banks creep me out." She has already looked into them. The anonymity scares her. And who wants to pay three hundred dollars a shot for frozen sperm? "Are you Irish?"

"Irish?"

"Your eyes. The way you can see the whole iris," she says. Blue, but losing some intensity behind white lashes. A little mascara would heighten. What her mother calls "the Kennedy eyes." If you can see the bottom arc of the iris, trouble; if you can see the whole iris, glorious trouble.

"Nah. Maybe half," Sylvan says. He has good teeth, one dimple, several moles on his neck. "I'm your basic American mix."

She tries to picture his parents, gets a vague image of a couple smiling for an Instamatic, tweeds and a linen dress, Volvo station wagon, Irish setter going gray. "Any brothers or sisters?"

"One sister, Emma. Incidentally, she's pregnant, just." Sylvan chuckles. "This a background check?"

"So what would you say, if someone asked you?" She has to laugh at herself. Here she is, practically signing him up for this ludicrous fantasy when she should have told him *no*. No, Sylvan, you can't have your job back. All those accidents last year—the easel that caught fire from the lava shooting out of the model volcano, then Solomon spraining his thumb in that box o' tornadoes, and Adonis vomiting up half a banana slug because he didn't understand it was only a name. And today's mishap with Teo and the bull. Of course the kids love him.

"I heard of this lady who was on welfare, she sold one of her kidneys for ten thousand dollars," Sylvan says. "Why are you laughing?"

"So you're saying you'd want to be paid."

"Are you serious about this?"

She looks away, at Teo, who's snoring. Been a long day. Ten hours of signing up kids, explaining curriculum to parents, organizing teachers' work schedules; everybody needs personal reassurance. Phyllis rests her eyes by letting the focus go slack, how a toddler sees the world, swirls and eddies. "I'm twenty-nine." She rubs the bridge of her nose. "And I've spent almost ten years caring for other people's children."

"And Teo's five and a half, and I'm twenty-two," Sylvan says, sitting down but standing right back up. "Everybody's awfully sensitive about their age today."

Phyllis begins closing cupboards and locking windows. Sylvan helps out with the higher ones, though she's only two or three inches shorter than him. They probably weigh close to the same, he's such a rattlebones.

"Well?"

"No," Sylvan says. "If someone asked me, I'd tell them I'm not ready. First of all, I couldn't afford a kid, financially or emotionally, and besides, I'm too normal. The—"

"Financial support isn't necessary. And neither is emotional." Phyllis laughs off Sylvan's stare to keep the tone hypothetical.

"I'd also have to wonder why me."

The phone rings and Phyllis jumps, feeling strangely pinned out, but also not wanting the noise to wake Teo. It's Sam, worried, asking why she and Teo are so late, and then for a favor. "Bring home tomatoes, milk, also tampons. Please."

Sylvan has his shoes in his hand and is mouthing good-bye. Phyllis holds up her hand, wait, but he walks away as though the floor were a trampoline. After she hangs up, she runs out the door. He's nowhere.

Is it possible he thinks she was joking? Was she? She *did* hire him.

Phyllis pulls over where the highway intersects the road that leads into the university. A Farm and Garden wagon is parked there, piled with tomatoes and broccoli and carrots, bunches of herbs, flowers, even a tumble of early pumpkins, smallish, green-streaked, one of them plastered with bumper stickers: TEACH PEACE and QUESTION AUTHORITY, and another with skull and roses, JERRYCISE. A disheveled man leads a pair of donkeys up the hill toward a row of tepees. Earlier in the day these same donkeys pulled the wagon-wheel cart down here and parked on the corner in front of an old limestone ranch house. Now BMWs, buses, mopeds, and mountain bikes clog the intersection. The whole scene is like a vision from another time in a movie with bad art direction.

The tomatoes are likely to burst if you touch too hard; spicy smelling, the green leaves, mildly abrasive like superfine sandpaper, still attached. Phyllis chooses seven, her good-luck number, and puts them into an old Albertson's grocery bag turning slightly chamois from so many recyclings. She decides on some corn too, and a bouquet of red and blue anemones for Sam.

The girl who takes her money (the five-dollar bill suddenly absurd, even embarrassing in Phyllis's hand) is barefoot, wearing khaki shorts several sizes too large, and a tie-dyed spaghetti-strap top that barely conceals loose breasts. A string of beads sets off a peace sign at her throat. The last person Phyllis saw wearing a peace sign was Aja, Sam's separatist friend. "What's a separatist?" Phyllis had asked. "You're kidding," Sam said. When it became apparent she wasn't, Sam explained. "A woman who considers herself an altogether different species from man." Aja's peace sign had been supplemented by a macramé noose earring and taxi yellow hair.

"Nice, huh?" the girl says, breathy, nodding at the tomatoes. "And the corn too. Wonderful. A gift. The summer was good to us." She has bright eyes with that faraway glaze of alcoholics and people born again. Phyllis's father's eyes. Full of speeches. He had moved the family from Los Angeles to Tulsa because "Oklahoma is the buckle of the Bible belt." A phrase Phyllis always thought slightly lewd, if you carried the imagery one step further. The whole way there he'd refused to let her mother drive. "The family unit is like an automobile; there's only one steering wheel, and I'm behind it." Years later when Phyllis got suspended from Tulsa High School for saying "fuck" in biology class, he'd told her, "Look to the Bible, child. It is a road map to show you the way."

The girl has wild roses woven into random blond braids. Her hands are callused from farming. "Do you live in one of those tepees?" Phyllis asks. She sees them every day as she drives past the campus, but has never met anybody who actually lives in one of them.

"Wigwam. I love my wigwam," the girl says, staring at Phyllis's eyes but talking past them, to the back of her head. Phyllis scratches herself there, and looks down. The girl's toenails are mud-caked but clean. Real soil isn't dirty.

"I've never been in one."

"You can visit. I'm the third wigwam from the top."

Top of what? Phyllis wonders. And what does this girl eat besides raw produce? And how and where does she go to the bathroom? And what about sex? Phyllis imagines campfires, an outhouse, seasponge contraceptives.

"Top of the slope. By the way, I'm Benita."

"I'm Phyllis." She's afraid the girl will hug her, relieved when she doesn't. Phyllis decides on a handshake.

"Aren't these anemones something, Phyllis?" Benita says. Her handshake isn't so much a shake as a touch. "Everything this year, best ever, like never before. Summer was good to us."

It's not so bad looking at everything as a gift, Phyllis thinks, except it must make you feel so owing.

Teo and Youngster are still sleeping in the backseat, and Phyllis can't hold back a yawn herself as she pulls up behind a long line of cars and flashing yellow lights. Roadwork. Craning her head out the window she sees men in hardhats and fluorescent orange vests up ahead funneling cars into one lane and diverting them right. Getting home will take forever. When she finally reaches the flagman, Phyllis impulsively turns left, causing oncoming cars to speed up and honk, teach her a lesson. She enters a quiet neighborhood, where she can navigate at her own pace, rather than be shepherded along that slow crawl of a detour.

This is the old part of town. Victorian houses, picket fences, and vegetable gardens instead of lawns in front yards. Trash cans are set out on wide sidewalks for the garbage collectors, as well as burlap sacks full of aluminum cans and some with bottles, since recycling has become the law. But the narrow one-way streets confuse her, and force her to make turns against her instinct. She drives faster, through a settlement of depressing stucco apartments, cars with important-looking hubcaps parked out front. Uh oh. Where—?

Suddenly she comes out into a clearing. Now she knows where she is, the ghetto. The Duke Kahanamoku Community Center, an old adobe brick building with a mural on the wall, is its central landmark. She gave a lecture on Process Listening here once, her ideas becoming, in this neighborhood, suddenly hifalutin and false; may as well have been reading Romantic poetry. This afternoon she sees mothers picking up their kids from Head Start, while at the edge of a parking lot bums congregate under a huge magnolia tree. On an asphalt court, about thirty bare-chested black men are playing basketball. Bud tins and conga drums stand along the sidelines. On the grass a gang of hippies playing guitars.

It's clean for a ghetto, sunny, not too urban, but Phyllis still feels like a tourist here, an easy mark. She makes a left turn and then sees up ahead the road is blocked again. This time by furniture. Somebody's porch, apparently, only in the middle of the street. A grungy, sprung-out La-Z-Boy, occupied by a skinny Rasta man, stands next to a crate with newspapers on top, and a burly black man is squeezed into a bent lawn chair. She has to stop the car. For two minutes she idles there, wondering if they'll move on their own. They don't.

It's her prejudice scaring her. Broad daylight, plenty of people around, nothing to be afraid of. Teo, she can see in the rearview, is still safely asleep in the back.

When she does step out of the car, the large black man pops up and begins to bounce a basketball. He's got slicked-up hair. He wears a Hawaiian shirt and jams, several gold ropes around his neck.

"Sorry bout the dee-lay," he says, spinning the basketball absentmindedly on two fingers. "I'll just move my living room."

She smiles.

"Unless you wanna join us?"

She shakes her head, smiling. The skinny Rasta man still has his legs up. He nods at her, causing a headful of red-and-green-beaded dreadlocks to cascade over his eyes, leaving only a broad grin.

The fat man frowns, tucks the basketball under his arm, sticks two fingers in his mouth, and whistles. Several teenagers at courtside, all wearing beachy pastels and brightly laced but untied hi-tops, saunter over. "Let the pretty lady pass." They pick up the chairs, including the La-Z-Boy with the Rasta man still in it, and swiftly clear a path for the car.

As Phyllis drives slowly past, the fat man waves, and she wonders whether he really thinks she's pretty. Why can't Sam ever pay her that simple compliment? What does Sylvan think? Why should she even care?

The ocean has that flat look, slick with light, kelp matting the surface, meaning low tide. An otter floats on its back just beyond a row of surfers sitting astride their boards, waiting. She can make out Carmel across the bay, south, although it feels like looking west.

Relieved to be out of traffic, free of the Duke Kahanamoku neighborhood, Phyllis feels lucky to be living in Santa Cruz. Every day a different sky. This evening's like spilled orange juice.

PREGNANT?

We have loving, childless couples who want to adopt your child. Heavenly Cradle Adoption Services. Call 423-BABY

says the ad on the bus stop bench that she first noticed at the beginning of the summer and has been wondering about ever since. Her own adventure at an adoption agency ended in a paneled office when the adoption agent, a woman with frosted hair and wearing Jordache jeans, gave Phyllis three clipboards of paperwork to fill out. Four weeks and a background check later, Phyllis would learn whether she qualified for an interview. If she passed her interview, she would get put on a six-month to four-year waiting list. Four years. Phyllis couldn't sit tight waiting four years for a phone call.

Besides, the baby-brokerage business is expensive. Eight to twenty thousand dollars for a legal adoption. Thirty to forty for a black-market baby. But what finally turned her away from adoption was that the urge to have a child began in her own body. And there's no reason why she can't answer that urge.

"We're home, guys," Phyllis says as she pulls into the driveway, a strip of dirt road, dusty now, one long mud puddle in the rainy season, that leads to a settlement of whitewashed bungalows all separated from each other by colossal fuchsia bushes. Hers is the most private, half an acre her own.

Teo's playing possum, refusing to wake up in the backseat because he wants to be carried. Phyllis likes this game, though lately he's starting to get heavy.

"Hello?" she calls as the screen door shuts behind her. "Hey, Sam, look what I've got." But Sam doesn't answer, must be out taking a walk or gone to buy the evening paper. Sam's addicted to newspapers. On Sundays she buys four different ones and spreads them out on the living room floor. Phyllis prefers mail. More personal. She deposits Teo on the couch and goes out to check the box.

A letter from the Red Hourglass Network addressed to Samantha Timoteo (they still refuse to acknowledge her married name), a brochure labeled OCCUPANT offering dichondra and special cheese graters, and a package from Doggy-Dent International, which Phyllis opens. Dog-O-Dontics toothpaste, Happy Breath Mouthwash (fennel), and liquid Beautycote in an amber jar. Recently Grampa's fur has begun falling out in tufts under his arms and on his belly, revealing rashes that smell like dishrags. This stuff is supposed to help.

Sam will laugh. Rowing Overboard, she calls it when Phyllis brushes Grampa's teeth every other day, and Beyond the Hall of Duty when Phyllis brings him into the shower with her, where he sings. Basenjis are barkless dogs, but they do yodel. At least Grampa does. Once you get him started, he can do a throaty a e i o u, and sometimes y.

"Hey there." A man's voice.

Phyllis turns, surprised. Jack Stark, her next-door neighbor. He's got a face like a hardware store—handlebar mustache and steely eyes. He waves hello by making a finger gun and clicking his tongue. A gorgeous young Afghan—his recently acquired prize possession—strains the leash in his other hand, giving Jack an excuse to flex a bicep. "How's Stinko?"

"Grampa's fine," she says, trying not to stare at the Afghan.

"Glad to hear it." He clicks his tongue again, getting the Afghan to heel. "Be sure and keep him away from my Princess."

Phyllis turns to go.

"And say hi to the other." He means Sam, whom he has a slight crush on and refuses to believe is "amazon." Phyllis turns again to watch him walk away with the new Afghan and can only think, Trouble for Grampa.

In the kitchen, she puts the tomatoes on the table and arranges the flowers in a black vase so they will be the first things Sam sees when she comes in. Then it's time for Grampa's skin treatment.

But at the window she stops. Outside, Grampa is sitting, attentive, panting at several pieces of leftover turkey stacked in the lap of the Buddha statuette by the back door. Sam leans over him and tears meat off a drumstick. A peaceful scene: full-page glossy selling life insurance or, with a sexy lift of Sam's back leg—she has the nicest calves, Phyllis's own are too fat—a new diet soda or sports car.

Phyllis stays put, content to watch.

Samantha Wilcox (nee Timoteo) was born with a grace and beauty that only complicated her life. After two years of study-

ing Communications at the University of Texas, she had real-
ized she'd rather travel than sit in class, and had dropped out
to become a stewardess. As jobs go, it wasn't bad (especially
when she was working first class); free flights to New Zealand
and Paris outweighed having to serve bossy passengers and
lecherous businessmen. Eventually the airline she was working
for began losing money and decided, as a public relations stunt,
to conduct an in-house search for "an exemplary flight atten-
dant" who would become their national spokesperson. Sam
was delighted when she won.

Her first project was getting photographed christening new
jets by smashing bottles of champagne on their noses. Her second project was getting photographed handing airline-donated
vacation vouchers to orphaned children. Her third project—it
too involved getting photographed—was the one that got her
into trouble. Sam's picture was featured on thousands of bill-
boards across the country as part of an ad campaign that was
unprecedented: Instead of smiling, Sam was pouting. The
expression, a wistful, brooding appeal, distinguished Sam's airline as the only sincere one in an industry of high profits and
phony smiles. An innuendo-loaded slogan accompanied her
300-square-foot pout: "COME FLY! When lip service alone
won't get you home." The campaign was enormously successful for the airline, extremely humiliating for Sam.

"Here ya go, Grampa," Sam says. "A treat."

Looks shouldn't matter so much, Phyllis thinks, and wishes
she weren't so vulnerable to Sam's. Cheekbones, light eyes
exotic against dark brows, and hair so shiny and black it looks
purple. But it's the shape of her head, really, that makes Sam
so beautiful. A perfect skull, no faking that. Plus she can eat
anything and never worry. Phyllis wants a hug. More than a
hug.

"Poor Grampa, always hungry," Sam is saying, feeding
Grampa a strip. "Now, shake." His face looks quizzical. No-
body has requested a trick from him in years, and he refuses.
"Never not hungry," Sam says.

When Grampa takes a few steps, Phyllis notices he's still roped to the cypress. Thursday is trash day, and unless he's restrained, he chases the garbage truck. But the cans are empty. Why is he still tied up?

Sam's having trouble with a stubborn piece of gristle, and finally bites it off in a kiss of the fingertips, managing to make even that gesture sensual. The natural beauty in her. She can make taking a pee graceful.

Passengers had eventually begun giving her a hard time, requesting "more than lip service" here and now, or telling her to "Smile, honey," or asking her to autograph in-flight magazines (sprinkled liberally with pictures of the famous pout). When it became impossible for her to continue working, she was no longer "exemplary," so the airline released her.

Pissed off, degraded, and broke, Sam sued. Headlines. Editorials. Notoriety. Strangers on the street began accosting her. "Look! The Billboard Stewardess." An out-of-court settlement made her financially secure for life, but at a great cost. "They stole my identity."

"People make you beg, don't they?" Sam puts a bit of meat inches beyond the reach of Grampa's rope.

Either Sam is being mean, or Phyllis doubts her own perceptions. But, then, Sam has been a little icy lately, not even bothering to make excuses.

Grampa's blue-blotched tongue ("Did he get into some ink?" people always ask) swipes at the turkey, but gets only dirt. Phyllis forces herself to stay put. She hates being the police for one thing, and Grampa, tail a spiral, thinks Sam is playing. Maybe she is.

"Sing for me and it's yours," Sam says, pointing to golden turkey breast in the lap of the Buddha statue. "Aahoo!"

Grampa won't sing. A string of drool hangs from his mouth. Sam wiggles a tidbit and howls. Grampa runs and leaps, but the rope snaps tight around his neck while his body whips forward, and he lands on his back with a thud.

Phyllis feels she should do something. But you have to give

people a chance. Like with kids, if you give them a chance to get themselves out of trouble, they usually will. Redemption is so often a matter of timing.

Grampa stands up, shakes himself out, jowls flapping against his gums, eyes blinking at the just raised dust. He walks sideways, hangdog, tail down, back to the cypress. Then he ducks his head and rubs it between his front legs, a human gesture of frustration, and frees himself of the collar.

Phyllis can't see exactly what happens next, only that Grampa jumps, Sam cries *"Ow!"* and shakes her arm free, and Grampa runs over to eat out of the lap of the Buddha.

When Sam walks into the kitchen cradling a bloody wrist, Phyllis already has hot water going in the sink, three squirts of dish liquid, soap-bubble rainbows.

"Oh, hi. You're here."

"Give me your hand," Phyllis says. Two punctures on the soft white skin of the inner arm, a nasty bruise on the bony wrist bump.

"He didn't bite me on purpose."

"On purpose?"

"You know, purposely. Like *on purpose.*"

One of those phrases Phyllis hears everyday at Tres Ojos. Kids just learning to camouflage their motives.

"Ouch."

For the second time today, she's playing nurse. "Always needed, never wanted," as her mother says. Back in Tulsa she's head nurse in the operating room at Mercy General, or General Mercy. "That's a nurse's lot, until virulence and violence learn the meaning of Sunday." Sunday meaning roughly heaven on earth. Ambitious for salvation, Mother is a stockpiler of good deeds. Phyllis could have killed her for sending money to Oral Roberts when he claimed God would call him home unless his flock sent in eight million fast. "Mother, he's a self-terrorist,"

Phyllis said over the phone. "The money goes to a medical school, honey, a good cause." Causes and high-mindedness in her mother, Phyllis knows—because it's also true for herself—are an escape, not altruism.

"Ow!" Sam cries, childlike.

It's Phyllis's habit to spot the kid in the grown-up. She can see it in Sam's pout, the freckled nose, and the lips curled around a strawberry or a beer. And now in the "on purpose" and the teary eyes. It is this side of a person Phyllis likes to address herself to, the one she considers in the deepest sense most responsible.

"I'm such a jerk," Sam suddenly says.

"It would be like me teasing Teo." Where did that come from? A selfish, bitter comparison; Phyllis is sorry she opened her mouth. But anger will find a way out. How much of it does she have anyway, and where is it coming from? She decides now is not the time for self-examination.

Sam looks scared. "You were watching?"

Her wrist cleaned and bandaged, Sam goes to check on Teo, who's still conked out on the couch. She licks her fingers and wipes a smudge from his cheek, then carries him into the bathroom and makes him take a pee before putting him to bed. Meanwhile Phyllis takes the Beautycote to the backyard, where Grampa wags his whole hind end, jumps on her, and goes wild howling.

"Did you remember tampons?" Sam calls from the bathroom down the hall. She's doing a hand wash—underwear and bras.

"Oh, God." Phyllis looks up from *Childerness*, a magazine dedicated to "the Now Age Parent." She's sitting at the kitchen table, the top made of varnished children's art, a gift from a group of Tres Ojos parents a few years back, just ugly enough that she feels protective of it. The flowers are beginning to close up, and Grampa is beginning to snore under her chair. "Sorry!" When Phyllis yells, her voice squeaks. "I forgot."

"I'll go out," Sam says, buttoning up her jeans as she enters the kitchen. She puts her underwear and bras in the oven to dry by pilot light. Quirky but practical. On even the hottest days the evenings here are dew-drenched, ocean air. Things never dry on a line. "Gotta have 'em."

Any day now Phyllis will need tampons too. It didn't used to be like this, but in two years of living together their periods have begun to come within days of each other. In this case, the old wives' tale is true. "Do you think temperament is destiny?"

Sam scratches Grampa's ears, he groans in pleasure. Neither seems to be holding a grudge. "Did Humphrey Bogart say that?"

"Do you think it's true?"

"I don't know what it means. Who said it?"

"Gertrude Stein." Phyllis points to the article about Gertrude Stein's childhood.

"Yeah, then it's definitely true." Sam leafs through the mail. "Hourglass?" She squints suspiciously.

After the Billboard Stewardess hoopla had died down, Sam had moved to Santa Cruz, finished up her degree at Mills College, and founded the Hourglass Network, a nonprofit educational corporation committed to "the pursuit of happiness." She put up some of her own lawsuit earnings to charter the organization, which was primarily for women. Membership grew, grants started coming in, and with the infusion of new money came internal power struggles. The organization's emphasis shifted from providing financial support for women's health collectives and instituting literacy campaigns for the children of migrant farm workers to advocating radical feminism. And then when Sam, accidentally pregnant, married Salty Wilcox—a semiprofessional surfer whom she had met on a Honolulu-bound flight before she was the Billboard Stewardess —and took his last name for her own, she earned the wrath of the militants. They claimed she was an inept administrator and, after a hostile takeover, kicked her out, bestowing upon her the consolation title of Honorary Founder, which she declined to accept when they added the Red to the name. The Red Hourglass Network became renowned for ripping up issues of *Hustler* and *Penthouse* in liquor-store parking lots (sometimes acting in league with Fundamentalist groups), giving public slide shows on the difference between erotica and violent porn, teaching self-defense classes, and lobbying local politics.

"The nerve," Sam says. "They're asking me for money. Me." She still has a grudging respect for the Network. Phyllis, though, is a skeptic. Red Hourglass commits the sin it's out to expose, using pornography to protest pornography. Once they masturbated a two-foot rubber dildo till it came Jergens lotion all over centerfolds. Another time they threw baggies of their own blood at a Playboy Club in San Jose. Why not do something constructive? Build day-care centers, for instance.

Grampa comes to Phyllis for a fresh dose of affection. Ears back, tail wagging, he noses her crotch. She wonders vaguely what he smells. Her period on the way? And after this one, how many more?

On public TV Phyllis once saw a uterus through a laparoscope—a thin fiber optic tube used for spying on internal organs through a small hole in the skin. The ovary, a healthy young one, looked battered and pockmarked. Every fertile cycle entails the release of a single egg from the surface of an ovary, which swells with a spot of bloody fluid before it bursts open to disgorge the ovum. A messy, violent process. And there are only so many eggs. A five-year-old girl—Heaven, for instance—has as many now as she'll ever have, actually more, because eggs are steadily lost from birth onward. Twenty-nine years old is getting up there, perhaps as few as five or six dozen viable opportunities left. And those eggs that do survive until the age of thirty-five are more likely to be freaks, having an extra chromosome that can result in Down's syndrome or worse. Really not fair, when you consider that a man generates several hundred million sperm a day till age one hundred, if he lives that long. Not fair at all.

"Maybe I should freeze an egg," Phyllis says, and catches herself tugging at her fingers, a nervous habit she can't seem to break.

"See if we can eat it when it thaws?" Sam asks, probably picturing a hard-boiled.

"No, an ovum egg. They freeze sperm, why not ova?"

"Seems to me fresh would be better than frozen," Sam says. She's got a gift for saying the obvious, a talent Phyllis herself lacks and fails to appreciate. "Like fish."

Grampa murmurs, closes his eyes, and rests his chin on Phyllis's fingers. The cords in his throat are vibrating. The more she thinks about it, the more she thinks Sylvan is the perfect candidate. Is it possible that right now he's thinking about . . . what she (can't believe she) asked him?

"Flowers?" Sam has just noticed them. She kisses Phyllis's head, then sniffs at a red anemone. "Well, bo and lehold, corn too." She examines an ear. "Hey, Phyllis?"

She does this often (and not *on purpose*), asks, "Phyllis?" then won't go on until Phyllis says, "What?" But this time Phyllis decides to hold out; same as Sam has been doing lately.

"Phyllis?" Sam asks again, raising her utterly innocent violet eyes. Wistful. Frank. Eyes you believe before your own.

At least Phyllis does. She just can't help it. "What?"

"Did I tell you Aja is microsurgically needling an ovum in a petri dish up at Berkeley?" Aja the separatist, with the peace sign and noose and taxi yellow hair, doubtless does not do the needling herself, but the funding of the needling. She's one of the "womyn" who helped turn the Hourglass Network Red, and is now a spokesperson.

"And?"

"She's trying to get it fertilized without sperm." Sam is lacing up her shoes.

"Yeah, well. Mom of Frankenstein." Phyllis is half-reading a

Childerness exclusive about an educational film company that constructed a lemming-flinging device, like a merry-go-round, to toss the tiny arctic rodents over a cliff in a mass-suicide scene. How awful! Phyllis has shown this very film to her kids at Tres Ojos. The lemmings appear to be jumping of their own volition. Fiction as Documentary is nothing new, but always a bad surprise.

Outside is totally dark now, and Phyllis is hungry and tired and needs a shower. Instead she gets up to boil water for coffee. "You know how we've been talking about me having a baby?"

"If you can wait for Aja—"

"I asked a guy to be my sperm donor today."

Sam tries not to smile. "Who?"

"That guy Sylvan. Remember the blond kid at Tres Ojos, taught Outdoors last year? You met him at Teo's birthday party."

"Real curly?" Sam has an elastic between her teeth. She flips back her hair. "Gawky, kind of?"

"I asked him."

"No you didn't." Sam giggles.

"No, I did."

Sam blinks rapidly, pushes out her lower lip, blows a strand of hair from her eyes. The famous pout. Every once in a while Phyllis will come across an old magazine at a rummage sale or used-book store, the back-page glossy of Sam using this expression. "COME FLY! When lip service alone won't get you home." Phyllis always buys them.

"But," Sam says, "all that research we did?"

"What research?" Phyllis asks. "We read some books." And a few legal and medical journals, and a firsthand account written by a lesbian couple who used what the Vatican calls "new reproductive technologies." A Mason jar and a turkey baster.

"I sort of thought we were . . ." Sam pulls back her hair, better showing off the fine shape of her head. "Partners."

"But, Sam. I thought you'd be happy. It's not you, I love—"

"What, me?"

Phyllis nods.

"Me? Or some idea of me in your head?" One tear hanging. "Is that what the flowers are for?"

"We can't, I mean, I—" Phyllis is rescued by the whistling teakettle. Words are scary just now. A cup of coffee can't be itself when you call it a cup of coffee. Even more difficult with something like *love*. Phyllis takes her time brewing a pot, trying both to lose her fear and to find herself in the warmth, the aroma. "Sam, I was holding a baby in my arms today."

"But shouldn't my wishes count too?" Sam says, the tear still lingering on her lashes. Her eyes and mouth seem governed by different emotions. "How do you think it makes me feel to—" The tear falls, runs along the contour of her cheek, leaving a faint mascara trail. "What did he say?"

"No." She puts down two cups of coffee, then lifts one and takes a long sip. Caffeine she'll have to cut out when she's pregnant. Other pleasures. Beer. Too much of anything, salt and sweets and scares like roller coasters. "He thought the question was hypothetical."

Sam wants proof. "How did you ask him?"

Phyllis prepares a sigh, but decides against it. "Like, what if?"

Sam traces the lines on her palm with a fingernail. The hand looks lonely, untouchable, and for that reason Phyllis reaches for it. Sam doesn't squeeze back.

"Don't you think an Unknown Donor would be smarter? I mean, fewer problems, no conflicts of interest—"

"He's so perfect," Phyllis says. "Young, healthy, good-looking"—though that's debatable, kind of a cross between Dennis the Menace and a jackrabbit—"smart, and, most important, he won't want any involvement." Phyllis isn't sure this is true, but she says it anyway to appease Sam.

It works. Sam perks up.

"Hon, it's just that for this I need a man," Phyllis says between sips. "Sperm."

"Ick!"

Phyllis sings in the tub. The bubbles are breaking up, and the bathwater is no longer steamy, but tepid, just about body temperature, perfect for making her voice do tricks. She bounces it off the porcelain tiles, pitching it to sound like her father's, her mother's, then Sam's, telling herself things she's always wanted to hear from each. Then, because nobody lives forever and, at twenty-nine, she's finally ready to get what she wants, Sylvan's.

"Spinach-fluoride bones!" Sam sings, sailing into the kitchen. "For Grampa. And shrimp for us!" Fresh, pink, a large pile spilling onto the table. "And these for me." A bottle of aspirin. "And this for you." She hands Phyllis a small pamphlet: *Name That Baby.*

"I'm starved," Phyllis says. Shrimp is her favorite food. She hurries Sam, who has promised "to cook you dinner," by rinsing it and preheating the oven.

"My favorite is still Heaven," Sam says. She associates the name with the child, her favorite at Tres Ojos, Phyllis knows, because she's so photogenic.

"I like Heaven," Phyllis says. "For a middle name. As long as the first is Helen."

Sam doesn't get it, keeps reading. "Oooh. 'Phoebe: the wise, shining one.' "

Phyllis chops the garlic and tomatoes.

"Hey, I'm 'the swift one,' Samantha."

Apt, Phyllis thinks, those calves.

"You're 'a green bough.' "

Phyllis bends over and kisses Sam's ear. Sam closes her eyes and smiles. A green light. Phyllis slowly runs a hand up under the shirt, all the way to the nape of the neck. Another green light. Dinner can wait. Sam lifts her chin, swallows, exposing her throat for Phyllis's lips.

"Bed?" Phyllis asks, beginning to unbutton Sam's shirt.

But Sam holds the hand, kisses Phyllis's eyelids, and whispers, "Dinner?"

Phyllis keeps her eyes closed tight, sees a roomful of babies, Jack Stark's Afghan, Teo flying a kite, Sylvan—

"My underwear is burning!" Sam shouts. Smoke is seeping from the oven door. She flings it open and, with a barbecue fork, extracts several burnt-crisp bras and pairs of panties.

"We have a clothes dryer, you know."

"I'm not going to have this argument again," Sam says, dousing the underwear in the sink.

They ignore an awkward silence by chopping vegetables and avoiding eye contact. Phyllis wonders if she did it, at some level, *on purpose*. Then she looks at the shrimp, decides their color is innocent.

"A hug?" Sam finally asks. But Phyllis knows exactly what kind of hug it will be, as if they were both wearing layers of winter clothing.

3 Shit
Happens

A roommate, like a brother, you can't choose yourself. And by the look of the redheaded guy nailing a boot heel to the bedroom door—a harmonica fitting snugly in the faded slot in the back pocket of his Levi's, a pack of Camels rolled up in the short sleeve of a T-shirt with the words SHIT HAPPENS stenciled on the front—Sylvan thinks somebody upstairs has made a mistake. Or pulled names out of a hat.

"Alabama," the redhead says, offering a freckle-covered hand.

"Napa," Sylvan says. "Fifty miles northwest of Sacramento, if you know where that is."

"No, I'm not from Alabama, I'm from Tennessee. I'm called Alabama on account of my accent."

Like a rubber band, Sylvan thinks, stretched out and snapping on the b's and t's. Maybe a Tennessee accent has more twang, maybe less. Somebody once told Sylvan he had a guitarist's accent, whatever that is, and he doesn't even play. Alabama does, if that amplifier blocking the hallway is any indication. Sylvan hopes he's not a bar-chord-and-blues-scales man.

"Sylvan," Sylvan says. They're still shaking hands. "Sylvan Park."

"Your parents hippies?"

"They both have short hair," Sylvan says. "But my sister kind of is. Or used to be." Beads and Joni Mitchell and *One Flew Over the Cuckoo's Nest.* Now she's grown-up, a first-year resident at the UCLA medical center. And soon to be a mother. "Uncle Sylvan" has a ring to it, but implies . . . something. Oldness, hairy arms, ironed clothes. "Why, are yours?"

"No. It's just that your name sounds lyrical."

Lyrical? Sylvan realizes that his own name probably seems to Alabama as exotic (or Californian-hippy-dippy) as, say, Gaia, Wolfgang, or Heaven.

"I guess Sylvan is better than Otto. Get it? Auto Park? Ha!" Turns out Alabama's an exchange student, here to finish up a degree in English, a language he doesn't really speak but heck they were handing out fellowships. His real name is Thoburn Downs Whitaker III, which sounds to Sylvan like a sports page headline, and he grew up in a mansion outside Nashville, with two brothers, one sister. His mother is a congresswoman and his father runs a chain of tanning parlors, he thinks.

"What do you mean, you think?"

Alabama shrugs, sucks his cheeks furtively, looks kind of sullen. "He's got his fingers in lots of pies." Many other students at this school brag about their fathers' being in one version of Mafia or another. But usually they're not so sheepish about it. Why the big mystery?

Alabama changes the subject, grins broadly again as he tells Sylvan he's an exchange student from Princeton, knows Latin and Greek, hates the Romantics except for Blake, and came to California because he wanted to see if people really say "gnarly" and "bitchen." "Long drive, though, and when I finally make it here, paradise, but my car door won't open."

Too much information for Sylvan to absorb at once. Somebody upstairs definitely screwed up. Here he is, seriously Earth Sciences for one thing, a nonsmoker for another, the opposite of—what Alabama says he is and appears to be with his grizzly red whiskers, arms pumped up from hammering the boot heel, and now jumping around on one leg and blowing metal noise from his blues harp. What kind of SHIT HAPPENS anyway?

Maybe he should have moved off campus this year. But student housing is close to the labs and not that far from Tres Ojos, convenient, still the best deal in town. The campus is so spread out. The university has a policy of no-buildings-higher-than-the-redwoods, so you come upon them like a discovery. Ansel Adams was a creative consultant in designing the campus. Mood was his thing. "Consider public safety but also consider the basic mood of the place." Sylvan likes that, *the basic mood.*

This particular cluster of apartments was built just two years ago, mod. Crisp lines, all white walls with purplish pipes, the exposed plumbing and skylights keeping things honest, roofs all slanted the same way and spotlit at night, making the place look like a Hollywood studio lot, all props and facades. Especially this week, with orientation booths giving out cookies, lemonade, and safe-sex kits, banners decorated with banana slugs saying WELCOME, music coming out of every open window, and blue and yellow helium-filled condoms riding the breeze. New students in shorts smile at each other, everyone carrying boxes of books, stereos, sleeping bags, personal computers, and houseplants. Mood.

"Fine sight." Alabama stops playing harmonica. He's looking out the window at a pair of legs. The girl they belong to is bending over a box packed with Cheerios and peppermint tea, toilet paper and a teddy bear. "You sudsworthy?" Not waiting for an answer, which he won't get anyway because Sylvan doesn't understand the question, Alabama jams the harmonica back into his pocket, does an emptyhanded drumroll on a dictionary, and walks toward the kitchen.

The whole inside of the apartment is open, kitchen and living room and dining room combined into one, clean with the smell of paint and sunlight. Probably not for long.

Alabama opens the refrigerator, which contains a case of beer and a hunk of cheddar, along with Sylvan's package labeled SEAWEED. He tosses Sylvan a beer, the can cold and sweaty. Bubbles tingle the back of Sylvan's throat, the quenching making him thirstier.

"Always this hot?"

"Gets hot a lot here. Even hotter yesterday," Sylvan says, remembering the bull episode with Teo. What a nightmare. At least he got his job back. Even if Phyllis was being weird. Asking him about his sperm like she was serious. Why him? Millions of stud types around; millions. One right here, as a matter of fact, this roommate who's unrolling cigarettes from his sleeve.

"Smoke?"

"Rather you didn't inside."

"Why not?"

"I like fresh air."

"Understandable. Good to nip these things in the bud." Alabama rolls the Camels back up into his sleeve and begins eating sunflower seeds instead, spitting the shells into a sack, sometimes missing.

Vacuum cleaner headaches and slimy carpet. Oh well, there are worse things. What is it Sylvan's mom tells him? "An ideal situation teaches you nothing." "You know yourself by the concessions you make." "Heaven is for dead people." She's always making up aphorisms along with the *et als.* and *comb. forms* and *fill in the* _____s for the Sunday crosswords she composes for the Oakland *Tribune*.

"Geology?" Alabama asks, pointing to the bookshelf bending under the weight of Sylvan's textbooks. *Geology, Hydrology, Volcanology,* and *A Look at Planet Earth*, all thick as dictionaries. "Or fossils?" He jerks a thumb at the Napa Park Wines crate packed with Sylvan's special collection: deer antlers, a string of pink and green iridescent feathers, a single human vertebra, and a chunk of molten glass. Other stuff is tucked underneath: a box containing a bluebelly lizard pelt and a rattlesnake rattle, a tin of shark teeth, his own baby teeth, a pearl shaped like a tiny peanut, various quartzes and pumice stones, the talon of a white-tailed kite, and a large magnifying glass.

"Museum of Natural History in a wine crate, goddamn."

"I just collect this stuff. But yes, my major is Earth Sciences." Sylvan tells him how he has just spent the summer in the White Mountains mapping terrain and charting wind erosion. Now he's back in Santa Cruz to finish his senior thesis.

"Earthquakes?"

"Yeah. Volcanology and sand migration and seismology. You know, plate tectonics."

"Toast. Here's to the collision of continents." Clunk of half-full beer cans. When he smiles, Alabama has perfect teeth except for two, the front and canine turned sideways, an imperfection making him seem, in some way, trustable.

"Hate to do it, but I gotta ask a favor." Alabama swallows the last of his beer. "Orientation meeting started five minutes ago, and I don't know where the English Department is yet. How 'bout a tour?" He picks up his dictionary as if to take it along, but then sets it back down.

On the way across campus, Sylvan points out the library that looks like a giant microchip plunked down in a redwood glen, piano-equipped practice rooms, the sorrel clover that tastes sweet this time of year but sour in the spring—the same plant they pour vinaigrette over in San Francisco and call New California Cuisine—and the exact spot under a fallen madrone where last year he found an Amanita Muscaria, bright red with fuzzy white polka dots, violently hallucinogenic.

"Smell this." He hands Alabama a bay leaf, half limy, half minty, and ultra aromatic. If you inhale deeply several times in a row, sparks go off in your head. Sylvan knows because little Teo tricked him into doing it last year. "Crumple it up first."

Alabama shuts his eyes and takes long, nose-drawn breaths. Suddenly he gasps, squinches up his face in a closed-mouth yawn, and puts his hands against his temples. "Speed of light."

It's a couple of moments before he can open his eyes. And grin. "More kick in this leaf than in the smelling salts they gave out for high-school bootfa—football." He sniffs again to make sure, yep, oughtta get his pop to package it, make a mint, get it? and retire for life. He stuffs several in his pocket. "Gonna send 'em home, seriously."

By the time they reach the English Department, students are already coming out the door with syllabi, bibliographies, course descriptions, wine and cheese. Alabama lays a hand on Sylvan's shoulder, raises an eyebrow toward the girl they saw earlier, the legs, the Cheerios, the teddy bear.

"My lucky day. She's English."

He introduces himself, pouring on the Southernese, and asks what he missed. Nothing. He didn't think so, but what about those papers? Plenty more inside, wine too. Her name is Monica, and she's got big eyes, brown, polite and bored. She's obviously used to this, deflects lots of unwanted attention, gives directions to strangers too often. Alabama hands her a few bay leaves to smell.

"O my fucking God—"

What language, and a face that looks about to explode. Now she watches Alabama with different eyes, and agrees to come over tomorrow night. "Be neighborly," Alabama puts it, and "Bring your roommate."

Sylvan takes Alabama, who won't know the difference, the long way home. There are so many trees and ravines and curving paths that you can't see much sky. Hard to tell what direction you're heading when there are no shadows to judge by. People know this without knowing it. Getting oriented can take several weeks on this campus—huge, sprawling as a natural park, but better, fewer rules, more mood.

Sylvan has gone to progressive (though now the word is its own antonym) schools all his life. Hardly any rules at all. He learned video editing and t'ai chi, as well as the basics, in classrooms furnished with air pillows instead of desks.

The path comes out on an open hillside that has a view of all Santa Cruz. Tres Ojos, in the distance, looks close enough to touch. Kids are playing on the playground. He can make out Wolfgang (red hair), Astrid and Humberto (inseparable), and Adonis (trying to climb the fence and escape). No sign of Teo or Phyllis.

"I work there starting Friday."

"Baby-sitting?"

"No." The guy obviously has no concept. "I take the kids on field trips."

"Cool." Alabama squints.

"The lady who runs the place—" Sylvan stops. Maybe she doesn't want anybody to know. Artificial insemination could be kind of a scarlet letter. The only reason he could ever treat it lightly is because he knows he's not going to say yes. "She's a nice lady."

"Nice or *nice*?"

"She's an okay person." An okay person?

Beyond Tres Ojos: more hilly neighborhoods, then downtown itself, highlighted by the roller coaster standing like a Tinkertoy structure on the boardwalk overlooking the bay, which shines today like brushed metal.

"Injuns?" Alabama points to the row of tepees in the foreground, setting off the campus farm. "Or just decoration?"

"They grow organic stuff."

"Organic stuff gives me the farts." Suddenly Alabama's leg skates out in front of him and he almost goes down. His heel leaves a slimy yellow skidmark. "Mercy!"

"Banana slug," Sylvan explains. "They're pretty common around here." Bright yellow like ripe bananas—though farther north they're often green—and about six inches long, banana slugs creep about the redwood forests leaving behind glazed trails of slime. The slime, now smeared across the path, and all over the bottom of Alabama's sneaker, works as both an adhesive and a lubricant. A slug can stick to Teflon, and slither unscathed over the sharpest barbed wire.

Using a handful of leaves, Alabama cleans the yellow remains off his shoe.

"It's the school mascot," Sylvan says. "Major issue, though, even made *Time* magazine." The chancellor wanted sea lions, but in the end, the students voted seven to one for the slug, calling it symbolic of the university's philosophy: noncompetitive, no grades, emphasis on tutorials, mostly liberal arts, but with access to the finest scientific laboratories, which in Sylvan's case happens to be California itself.

Banana slugs' sex lives are extraordinary. And, given Phyllis's strange request yesterday, Sylvan thinks that particular characteristic may somehow reflect Santa Cruz's image as well. Although banana slugs are hermaphroditic—each slug possessing both male and female sexual organs—they must mate with one another to reproduce. Finding a partner is like hunting, and occasionally a slug will shoot dartlike spears into a potential mate. Slug penises grow as large as half the body length, and sexual entanglements may last a couple of days.

"You have the banana slug, at Princeton we had Brooke."

"Careful." Sylvan points out some poison oak, dry now, the glossy red leaves turning brittle, but not harmless. It will be just sticks in a couple of months.

"So that's the stuff." Alabama has read a warning in a campus brochure. "Do firemen really die from breathing the smoke when it burns?"

"From the inside out."

"Hey, I like that." He takes a pen from behind his ear and writes on the back of a syllabus. "Not the concept, but the turn of phrase."

"Are you a writer?"

"I'm writing, aren't I?" He bends over, closer to the oak, eyes going wide from a squint.

Even in the fall, the plant is dangerous. Sylvan has seen people messed up. His field partner Rusty, for instance. Last year when they were measuring the sediment (which Rusty spelled "sentiment" in lab reports) pouring out of Waddell Creek for a sand-migration study, he got wrapped up in a whole plant that must have come unrooted during the storm and was floating downstream along with blackfoam, logs, and twenty-seven gallons of silt per cubic foot per minute. Sylvan had to rip the plant off, thankful for his thick neoprene gloves, and help Rusty to the shore, where he stripped and went right back into the river to wash off the oils. To Sylvan: "Any soap?" To the bush: "Fuck you. Not really." To the sky: "Please, no."

Three days later Rusty was laid up—"the bed feels like nails" —his head the size of a basketball and his eyes puffed almost shut. What little of them Sylvan could see was red like split tomatoes. And his lips, cracked, secreted the same yellowish crusty stuff that came from the sores on his arms. Doctors gave him cortisone injections, but those didn't seem to help. The red scars lasted for months. Eventually they healed completely. Hard to believe that something so evil-looking could vanish without a trace. That Rusty's head, so deformed, had returned to normal.

Now Alabama is putting his hand in the oak.

"Don't!" Sylvan says. Great. A fool for a roommate. He can see it now: Alabama fat-headed and sick for weeks. Oozing all over the apartment.

"Wondra!" Alabama extracts something from inside the plant. He delicately holds a piece of green paper as if it were a butterfly wing. "Fifty ducats." It's a fifty-dollar bill. Unbelievable. "Charter our party fund." He walks on his toes, giddy now, more with the discovering than the discovery, eager to "go exploring." He wants to follow the "real life" deer trail that Sylvan knows loops around the firehouse and leads back to student housing.

The trail winds down a hillside through a fern grotto, the glades brown-fringed and dry. The air gets dusky under a canopy of madrones, gauzy-lit, and smells like dried sap. Sylvan probably wouldn't have noticed but there's also a heavier scent, wet wool, from behind a charcoaled tree stump. A wild animal skeleton lies stretched out on its side, the flesh having sunk into the ground, where clusters of deathcaps feed on its compost. Hide and hair stick to the ribs and in tarry patches along the spine. The skull is pretty clean though, the teeth enamelly and predatorial.

"Bobcat. Didn't die of old age." Sylvan wouldn't mind saving the thing, reassembling it with wire, showing it off in his apartment. In fact, that's what he's going to do. "I gotta run back and get a bag to collect these bones."

"I'll hang here." Alabama squats and scribbles more notes on a folded syllabus.

It's dark before Sylvan has labeled each bone, bagged each paw separately, and numbered each rib and vertebra. While he finishes up, Alabama sits cross-legged under a tree and smokes. "Mama or papa cat?"

"Don't know."

"What do they eat?"

"Prairie dogs, jumping mice, lizards, stuff."

"How'd it die?"

"Don't want to know."

"Why not?"

"Don't know." Sylvan places the ziplocked bags inside a green tight-mesh net and puts that inside a backpack.

"Rubber gloves freak me out," Alabama says, watching Sylvan peel them off.

"I'm used to them from the lab. Give me those." He points to a couple of cigarettes Alabama has crushed out in the dirt. Even one butt would ruin *the basic mood* of the place. He crumples them up into the disposable rubber gloves and bags the whole mess.

"I would have offered to help."

"I know that," Sylvan says, glad Alabama didn't make him have to say no.

* * *

"Can't you make that look somehow normal?" Alabama asks.

Sylvan is boiling the bobcat skull and teeth in a soup kettle. He has already boiled the rest of the skeleton, and various bones are soaking in bleach trays set out on his bedroom floor.

"Monica's coming over." Alabama's spitting sunflower shells into an empty beer can.

"So?"

"She's a pretty girl." Girl, the way he says it, rhymes with virile. "I just don't want her to get the wrong impression."

"Then why disguise things?"

"She's bringing her roommate." Alabama winks. "Besides, it sorta stinks. How 'bout it? Make it look like soup."

Sylvan can't smell any stink, but Alabama's pinching his nose and fake-barfing. "All right, all right, it's soup." Why waste a chance to be a good roommate? He throws a clove of garlic, an onion, and some carrots into the pot. Curious how doing somebody a favor makes you like them more. Vegetables won't damage the bones in any way he can think of, and they'll make the apartment smell good.

"Boastable?" Alabama asks.

"What-able?"

He underhands Sylvan a beer, then "boasts" one himself from the stockpile of imports paid for with the "party-fund fifty-spot." Alabama has his own language. Last night he "bagged up" at bedtime, and this morning he "bogged down" in the bathroom. Anything undesirable is a "cheese product," and the opposite is "a wondra" or "a boon." When he's let down it's "much to my dismantlement," and he's fond of "-ism" and "-worth" as suffixes, so when he's hungry he's "munchworthy," and when he's philosophical, "that's lifism."

Now, while Sylvan stirs with a wooden spoon, Alabama

chants: "Double, double, toil and trouble, fire burn and cauldron bubble. Shakespeare. Now comes the good part. Cool it with baboon's blood, then the charm is firm and good." Alabama empties Sylvan's package of SEAWEED into the soup.

Fifteen minutes before nine, Alabama pump-sprays some mousse and runs an Ace comb—the fine-tooth black rubberized kind Sylvan used to carry in his back pocket before he stopped combing period—through his hopeless red hair. No two strands the same length, each hair has a different curl. The total effect is that of an exploded seedpod.

He pulls on a pair of turquoise cowboy boots, tucking in jeans that have a crease like a chalk line down each leg. With a sleeveless T-shirt finishing off the outfit, Alabama looks tight and together, and standing next to him, Sylvan feels tall, clunky, out of control in the elbows. Hard to believe he used to be a shrimp—the shortest person in the fourth grade, and fifth, and sixth, all the way up to high school, when he suddenly had a "growth spurt." Almost a foot in two years, leaving stretchmarks on his knees and hips. He spent most of those two years sleeping or eating multiple helpings of roast beef. Now he's more than six feet tall, sensitive in the ribs, always too hot or cold. He also has perpetually bruised shins from knocking them on lab stools, and he can't sleep on his side because of pointy hipbones.

Alabama caps the mousse. "You don't need any of this."

Sylvan's hair is curly and yellow and "too pretty for a boy," women (but thankfully not Phyllis) have told him all his life. His eyelashes are the same yellow, now bleached white from a summer above timberline, and he can see people looking at them instead of his eyes during conversations. Alabama may have the same problem with those reddish lashes, but at least his eyes themselves are darker—hazel with green specks, and on his right eye, a green fleck even outside his iris.

"What?" Alabama blinks rapidly. "Do I have a pimple or something?"

"Nothing." Sylvan looks down. His jeans are bunched at the knees and hips, they sag at the crotch, and the cuffs pile onto his hi-tops. Outdated and sloppy, but all clothes are like that on him. Except for cutoffs, anything he wears looks, somehow, borrowed. He takes a tooled leather belt from Alabama, who cautions him that vanity is the worst insecurity but running a tight ship is a different story, and tucks in an old Hang Ten shirt, red with thin white horizontal stripes. Less awkward-looking now, but still so damn tall. Why would Phyllis choose him? Unless she wants a geeky kid.

The windows are steaming up and the room's beginning to smell good.

"Home cooking," Alabama says as the doorbell rings.

Monica comes "via UCLA" and is here to do graduate studies in Comparative Lit, which, Sylvan thinks, is an airy thing to study. Real dissections of imaginary frogs. She has an ambassador for a dad, and a certain prettiness that turns to beauty in photographs. Snapshots are lying all over any available table, since Alabama somehow, and for some reason, persuaded her to go next door and bring back her photo albums. God knows why. He seems kind of hung up on Family.

Monica's roommate, Dawn, wants to talk politics, especially since it appears Monica has lived in more than a few geopolitical hot spots, but nobody's interested.

Here she is seven years old, eating papaya in Grenada. Here she is at fifteen riding a camel in the Sudan. And later, a seventeen-year-old standing on the White House steps with Dad and the president of Yemen. She acquires a strong jaw and cheekbones in the photographs that she doesn't have in real life, and her brown eyes look as if they're asking your name. Twenty-two and very right in a bikini.

"No brothers or sisters?" Alabama asks. She shakes her head no. "I got a whole slew of them." He looks at Sylvan. "Hear that, buddy? Three brothers and a sister. Expect visitors."

"I thought you said two brothers."

"Did I?" Alabama points to his own temple and shakes his head. Then he holds up a snapshot of Monica blowing out eleven birthday candles.

Damn. Sylvan remembers it was Emma's birthday last week. He always forgets hers, she never forgets his. And now that she's pregnant he wants to be extra nice to her, as if she were his younger, rather than older, sister. What could he get her? Baby spoons? A rattle or something? Or maybe something doctorish, since she's a full-fledged resident now.

"Mmmmm," Dawn says. "Smells good in here."

Sylvan watches Alabama force back a grin by concentrating on Monica's pictures. "All these exotic locales and you're not smiling in a single one."

She explains by smiling. Bulging cheeks, ears that tip back, one eye squinting shut. Goofy.

"Heavens," Alabama says, employing the accent. "Not your run-of-the-mill saycheeser."

She goes into a seizure of laughing—swallowing giggles and spraying a fine spit mist that everybody politely ignores, except for Alabama, who makes a show of wiping his cheek with the back of his hand. Now they all laugh, laughing at themselves for feeling bad about laughing at her.

But when the laughing stops, they all avoid each other's eyes.

"What's that high-pitched buzzing?" Monica asks. A thin, fried-sounding whistle comes from nowhere, everywhere, impossible to say how long it's been ringing before she noticed.

"It's the light." Sylvan points to the fixture on the ceiling.

"Smoke detector," Alabama says.

"Sure is loud," Dawn says.

"Why'd you make us all hear it?" Alabama asks.

"I couldn't stand to bear it alone," Monica says.

Dawn has the face of a dog straining at the end of its leash. She follows Sylvan into the kitchen, where he's going to get another round of beers and some chips. She's wearing denim down to the boots, which have pockets sewn over the ankles. A copy of *The Female Eunuch* by Germaine Greer sticks out of one. Dawn's a History of Consciousness student specializing in Women's Studies. Born and raised in Fresno, she moved to Santa Cruz because, she says, "It's an antenna for the country as a whole, the westernmost point on the frontier of Western civilization, picking up on the first tremors of new cultural zeitgeists."

In the other room, Sylvan can hear Monica saying something about "Bugs Bunny speaking Swahili." And Alabama saying, "In Nashville when it rains the sidewalks get foamy." Dawn meanwhile has Sylvan cornered while she explains her "White Blob Theory of Western Civilization." The white blob standing for men, virginity, the president's residence, sperm, the vast middle class for Chrissakes, everything powerful and oppressive. While she talks, the fingers of one hand pick at a janitor's key chain holding at least two dozen keys. "It's the subject of my dissertation."

"Congratulations." Sylvan can get away with saying this and not sounding mean. After all, she's right, in a way, about women getting the short end. He basically agrees with her. But just now he's thirsty and she's standing between him and the refrigerator. He squeezes past and takes out four beers, grabs a bag of chips off the counter, and walks back into the living room.

Monica is talking about growing up an only child, living in hotels or in houses just like them, sandbagged for protection against exploding trucks. The only thing to do was watch a lot of TV (emphasis on the T) and read. "I read *Peter Pan* in four languages."

"Wasn't Peter Pan allegedly murdered by a crazed individual right here in California?" Alabama asks.

It had been all over the newspapers during the summer. Peter Pan, age unknown, a San Francisco address. One of the casualties in a mass murder reminiscent of the Night Stalker, the Hillside Strangler, Helter Skelter, etc. This one involved videotaped tortures and meathooks. Sylvan doesn't want to laugh, but can't help it. The way things connect up is very strange.

"Murder capital of the world right here," Dawn says, referring to Santa Cruz's string of never solved ax murders, a series of hitchhiking dismemberments, and a psycho who went on a rampage with a homemade bazooka (six tennis-ball cans soldered together shooting wood screws and nails as shrapnel) at City Hall.

"But before I read *Peter Pan*," Monica is saying, off on her own track, "I always thought of grown-ups, who I spent a lot of time with, all of it really, as g-r-o-a-n u-p-s."

When Sylvan was four his father had brought home a red lump of hard plastic and put it on the kitchen table. It had ugly blue and yellow veins. This, Dad explained, was a heart. The size of your fist. Chunks of it pulled away, revealing, in cross section, ventricles, valves, the aorta. Not at all the heart Sylvan had pictured beating inside his own chest, a sweeter color red valentine that had nothing to do with blood. What a disappointment this was, the plastic human heart lying next to the salt and pepper shakers. What you had to look forward to in life.

"What's 'rimming'?" Alabama asks nobody in particular. He's pulled a safe-sex pamphlet out of a pile of books and papers on the floor next to the couch. "Oh, I see. 'Applying the tongue to the anus.' Considered unsafe."

Sylvan watches Monica and Dawn try to retain their composure. They do a good job of it, mainly keeping their eyes to themselves.

He wonders if there's anything in the pamphlet about artificial insemination. Safe unsex. Sylvan chuckles to himself, wishing somebody were here to share the joke, and wonders what Phyllis is doing. Is she still at work? What does she do in the evenings? What's her favorite food? Her sex life like? What *do* lesbians do? He should take a look at that pamphlet.

"I'll be." Alabama's crazy without being rude. He scratches an eyebrow. "Wouldya look at—hum, never would've thought of doing *that*. Imagine putting a telephone—forget it." A moment later he snaps shut the booklet. "Practically every kind of relations—even normal ones between consenting adults—is considered high-risk behavior."

Everybody looks down. It is impossible to be silent now without hearing that high-pitched buzzing.

"My, doesn't that soup smell wonderful," Dawn says. "Aren't you gentlemen going to offer us any?" She's pressing her fingertips down on the last crumbs of potato chips at the bottom of the bag. Anybody else, and this gesture would be endearing.

"Absolutely," Alabama says. "By all means. It'd be a pleasure. We would have already offered, but truth is, we haven't unpacked any bowls or spoons yet!"

He has to be joking, rubbing his stomach like that.

"Don't bother," Monica says. "We'll just go next door for them."

"More chips too," Dawn says. Even her eyes look denimy.

"What next? Open a can of Campbell's?" Sylvan asks. They'll be back in five minutes at most.

"She's fully me." Alabama is still looking at the door.

"You can't feed them that stuff. Make them sick." Though it probably won't. The skull, clean to begin with, has been boiling long enough to kill any bacteria, viruses, or single-celled etcet-eras that may have been malingering.

"What do you think of Ms. Denim?" Alabama asks. "She your type?"

"Include me out." Sylvan's beer is empty, but he lifts the can to his mouth anyway, and watches the skew fleck of iris drift across the white of Alabama's eye.

"What are you looking at?"

"Germs. Patches of hide. Clots of who knows what. Go ahead, eat it if you want, but I'm not having any." He settles back into the sofa. Maybe Alabama's bluffing. "Boast me."

"Dare me?" Alabama asks.

"Just throw me a beer."

Alabama tosses him one, and gets one for himself. He also takes out a head of broccoli and adds it to the pot along with salt and pepper. "Smells like heaven."

"Heaven is for dead people."

He slurps from a wooden spoon, dips for a carrot, brings it to his lips, blows on it, eats it. "Not bad. Needs a little more salt."

Watching, Sylvan's stomach growls.

"Did you see how I made her smile?"

"You're going to feed her that soup, aren't you?"

"She's hungry. I like her." Alabama can get away with it. They'll eat it and love it and never know the difference.

Sylvan remembers going fishing one time with his cousin Gary, who was six feet eight and big in every way. Sylvan was seven years old, a shrimp, and not having much luck, not having any luck with his line. So he went in search of a new spot. On the far side of the cove he found a foot-long catfish floating belly up in the shoals. He grabbed the fish and shook his wrist so it appeared to be wriggling violently. "Gary! Gary! Look! I caught it with my bare hands!" He ran towards his cousin, but just when he got close he fake-tripped and let the fish go flying. It splashed into the lake with a hollow plop. Fantastic, Gary had said. Bare-handed. But after being so easily faked out, or, worse, letting him get away with the lie, Gary seemed not so big anymore.

"You tell them or I will."

"Absolutely," Alabama says, smiling, displaying those sideways teeth, trustable.

Monica's got a box of Figurines and two crocks, and Dawn has chips and another pair of crocks. Sylvan does not like this pairing-up dynamic—Monica holding her own and Alabama's is okay, but Dawn holding hers and his is not. That everybody acts as if they don't notice makes it seem even more absurd, and slightly insidious.

"You girls have yourselves a sit," Alabama says, setting the coffee table. "I'll dish you some soup."

"Women," Dawn says.

"Pardon?"

"*Women*, not girls."

"Doesn't take special powers to see the obvious."

"It's just that we're not *girls* any more than you're *boys*."

Alabama sucks his bottom lip, considering. "How about 'faces'? Hey, Face. How's that?"

Monica changes the subject. She starts talking about the crickets and Indian summer, how outside the air smells like toast, which reminds her how hungry she is. She hands over the crocks and makes her eyes go like butterflies. "What kind of soup is it, anyway?"

"Bobcat," Alabama says.

"Hmmm," Monica says. "I think I had that once. Now I remember, at the World's Fair in Vancouver. Or maybe it was venison."

"Made with real bobcats?" Dawn asks.

"Don't worry," Alabama says. "They're not on the endangered list, are they, Syl?"

Sylvan catches up with Alabama in the kitchen. "Stop this."

"I told them the truth."

"No."

"What no?"

"No no."

"Dude." Alabama shakes his head and clicks his tongue. "I wouldn't serve them anything I wasn't eating myself."

"You're serious."

"A girl with a normal appetite is rare nowadays."

"You're—"

"I'm told people tell me I'm crazy."

Monica and Dawn come into the kitchen, ask if anything's the matter. "Can we be of help?"

"Sorry. Can't eat the soup," Sylvan says, uncrossing his arms, trying to look relaxed, like he knows what he's talking about without having to talk about it. A trick of body language he learned from Phyllis, the way she deals with a classroom of four-year-olds.

Monica's openmouthed, Dawn's stewed, and Alabama's examining a thumbnail. Nothing makes Sylvan feel worse than putting somebody under the gun, having to see them squirm. He'll do anything to prevent another person's humiliation. Alabama deserves this, though. Monica may hate him, but at least she'll see him for what he is.

"Because—" Sylvan says. "I made it special. It's mine."

Alabama smiles the smug smartass smile of a successful bluffer, the women collapse into bad posture, and Sylvan feels like the Bad Guy who's really the Good Guy. There's no way he can say anything now. About the bobcat skull, the real situation here (what kind of person would salvage a bobcat skull and then boil it with vegetables?). How nothing is the way it seems. How this kind of shit happens when a wrong impression gets out of hand.

"You coulda told us before," Monica whines.

Dawn says, "Finally, a man cooking, and he hogs it all for himself. It figures."

"All right, all right. Go ahead." Partly because they're being such whiners, but mainly because now he wants to see Alabama eat it.

"Yum!" Dawn says.

"Are you sure?" Monica asks.

"Absolutely." Shades of Alabama in that assurance.

Alabama himself now looks a little freaked. His lips are parted in an involuntary, barely perceptible sneer. And his eyes are wide.

"Really. Alabama'll dish it up for you."

They all sit around eating bobcat soup, except for Sylvan, who has poured himself only half a bowl and pretended to eat one spoonful. But even when Alabama gets to the bottom of his crock and is forced to accept seconds from the girls, so helpful, Sylvan can take no pleasure in the revenge. He's too old for this, should be moving past dorm-room pranks, past hanging out with people not of his choice. Toward doing exactly what he wants with people he can, well, call his own.

4 Sylvan Loses Control of His Face

I need a first sentence." Alabama holds a piece of paper against the hood while Sylvan rolls back the convertible top of the pink Corvair. "How about—'One must be plastic in one's understanding of Neorealism,' " he reads aloud as he writes. Even though they have both been up all night working on midterms, Alabama still hasn't finished his essay on Fellini's *8½*, a draft of which he has with him, along with the dictionary he reads every day the way some people read newspapers. "Or, 'In the analysis of film language, a picture generally *is*. But in Neorealism, a picture must *refer*.' " He looks up questioningly. "Nah. Curds and whey." Meaning cheese product, meaning he will scratch it out and start over.

Sylvan, on the other hand, has finished his assignment, a study of igneous rock, and when Alabama said he was motoring downtown to buy Wite-Out, Sylvan decided to come along for the ride. Fresh air feels good after being cooped up working all night. And after being cooped up with the kids at Tres Ojos before that, rain having kept Outdoors in. Sylvan had read aloud from *Bambi.*

"Phyllis brought up sperm donorship again." The fourth time in three weeks. After the second time, Sylvan had to tell somebody; Alabama was a pair of ears. "Said her 'biological alarm clock' is ticking away." The canvas top won't snap down. He tries forcing it; when he lets up, it stays in place.

"An opportunity not to be wasted," Alabama says. "Get your chromosomes out there and populate." His hair is wet-combed, actually parted on the left. Looks spring-loaded. He's got on his turquoise cowboy boots, purple houndstooth slacks, and a red flannel shirt. "But as long as you're going to knock her up, why not enjoy it?"

"Vulgarian," Sylvan says, not caring though, since he is done, and has the whole afternoon free, and it's sunny. He wears safari shorts and a T-shirt, no sweater on purpose, as if not bringing one is insurance the weather won't turn cold.

"Why'd she ask *you?*" Alabama tries to light the wrong end of a cigarette. "She know genius runs in your blood?" He's referring to Sylvan's great-great-grandfather who invented syncromesh. Who also discovered the tenth planet no astronomer since has been able to spot, and named it Dwanna. Alabama finally gets his cigarette lit and is removing a spot on the car's finish with his thumbnail. He loves his Corvair, calls it his Magic Car-pet. Once an old man pulled up alongside him at a red light and offered fifteen K, but Alabama told the guy he'd rather part with his left testicle.

"She hints around all the time, too. Asks me if I think frozen sperm goes stale."

"Falling in love behavior."

"She wants a baby, not a man," Sylvan says, liking the sound of it, but not quite convinced. She has been treating him differently, going out of her way to be nice to everybody else, then getting mad at him for no reason.

The car starts right up, as always, and, as always, Alabama

lets it idle awhile. This annoys Sylvan, sitting in a car with the engine running and not going anywhere. His life.

"You think it's just your jam she wants?" When Alabama's eyes are bloodshot, the green stands out, that skew fleck sparkling like a bottle chip.

"She lives with a woman named Sam."

Alabama flips through the pages of his Webster's, its pink fiber cover frazzling. "Lez-be-un. J, K, L, what do you think, wine dark sea, island teeming with toga-clad poetesses?"

"Dykes in work shirts and boys' haircuts more like."

"I've got some of 'em hard-core in my classes saying we should read more of their brand. Lesbian Fiction. Radical Feminist Verse." Alabama frowns to himself. "Genre, not the author, that matters to 'em. Plus they're always complaining."

"If you've got a belief structure, may as well go out and get it in print."

"Is that a mom-ism?"

"Static river, flowing bridge."

"Fuck you, I'm trying to say something here." Alabama gives up on the dictionary, rolls a kink out of his neck and tugs an earlobe. "How about 'The Redhead Experience'? Huh? How about that? We're a minority too, you know." Grumpy from no sleep, he's clicking and unclicking a pen into a spot between his eyes.

Staying up all night makes Sylvan light-headed. Colors have edges, and you can see the curve of the earth on the bay. A few nimbocumulus clouds, their bottoms flat as if they sit on an invisible shelf, cast shadows that move like schools of fish across the water. Beautiful. Just looking feels nutritious.

Alabama puts his pen to paper. " 'Does Truth reside in language or the real world?' " He pauses, studying it. Then drawls, "Cheese Whiz."

The wind has liberated Alabama's hair, and he hunches over the steering wheel, upshifting, downshifting, jiggling the broken "manual" blinker, and tapping his foot to some internal rhythm.

"You drive with your whole everything."

"You have B.O."

"You sound like my mom," Sylvan says. She gives him a bottle of Ban Roll-on every Christmas, and every New Year when he goes back to school he leaves it behind. Plugging up your pores is repression, he tells her. Now there are about six unopened bottles in the medicine cabinet. He tries to smell himself anyway.

"What are you going to tell her?" Alabama asks.

"Phyllis?"

"No, the Virgin Mary."

"No."

"No?"

"Yeah."

"That's better."

As they drive through the pasture, Sylvan spots El Toro. The bull is alone, fifty feet from the road, and seems to be looking right at him. The pair of golden eagles rides the thermals, circling the sky directly above the cave. The feeling passes.

At the red light at the campus exit Alabama waves to a pretty girl in tie-dye and haphazard braids selling produce from a donkey cart. One of the organic farmers who live in those tepees. Sylvan has heard all kinds of rumors—about harvest moon orgies and strange hippie sex rituals—which he now happily spreads to Alabama.

"Owdacious."

The pumpkins are bursting and orange, "thanksgivable," some plastered with bumper stickers. HUGS ARE BETTER ~~THAN~~ WITH DRUGS, and I'D RATHER BE GRATEFUL AND DEAD THAN STAYIN ALIVE, as well as the usual Nicaragua and No Nukes ones. They remind Sylvan of his high school days when he'd Scotch tape a Mothers Against Drunk Driving sticker—MADD—to the rear of his car as cop repellent.

"Sapient maneuver," Alabama says. "I'll try it sometime." The light changes and when he steps on the gas the glove compartment door springs open and a can of mousse and an anthology of Latin American fiction spill into Sylvan's lap, along with a box of rubbers, ribbed, "For the Feeling of Feeling in Love."

"Shouldn't keep them in here. They'll melt."

"More action than they'll get with me. Ha!" Alabama scribbles a note. "Speaking of which, what technology's involved?"

"Technology?"

"As in reproductive technologies. Test tubes, turkey basters, beating off into a bell jar, what?"

"If you're so interested I'll give her your number."

"It's the same as yours." Alabama readjusts the sideview mirror, throwing it a wry smile, then smooths an eyebrow in the rearview. Both mirrors are aimed at his face.

Downtown has crowds, gridlock even, a condition that should have ended with the tourist season a couple of months ago. Clusters of out-of-towners are jaywalking and pointing into store windows, the men in suits, the women in gowns all done up like desserts.

Alabama lays on the horn. "Who are these people?"

"There's a place."

"Curb's green. What's green mean?"

They decide it means pay money and keep searching, driving several blocks out of their way into a neighborhood of one-way streets and scaled-down Victorian houses, some with gingerbread trim and vegetable gardens, here and there stucco apartment complexes with palm trees growing in their chained-off parking lots. Sylvan spots an open space right along the curb beside the Duke Kahanamoku Community Center. Named after the famous surfer and Olympic gold medalist freestyler, the Duke Kahanamoku is an old adobe building, therefore not earthquake safe. The city council is making enemies trying to shut it down—The Only Place for the Poor and Now They Want to Close It kind of thing. One outside wall is covered with a giant mural depicting people of different ages and colors and creeds all in the act of painting the very scene they're part of. Beyond the wall is a huge grassy yard where there are picnickers, and a basketball court where a game is in progress.

As Alabama slows down, the game comes to a halt. Every player, all ten of them black men wearing shorts, stares. So do the bystanders, an additional fifteen or so teenagers huddled around a sprung La-Z-Boy and lawn chairs on the sidewalk, all drinking Big Gulps and listening to rap.

''Yo!'' says one of the largest players, a power forward whose neck is so thick it looks like his head is capping it off. ''Yo, Red!''

Alabama's hair is fully exploded now, very shiny in this autumny sunlight. Sylvan wishes Alabama would stop grinning and waving like some parade grand marshal. "Maybe we should keep moving."

"If we go much farther, we'll have to take a goddamn bus back into town." He jams it in reverse, begins to parallel park.

"Show ass, Red," the power forward says. The others, all twenty-five or thirty of them, gather behind him as he walks toward the car. Sylvan checks the park for allies. A group of kids and moms are having a barbecue and playing a game involving balloons and clapping. A circle of Rastafarians stand around a pair of congo drums under a magnolia tree where several bums are sleeping among newspapers and empty bottles. A skinny, bearded man wearing a series of robes is playing a ballad on a guitar, singing something that sounds like "Just because, oh, oh." And, finally, a bag lady who can't stop crossing herself.

"Fresh wheels," the shortest player says. He's a point guard, and has a T-shirt jacked up over a belly that jiggles.

"See, they like it," Alabama says in a low voice as the back tire chafes the curb.

"Like I say, fresh. You wanna keep it that way, Red, park somewheres else."

"I don't see a problem," Alabama says. But Sylvan does, and fights an urge to sink down in the seat as more than two dozen black people circle the car.

"Boy, this be Maximus Loach's personal parking place," the power forward says, voice like a record played at sixteen. His arms are thicker than Sylvan's thighs.

"Now I don't have no problem with you, Red," the guard says, scratching his bellybutton. "I like a honky drive a rig like this." He runs a finger along the rear fender. "But parkin here be askin for shit."

"Am I mistaken or is this a city street?" Alabama finishes off the parking job with a whip of the wheel. Very effective bluffing, or very foolish behavior, Sylvan can't decide which.

"You gotta hearing problem or you just want your face totaled?" the power forward croaks, head and neck covered with thousands of tiny drops of sweat, as if the threat in the air were condensing there.

"Finders keepers, man."

"Are you insane?" Sylvan whispers. "Let's get outta here."

When Alabama makes no move to leave, twenty men search the car for handholds. "Consider we be doin you a favor." They lift the car. Unbelievable. Sylvan looks around, down. Kids clapping for balloons. Rastas getting stoned. Aging hippie singing, "Just because, always was, oh, oh." No help there.

The Corvair bobs like a rowboat as they carry it across the street. Sylvan feels he should sit still, that if he moves sharply he may cause the weight of the car to shift, throwing somebody off balance, and even if they are his enemies, he doesn't want anyone crushed.

Alabama, on the other hand, screams, *"Put me down!"* Then, *"Bootlickers. Knobtwisters. Who—"*

Just then a lime-green Cougar, jacked up and with chrome

headers, squeals around the corner and blows a horn that plays two bars of "Yankee Doodle." It pulls into the just-vacated parking spot. On each mudflap Yosemite Sam holds up a pair of flintlock pistols, BACK OFF. A black man gets out. He's wearing shorts too tight, a Hawaiian shirt with sea turtles on it, and three gold ropes around his neck. "Niggers, put them boys down. Car is not an aeroplane."

"Orange Julius here tried to snake your turf," the guard says, pulling at his flabby paunch. "Him and Goldilocks."

Sylvan's mad now, maybe because he's been bossed too much, maybe because now that the car has landed safely he knows they're out of danger. "But Jellyroll here thinks he's the parking commissioner."

The guard with the gut makes a move but the man who has just arrived stops him with a wave that turns everybody into The Audience—the other players, the picnickers in the park, even the Rastas, one of whom is walking over gimp-legged, together with the lady who keeps crossing herself.

"I—I was parked there," Alabama stutters. It's as if he and Sylvan switched circuits, now he's the scared one.

"Do I know you?" the man asks. He claps once and the power forward passes him the basketball. "I'm Maximus. Maximus Loach." He has gerricurled his hair so heavily it looks like shiny black meringue, and his brow seems to be melting into a permanent frown over familiar eyes.

"Al-abama," he says, flustered by the way Maximus Loach clasps, shakes, then slaps his hand. "Pleasure. But there's no law saying I can't park—"

"It's no law, Al," Maximus Loach says, dribbling now, between the legs, behind the back. "It's an imperative of awareness." He has a linebacker's body going soft, sausagey puckers at the hem of his shorts, the lower buttons on his shirt crabbing. A fat man deft with a basketball is an oxymoron, and Sylvan watches carefully to discover his trick.

"Think quick."

Sylvan barely catches a bounce pass off the left tail fin, and

Maximus Loach laughs. Liking him, Sylvan introduces himself, trying to remember the three-step handshake from the last time he used it back in grammar school.

"I remember y'all." Maximus Loach high-fives him instead and swipes back the basketball. "L M N O P?"

What is that supposed to mean?

"You don't remember me?"

A question he doesn't want to answer wrong, too much at stake, though he isn't sure exactly what.

"Beaujolais." Maximus Loach nods, his large head swiveling on two rubbery rolls that sandwich the gold chains at the back of his neck.

"Maximus speak frog," Jellyroll says.

Somebody from his dad's winery? Who? He does look familiar, the way the frown and smile sort of overlap.

The Rastaman limps up. He's not really a Rasta. Skin several shades darker than Maximus Loach's, eyes barely visible through red-and-green-beaded dreadlocks, his ethnic background remains uncertain. He looks brittle in baggy red drawstring pants, and around his neck he wears a string of things, maybe molars and seedpods and dried apricots, and definitely a miniature Old Testament. Stuff Sylvan wouldn't mind adding to his Museum of Natural History in a wine crate. The bag lady is one step behind. Her face has cellulite and she just keeps crossing herself.

"You'll wanna leave them fellas be if intentions have a say inna world," he says.

"Simba, shut the fuck up," Maximus Loach says. "Why you always button your head where it don't belong?"

"Coolify." Simba flips hair out of his eyes, the red and green beads clattering. "Fellas mean no harm. Here you startin off karmic chains thyself." A Caribbean lilt to his voice. He takes the bag lady's arm. "Idn't that right, Lady Light?"

She crosses herself and says, "I yo-yo. You yo-yo. My weight yo-yos."

"Your head look like a baby rattle," Maximus Loach tells Simba.

"The man has no cosmo politan," Simba says, a warm, dry handshake for Sylvan. The halfmoons of his fingernails are the same yellow as the whites of his eyes. Stepping back, he puts all his weight on the good leg and quickly rolls a fat joint using two leopard-skin papers.

"Spleefbrain." Maximus Loach dribbles the ball, the bounce echoing off the adobe of the Duke Kahanamoku.

"Open you up like a door, my friend." He seals the joint by licking it.

"Simba named himself after a soft drink named after a lion," Maximus Loach says. "He don't know he just another nigger." His use of *nigger,* a choosing up of teams and making himself captain, doesn't work on Simba.

"If a name idn't given, a name mistaken," Simba says. Sylvan's mom would like this guy. "The Lord give me mine and I stay with the song. Where you get yours, Maximus?"

"From my mama, same as everybody regula."

"Not him," Sylvan says, nodding towards Alabama, who is writing furiously, *a thing refers to a thing, or a thing refers to itself, both when—* in the margins of his essay. "He was named after a state."

"State a shock by the looka his shag."

"No, 'Alabama,' " Sylvan says for Simba's benefit. Alabama keeps his head down, not writing anymore but folding and refolding the paper. In front of anybody else, a girl especially, he'd take the spotlight and ham wildly. But now, no longer scared, he looks kind of squeezed out.

Simba passes Sylvan the joint and he takes a long hit—why not? Hasn't got stoned in months, a reward for pulling a successful all-nighter. He takes another. The pot tastes sweet, like burning pineapple, expanding inside, and it occurs to him that all four of them—Maximus Loach, Alabama Thoburn Downs Whitaker III, Simba, and Sylvan Park—have odd names, and an incredible range of skin colors, eyes, and noses. "We coulda stepped out of that mural," he says, immediately sorry that he opened his mouth.

Everybody looks over, examining it. Maximus Loach stops the dribble, Alabama cups the joint, Simba picks his nose with a pinkie fingernail and says, "Who the one minus the face?"

A figure in the mural has been literally defaced with a cloud of green spraypaint. Other than that, the scene is clean, graffiti free, except for a symbol in the far corner that can't decide whether it's an anarchy or peace sign.

A group of women comes marching down the street: they're topless. The breasts get everybody staring. Some pale, some pink, some floppy and blue-veined, some perky-nippled and tan, but all of them somehow fragile-looking in the sunshine. They bob and sway a half-second off the march step, giving the illusion (Sylvan's high is building) of syncopation.

"Am I havin a mirage or am I seein things?" Maximus Loach asks.

Alabama coughs up his hit and a look of pain crosses his face, then changes to mischievous. Sylvan's own face is taking over now too, a grin so big he can feel the sun on his teeth.

A muscled woman with high, tight breasts and a yellow mohawk aims a megaphone at the Corvair and, in a voice crackling with static, shouts, "Protest the objectification of women!" Another with breasts that nosedive is holding a placard that says NO MORE PROFITS OFF WOMEN'S BODIES. Still another's says, GIRLCOTT MISS GOLDEN STATE. "At the Greek, *now!!*"

"Great body on Yellow Mohawk," says Alabama, becoming more himself, smoothing down his hair with both hands.

"And a face to protect it." Maximus Loach licks his fingers, pinches out the roach, and swallows it.

The players on the court whistle and yell crude things. Children look up from their hot dogs while their mothers decide on explanations. The Rastas provide a drumroll and the bag lady at last gives up crossing herself.

"Let's join with the ladies," Simba says, and swings his bad leg over the car door to slide into the backseat. Sylvan wonders if smoking a lot of pot is what makes the whites of his eyes so keratinous. And what are those things clicking on his necklace?

"Caracol," Simba says, tugging at one. "Foot of the conch. You know the conch?"

Sylvan shakes his head yes, meaning no; he wants it to add to his museum.

"From the Caribe. I eat a ceviche with this one." He unstrings it and hands it over. "Yours. Now you got conchness. Ha ha!"

A rush of gratitude makes Sylvan feel he is moving very fast.

"Get out," Alabama says. "Please."

But Maximus Loach jumps in.

"Come on, you guys. Out. We have things to do." If you didn't speak the language you'd think he was asking directions.

"Slow up, Alabamamon. What thing exists onna planet can't ride awhile?"

"I've been up all night working, gimme a break." But he looks fresh, maybe the pot has rejuvenated him. He strikes a match to a cigarette, the right end this time. "We have to go to the store."

"What for?" Maximus Loach is standing tiptoe in the backseat, shielding the sun with the basketball better to watch the topless women. The sea turtles on his shirt are swimming.

"Wite-Out."

"Figures. The shit runs in their blood." Maximus Loach laughs.

"Go, mon."

Alabama's eyes come seeking, but Sylvan just can't stop grinning.

"My man!" Maximus Loach slaps his shoulder, massages it. "Mr. Beaujolais. Still pretendin you don't remember me?"

Sylvan nods.

Alabama starts up the car, idles it.

The sky is so clear, the magnolia leaves green wax, melty-edged, and the last woman marcher has the hugest boobs Sylvan has ever seen. He sits up straight, avoiding the glassy distortion of the windshield for a better view. Once he read in a physics text that glass is really a liquid, the ripple a result of time and gravity, and this windshield is older than he is. But the glassy distortion, he suddenly realizes, isn't in the glass at all, but somewhere between his eyes and brain.

The woman turns and cups her mouth and shouts something unintelligible, causing her breasts to bounce in opposite directions. She should be able to go shirtless same as any man. If you saw tits every day, in parks, on sidewalks, in lines at the bank, they would be no big deal. But as it is, looking, no, just wanting a look, makes Sylvan feel guilty, besmirched and besmirching.

"I'd like to bury my pecker to the hilt between those mamas," Maximus Loach says.

Police have barricaded the street in front of the Greek Auditorium for the Miss Golden State Parade. Hundreds of pageant-goers—the dressed up out-of-towners Sylvan and Alabama earlier had been unable to place—stand on one sidewalk, and on the other, across the street, stand hundreds of demonstrators, including the topless marchers and a woman wearing a box of Kellogg's Porn Flakes. A TV crew is setting up next to a bleacher sectioned off for the Ladies' Auxiliary Brass Band.

A cop waves Alabama on.

"Sorry, guys, party's over. Have to get out now."

But Maximus Loach says, "Stop here," and gets out to swing a police sawhorse over. Alabama sighs but takes the spot.

"Ringside," Sylvan says, now feeling responsible for Alabama having a good time. "Maximus Loach, parking kingpin."

Yellow Mohawk shouts through her megaphone: "A lot of

you are probably wondering why I'm not wearing a shirt. Well, it's a gorgeous day and I want a tan." A round of polite laughter. "We women have been hotwaxed, frosted, pierced, airbrushed, siliconized, tweezed, cellophaned, starved, and penetrated long enough!" Clapping like the first kernels of popcorn popping.

"Arson of the voice," Simba says, shaking his head gravely.

"The Red Hourglass Network is sponsoring the *Myth* Golden State Protest today to challenge the false ideal of womanly beauty being perpetrated on us by the major American corporations sponsoring the event across the street." Full-blown applause now, and more women taking off their shirts, chanting: WE NEED, WE NEED, WE NEED OUR BODIES FREED.

The chant takes Sylvan back in time, several years, to Loquat Junior High School, where during PE he used to watch the girls in their boxy blue gymsuits chanting WE MUST, WE MUST, WE MUST IMPROVE OUR BUST; FOR FEAR, FOR FEAR, THE BOYS WILL NOT COME NEAR. "The bigger, the better, the tighter the sweater, the boys depend on us."

"Say what, Mr. Beaujolais?"

"What the chant used to be."

A balding man in a sky-blue tuxedo says, "It appears there's a group of women against Beauty." The woman on his arm, in matching sky-blue eyeshadow, says, "Sour grapes. If I was a dog, I'd be a feminist too."

"Take it off!" a group of fraternity types yells. They're all wearing T-shirts that say BIG GUY, and have their own chant: TAKE IT OFF, TAKE IT ALL OFF.

Suddenly Alabama is honking the horn. "Face! Over here! Hey, Face! It's you!" He waves to Dawn, their next-door neighbor, who's crossing the street in front of the car. Sylvan barely recognizes her under all that white powder and black lipstick. Plus she's topless, one breast upturned and angry looking, the other hidden by a sash lettered MISS UNDERSTANDING. And she has chained herself to a bathroom scale.

"Been ages," Alabama says. "You look thin." Dawn's ribs

stick out, and neck tendons make a V where they meet at the collarbone. "Lose some weight?"

"Nah. I can still pinch an inch easy." She pulls at the skin on her belly.

"Where's Monica?"

"Oh, she's around. I had to drag her down."

Alabama scouts the crowd, hoping, hopeless. "Kissing her was like kissing toast," he'd told Sylvan the day he came home dazed from their one and only romp. "She put the zap on my head." Days, weeks later he was still obsessed. "I'm a little concerned at how concerned I am." Now the way he's looking over his shoulder for her is borderline pathetic.

"Wow, do you look stoned." Dawn's black lips make her teeth too white, the tip of her tongue like something plucked. "Hey, Spaceman."

It takes Sylvan a moment before he realizes she's talking to him. He grins.

"Are you guys here for the protest?" Those denimy eyes shift from Sylvan to Maximus Loach to Simba to Alabama. "Or kicks?"

"Neither and both." Simba introduces himself. "Why you shackled to the Sunbeam?"

Alabama is writing again.

"Eating disorders," she says, drawing blank looks. "The sub-theme of the Myth Golden State Protest." Still no response. She gestures with the bathroom scale; a bicycle lock holds it to an extra-large bangle on her wrist. "Some of us feel"—fighting a smile—"I don't know why I'm . . . it's not funny. I feel that a lot of women have low self-esteem because we can't compete with the svelte blondes in *Vogue*, and—"

"Compete?" Maximus Loach breaks her off. "Young lady like yoself already got em half beat."

Dawn makes a face like she is chewing sand. "So we don't eat. Or we eat like pigs, then go throw up."

Sylvan wonders if that's what she does. He remembers her being awfully gung ho about that bobcat soup. And Monica was the one who brought over the Figurines. Adonis, though, has them both beat when it comes to eating disorders. At Tres Ojos he eats scabs and banana slugs and takes stuff out of the garbage after other kids have scraped their plates.

"Number one problem with White Man," Simba says, yellow fingernails scratching his patchy beard. "And Woman." A gracious bow of the head toward Dawn. "He fraida his body and prouda his pain."

"What you lookin at?" Maximus Loach is both grinning and frowning. He looks like Buddha would look, Sylvan decides, if Buddha were a gargoyle. "Beginnin to recognize me, Mr. Beaujolais?"

"Napa Park Winery?"

"Who dat?" Maximus Loach, still in the backseat, dribbles the basketball on the street. "Try rattlersnakes in the campershell, along with a lady half naked." He nods and his neck rolls squish out. "You get me?"

Oh, oh yeah. Sylvan more than gets him. About three years ago, when he was a freshman, Sylvan borrowed his dad's pickup, the winery service vehicle, and asked his lab partner Laura to go to Yosemite for the weekend, check out Half Dome. The last night there she convinced him to tap the small cask of Beaujolais left in the campershell. Drinking wine led to Truth or Dare. Remembering makes his face get hot.

"The man's got a case a boilover!" Maximus Loach says. "Them cheeks!"

When Sylvan chose Truth, Laura, wearing only a bikini and thick glasses, asked him how old he was the first time he came. Then about wet dreams. This line of questioning seemed to be going all the way to the one Sylvan, then eighteen, didn't want to answer. Embarrassing now that it embarrassed him then. So he chose Dare.

She made him climb.

Bouldering under a smeary half moon. It wasn't a big rock,

open book maybe twenty feet till he came to an overhand, five-four tops, not that hard. Still, stupid to be doing it drunk. He stopped for breath and looked down. Laura was fully naked now, glowing white. What the hell. Legging up was no problem, and the beauty of it was that from this shelf he could fistjam a crevice seven feet home. But as soon as he put his hand in the crack he heard a tickaticka noise that sobered. Rattlesnake. He scrambled up, faster than going down, recklessly clawing rock to the top, where he stood and tried to control the shivering, granite somehow friendly under his feet, friendly because the same old take-it-for-granted granite.

On the way home, a tapped wine cask and a box of rattlesnakes in the back (there were two, and he had trapped them both in a shoebox so he could do studies in the lab), Laura made good on a dare owed. She was kind of pretty without her glasses, but as he remembers it, his imagination plays a strange trick on him, assigning her Phyllis's face. Laura's won't come back to him at all. Memory is weird that way, and loses credibility. Anyway, Laura (now with Phyllis's wide cheekbones, blondish hair, and green eyes) took off her glasses, then tugged his shorts to his knees and went down on him. He came quickly, explosively, messily, then smashed into the car stopped at a red light in front of him.

"Sylvan here was caught with his pants down," Maximus Loach is telling the story. "And when the Law rolls up, the girl be slappin at her boobs goin all sterical, wine smellin like vinegar. I says, 'Get her in the back, throw everything under the tarp, and leave Adam Twelve to me.' " He laughs. "I be feelin sorry for him."

Sylvan watched from behind the windshield as Maximus Loach gave the California Highway Patrol officer an extremely long tour of the Cougar, purple then.

"First time ever I didn't have no illegal substances on my person or property." Maximus Loach is palpating the basketball. "Damn straight I'm gonna toy with The Man."

When the patrolman finally got to him, Sylvan had his shorts on, and everything incriminating, including Laura, was under the tarp. And, as he remembers it, he even had the MADD sticker taped to the back bumper. But the cop made Sylvan walk a line anyway, touch his nose, and say the alphabet backwards, a test he couldn't pass unless he sang it first. Maximus Loach heard him singing his ABCs and laughed, really laughed, laughed so hard Sylvan started laughing, the air in his lungs turning rubber because then even the cop began chuckling.

"*Sssssshhhhh!*" In the middle of the street is a woman—Teo's mother, Sam!—wearing a silver crown and a gown made of lunchmeat. Sam! Sylvan recognizes her instantly, despite the Bride of Frankenstein hairdo. Phyllis might be here too. He scans faces quickly. If she is here, he prays, please don't be dressed in cold cuts.

"Wondra." Alabama is unconsciously rubbing his stomach. But when Sylvan tells him she is the Sam of Phyllis & Sam, he's crushed. "Such beauty, wasted."

Sam's crown sparkles and her sash says MISS TREAT. Yellow Mohawk, now MS. OGYNIST, approaches her and they kiss cheeks but exchange only a few words before Yellow Mohawk wipes her forehead with the megaphone and starts screaming. "Should have *consulted . . .* you are not *cooperating.* Just *go.*"

And Sam, "If I *can't dance,* I won't join *your revolution.*"

"She's coming this way," Alabama says, checking his reflection in the rearview.

The Ladies' Auxiliary Brass Band breaks into "When the Saints Go Marching In," and then trails off mid-phrase.

"Is that smile for us?" Maximus Loach asks, spinning the basketball faster and faster on two fingers, half showing off, half nervous habit.

"Whose praise she after?" Simba asks.

Dawn opens her mouth, rolls her eyes, and shakes her head from side to side.

Sam comes up to the car as if she hired it. "Hey there, Sylvan." Again, he is surprised by her eyes, actually violet like something tropical, extra bright under dark lashes. You can see

Teo in them, and in the nose and something else . . . the shape of the head. Sam has a nicely shaped head. She leans over and kisses his cheek. Strange.

"Where's Phyllis?" he asks.

"The wallflower," Sam says, as if it's an endearment. "She's at home."

In a way he's glad.

"I'd like to meet your friends."

Everybody is deeply impressed—except for Dawn, who's grunting her disapproval—that Sam and Sylvan seem to be good friends. The introductions remind him of the mural, and cost an enormous amount of energy, the lack of sleep creeping up.

"Absolutely stunning ensemble," Simba says.

The dress is knee-length, sleeveless—slices of bologna and salami, turkey roll, baked ham, liverwurst, and pimento loaf are threaded together in a scallop motif—and set off by a hot-dog belt. Looks pretty good, everything but the pimento loaf, and despite the earlier talk of eating disorders, it gives Sylvan the munchies. That's what he needs, food.

Sam models, turning on black spikes. Tan legs, hair there unshaven but sunbleached, shapely calves. She obviously has a nice body underneath that dress, which somebody could have fun unpeeling, slice by slice.

"What a second-rate imitator," Dawn mutters. "You're nothing but an Ann Simonton rip-off. She's the original Miss Steak, ya know!" As she stomps off, Sam shrugs.

"Phyllis sure knows how to pick 'em," Alabama says, changing the subject Southern style, charm incarnate. "I've heard so much about you."

Sylvan suddenly wonders how much Sam knows about the sperm donorship thing, and he wants to keep a careful eye on her for signs, but can't muster the energy. Too hungry and tired.

"You picked a winner here," she says. "Corvair's a beaut."

"My Magic Car-pet."

Simba has another joint going. *"S'il vous plaît,* come along onna magic carpet ride?"

She surprises everybody by saying "I'd love to," and taking a hit of pot.

Maximus Loach opens the back door for her. "Oooh. Some pair of eyes." She has to move delicately to keep the dress from tearing, and stays standing in the backseat, where she explains how the parade, which she wants to spoof, will start any minute, and what better car than this pink Corvair for spoof potential. "That is, if it's okay with you guys."

"Why should I?" Alabama says.

Maximus Loach and Simba jump on his back. "Aww." "You know you want to." "Come on, Al."

He sighs twice, then grins. "All right."

Sylvan is coming down with the yawns, each blink sticking a little longer, so when the ganja comes his way he takes two hits to wake up and three more for the show.

There are new arrivals to the protest: The Lesbian Thespians, including Miss Behavin, Miss Stress, and Miss Chief, all topless. And a group of shish kebabs—women wearing costumes made to look like chunks of skewered meat—jumping up and down on pogo sticks. Also a group of women wearing black leather and riding Suzukis, Dykes on Bikes. And about a dozen men looking fresh from the gym—just showered, overtrimmed mustaches—carrying a banner MEN AGAINST RAPE.

"They cream puffs or what?" Maximus Loach asks.

"I thought fudgepackers liked it rough," Alabama says.

"They mean women. Against the rape of women," Sam says. "And they're not . . . fudgepackers. Most of them aren't even gay."

"It says in here *rape* used to mean *turnip.*" Alabama has his Webster's open.

One of the Men Against Rape is shouting through a cone: "Stop Rape! Stop Rape!"

An easy thing to be against, Sylvan thinks. Nobody's going to come out in public pro-rape. What does rape have to do with a beauty pageant anyway? "I don't get the logic here."

"The logic of Neorealism." Alabama's writing again, as if he concentrates with his lips, puckering them like a monkey. There are freckles on the rim of his ear. Funny how you can live with somebody three months and then suddenly see him as a chimpanzee.

"Phyllis talks about you." Sam bends into the front seat, close. "She admires you." Her voice is practically a whisper. "And we both would love to have you over for dinner." Sylvan pictures a table set with china, napkins specially folded, gravy boats and sugar bowls, a carefully phrased proposal.

Alabama elbows him in the ribs. "No secrets allowed."

Sylvan grabs the elbow, probes with his thumb for the funnybone, knows he's got it when Alabama yanks back his arm, shakes it out, and, predictably unpredictable, asks Sam, "Are you Phyllis's agent in this issue of sperm donorship?"

Her earrings are mother-of-pearl lightning bolts. "We haven't decided yet which one of us is going to carry."

This can't be, Sylvan thinks. Phyllis would have mentioned it. Wouldn't she? Have?

Yellow Mohawk, screaming herself hoarse through the megaphone, kneels before a toilet bowl mounted on a plywood platform. "One in three women suffers from an eating disorder . . . anorexia . . . binging and purging . . . crash diets. They've convinced us we're fat. I'm here to tell you *fatness* is a state of mind!"

Maximus Loach shakes his head on those rubbery neck rolls. "My mama be two-hunnert-fifty pounder and that ain't *no* state of mind."

"That's Aja," Sam says. "She's angry. And a separatist." She explains that they used to be friends before the Hourglass Network (shaping a woman's figure in the air with her hands) went Red, and how Aja thinks women should withhold sex, therefore jeopardizing the continuation of the species, until men agree to change.

Black widows have red hourglasses on their underbellies; Sylvan gets it. The obvious point. Strange coincidence, though, that Sam is a widow herself. And poor Teo's fatherless. Both because of that great white. Hungry shark. Imagine the hugeness of appetite.

"She must get along with the Men Against Rape," Alabama says.

"She doesn't really get along with anybody."

"I will now do a public vomiting." Aja puts down her megaphone, crouches over the porcelain bowl, sticks her pointer finger down her throat, and vomits up what looks like M&M's.

"Sickness," Simba says, fingering the Old Testament on his neck. "Hatred got a hold on her."

"You have no idea," Sam says. "This goes on every day."

Maybe so, but it's still nauseating, and Sylvan smells, or imagines smelling, vomit. Watching Aja's ribs tense as she heaves, it occurs to him that she is living up to her title, a true Ms. Ogynist.

The color guard fires off a round of blanks, puffs of smoke preceding the rifle crackle, to start off the parade. The beauty queens, sitting atop expensive convertibles, look like copies of people already famous. Miss Redlands is a sanitized Madonna and Miss Sacramento an overinflated Christie Brinkley. Sylvan wonders what they think, being at the eye of the hurricane, so to speak, but then they don't look like they're thinking too hard about it, waving and smiling as if everybody had an Instamatic for eyes. Miss Oakland looks like Eddie Murphy and blows Aja a kiss.

"Gentlemen, start your engines." Sam flips back her kinky black hair, streaked white at the delicate temple whorls, and adjusts her crown. Probably the only time in his life Alabama doesn't warm up the car. He drives around the block and, honking at the Horatio High School Marching Band kids all doing funky leg kicks and mercy-lord flourishes, bullies his way into the parade.

When the pink Corvair, with Sam standing in the backseat wearing her lunchmeat gown, turns the corner to follow Miss Van Nuys's Cadillac, the Men Against Rape whoop. The Ladies' Auxiliary Brass Band plays "Dixie." The Dykes on Bikes kick-start their Suzukis and fall in line.

On the other side of the street, Tuxedoman's wife screams, "Ya oughtta be ashamed!" The five guys wearing BIG GUY T-shirts howl, one of them shouting, "Hey, Miss Treat, as long as I gotta face, you gotta place to sit!" Police chatter into walkie-talkies and start to mobilize. Sam waves and blows kisses.

Somebody throws an egg.

It splatters on Alabama's forehead, and he jams the car in park and gets out, stopping the parade. He's an eyeful in his purple houndstooth slacks tucked into turquoise cowboy boots, red plaid shirt clashing with a head of orange cowlicks, and gooey yolk dripping in his face. Maximus Loach jumps out of the car and wraps a burly arm around him. "Easy there, Al. Easy." Then, noticing Alabama's turquoise cowboy boots, says, "Shit, them are nice." Alabama has just risen several notches in Maximus Loach's eyes. He turns and, in the direction of the Big Guy who probably threw the egg, growls, "Cut that shit out! We trying to be peace-loving here!"

Sylvan notices Monica standing among the Big Guys. The bitch! She pretends to be invisible by closing her eyes and shrinking back into the crowd, but it's too late. Hanging out with the enemy. Why?

Alabama has seen her too. He is extremely humiliated. But compensates for it by clenching his jaw and rubbing a fist.

"Go home, nigger!" a Big Guy shouts. He's wearing a 49ers cap and his face looks boiled and peeled. With great effort, Maximus Loach ignores the comment.

"Niggers, dykes, fags, all o ya," Boiled Face yells. "Don't you know this is America?"

The Men Against Rape start across the street, backup. The Dykes on Bikes turn their Suzukis around and pull their leather gloves snug.

"Stay back!" Boiled Face screams. "Don't want no AIDS!"

Beer bottles and garbage fly. A police van, siren blipping, pulls in and unloads a dozen or so cops wearing helmets and carrying Plexiglas shields. The crowd quickly quiets as the riot squad lines up to form a border between enemy camps.

Maximus Loach escorts Alabama back to the car, where he tries to mop Alabama's brow with a page from his essay. Alabama looks about to cry.

Sylvan puts a hand on his shoulder. "You okay?"

Suddenly the press zeroes in on the Corvair, a TV reporter asks Sam for a statement. "If I can give just one person a moment of happiness," she says, impersonating a contestant, "I will have made the world a better place." Electronic camera flashes, hands sticking microphones in the car, faces pushing through faces.

Every gesture Sam makes now carries more weight. When she raises her arm to straighten her crown, the jewels scatter tiny rainbows. Sylvan suddenly envies her charisma. And the others, they all have something. Simba's Bible necklace, Maximus Loach's parking spot, Alabama's dictionary, even Aja, who at least believes something's worth a fight. But for Sylvan, being in the passenger seat is like being an extra in a film, just along for the ride. Shallow and thrill-mad, committed to nothing and tolerant of everything. Like that kid in the mural without a face.

"Hey, where are you going?" Alabama asks. His eyes are slightly pinched, maybe holding back tears, maybe realizing people are biological organisms, Monica included, and no amount of romance can stand up to that loneliness.

"Shopping." Sylvan shuts the car door and pushes his way through the crowd.

"Did you remember Wite-Out?" Alabama wants to know. The dictionary on his lap is opened to the L's. Love?

"Forgot." Sylvan has returned carrying a brown grocery sack on one arm just as the cops, wearing yellow rubber gloves, have begun arresting the Men Against Rape, prompting Simba to suggest, "Time we make an exodus."

They drive to the seashore and park at the end of the wharf. The roller coaster lights go on and a stiff wind is raising white-caps far out on the bay where the horizon is squiggly, the sun going down hot. Sea gulls cry and circle Sam. The lunchmeat.

"That cloud is a perfect example . . ." Sylvan blurts. "It looks like the Grand Canyon." Fatigue gone, the fresh air and more marijuana have left him clear-headed, almost extrasensory, and full of undirected generosity. "But you can't own a moment."

"Good to see you feelin aligned with yourself again," Simba says.

"Why'd you go off all in a huff, anyhow?" Maximus Loach asks.

Sylvan watches Alabama write: . . . *call it real life, and in film, it is.* Sylvan asks, "Anybody besides me hungry?"

Alabama looks up. "I'm a munchworth."

"Eat a goddamn supermarket," Maximus Loach says, and puts down his basketball in anticipation.

Sylvan pulls out a bottle of Napa Park champagne. "For the real winner, Myth Golden State."

"I want to thank you all so much," Sam says, faking a gush. "No, really," getting serious. "Thank you."

"Maybe our motives were selfish," Alabama cackles.

Sylvan is struggling with the cork when he notices Sam looking at him funny. Those violet eyes. That Bride of Frankenstein hairdo. Sperm donorship? Never. Even if it would make him Teo's . . . sperm uncle. But if she came asking naked would he turn her down? Those eyes, looking at him like she's reading his thoughts. He suddenly feels exposed. But then she winks, a challenge. She's daring him to resist her, *him*, not Alabama, not Maximus Loach, not Simba, all more than willing donors. She's wearing that crown and that dress for him, and he isn't sure why.

The cork blasts off, scattering the sea gulls.

"Food." Maximus Loach takes the bottle from Sylvan, guzzles, and passes it to Alabama.

Sylvan unpacks his brown paper sack: rolls, mustard and mayo, tomatoes, sprouts, Swiss cheese, potato chips, and five pickles wrapped in butcher paper.

Champagne spills down Sam's chin when she realizes they are going to make sandwiches out of her dress.

"I got it," Alabama practically whispers. He fumbles enthusiastically with his pen. "Reality, really the real reality, is not attended to in Neorealism."

5 Good for Goodness' Sake

A pretty girl is a public fantasy. Sylvan watches Sam in the doorway, backlit, her hair a purplish halo. She wears green and black, no zippers or buttons, Star Trek clothes that accentuate her loose shoulders and nicely shaped head. He feels, looking, as if he discovered her. Anyone would.

"Merry Christmas," she says, kissing his cheek twice, then the other. Phyllis still never greets him with kisses. And not another word about sperm donorship since Sam's cryptic remarks at the Miss Golden State parade. Mysteriously silent on the subject. Could what Sam said be true, they haven't decided which one's going to carry? "You forgot to shave half your mustache."

Just her way, he thinks, to pick out a flaw on your face and stare at it. "A very easy thing to do if you shave in the shower." It's only three or four days' growth anyhow, and blond. Like a milk mustache, only he can't lick it away. "Joyous solstice."

"Happy Hanukkah."

"Feliz Navidad and Año Nuevo." A problem, what to call this party.

Phyllis's ambition: a multiethnic, pansectarian, Tres Ojos combo-holiday bash. But, really, what's the difference between celebrating everything and celebrating nothing?

"Out with the old, in with the new." Sam puts a hand on his arm, suddenly hushing. "Have you seen the butterflies?"

Who hasn't? They come every year, though this year their population exploded. For two weeks torn-up looking clouds blew in from Alaska on icy squalls, and the ocean was so churned up and roiling that East Cliff Drive got covered with froth. Sylvan and Alabama had to motor through sea foam four feet deep, clumps sticking to the fenders, poofs shooting off the windshield wipers, headlights making hundreds of smudgy rainbows. Creepy. "Only on planet Earth," Sylvan had said to reassure Alabama, who was actually scared. "Fuck that. Only on planet California." Then with the sun the monarchs came out.

The door swings open, still not Santa (already a half hour late), but Heaven and Solomon and a couple more butterflies. The kids seem as bewildered as their parents, blinking at a fifteen-foot table laid out with tulips and Mexican hot chocolate, cider, tamales, potato latkes and applesauce, glittered cookies, the obligatory fruitcake, and a case of Napa Park cabernet that Sylvan has brought as a community gift.

Emma had a miscarriage last Sunday, and Dad suddenly began wildly giving away cases of wine. Mom's just depressed —long silences over the phone and crying. Emma herself sounds okay, "It's Mom and Dad I'm worried about." Paradoxically trying to cheer up those who should be comforting her.

The Joneses balk, overstimulated, until friendly hostess Phyllis greets them. "Merry Christmas, Ms. Mentone," the family says in unison loudly over the Vince Guaraldi Charlie Brown soundtrack. Interesting how a Bob and a Sally can turn out a Heaven and a Solomon and a Faith, no longer an infant—a full-grown four-month baby now. Most people consider the names stigmas, but Phyllis likes them. Bob studies particle physics and Sally bakes for the Staff of Life, responsible no doubt for the brilliantly red-iced cake Heaven's offering. They're one of the few intact nuclear families involved with Tres Ojos (only a third of the kids enrolled still live at home with both parents), therefore to Phyllis all the more precious. Religious and hardworking, clear-eyed and creamy-skinned, the Joneses seem almost fanatically happy. The kind of family Phyllis thinks her own would have been back in Tulsa, if only they had been perfect.

"That's something." She takes the cake from Heaven. It's heavy, a strip of sod.

"Beets." Heaven beams. She'll beam for anyone. Sally, with baby Faith holstered in a front-facing papoose on her chest, explains how the cake is "dairyless": no eggs, butter, or milk, but with tofu beet juice icing and "no sugar outright." Even the baking soda is "the kind without aluminum."

"I didn't know there was aluminum in baking soda," Phyllis says, trying to blink away a butterfly circling her head.

"I ran over a billion of these on my way over," Sam says, gently shooing it.

Phyllis suspects that Sam came to the party partly to keep an eye on Sylvan, whom she considers a threat. Lately Sam's been feeling rejected and excluded. Watching the most intimate of Phyllis's efforts go no longer towards her but instead towards having a baby has got to be hard on her. That Sylvan has entered the limelight makes it even worse: Sam's unable to compete with a man. Her nightmare. Phyllis feels a little guilty about this, and at home tries to reassure her. But she can't deny her feelings, which center more often than not on Sylvan these days. Today she doesn't want to let Sam out of her sight. Sam gets unpredictable.

"The windshield's plastered."

"They probably died laughing," Sylvan says, depressed by the thought of the monarchs living across the street from the new microchip factory that produces several toxic wastes, the most abundant (and perhaps least insidious) being laughing gas. "You know, the nitrous oxide."

"There's laughing gas in whipped cream," Sally says.

Nobody knows how much the gas affects the butterflies' sensitive pheromone sniffers—black dots on the back wings that give them enough sense of direction to fly thousands of miles over the Rockies every year to the same eucalyptus grove in Natural Bridges, where they overwinter, feeding on wild mustard flowers and mating. Sylvan takes the kids there for Outdoors. When clouds pour out the chimney of the chip factory, butterflies smack into walls and cluster idiotically on the streets. The factory itself is squat and unmarked, except for the United States flag, and California's. If a flag stands for anything, he thinks, California's, with the grizzly bear, symbolizes extinction. The last native wild one was shot dead in 1916.

"And cloven hooves in Jell-O," Sally is saying. And Phyllis, "They radiate green salads in hospitals." And Bob, "They've started giving away toys inside packaged chickens." A comment that expects some kind of reply about life in the late twentieth century—Sylvan's bed of roses. Everybody turns to face him, but he's spacing out, staring through the window.

"A total concept," Phyllis says lamely. "Well, make yourselves at home, and thanks again for the cake." The natural looks more artificial than artificial could ever look.

"Hi, Mom," Teo says, whining slightly. Sam hugs and kisses him six or seven times, then bestows a peck on Youngster, since Teo insists. Both he and the rat are wearing red velvet elves' caps. Sam sewed them herself. Phyllis admires this and looks forward to when she can do the same. Green knitted mittens with hat to match. Miniature denim jackets. Feety pajamas. Maybe she should ask Sylvan for an answer, he has been keeping her waiting. It's been hard . . . but she doesn't want to bully him as Sam claims she's doing. The other night she accused Phyllis of "cradle robbing" and "using" Sylvan, her "subordinate, her paid employee," suggested he's "too much of a boy" to make this kind of decision. "I ran into him,

you know, at the Myth Golden State Pageant, and he's totally
. . . naive." Sam had been so proud of her meat dress. Phyllis
thought it ridiculous. Embarrassing.

No, she'll wait, let him decide on his own. Or, better yet, let
him approach her.

Teo is holding on to Sam's leg, pushing his cheek into it.
"Youngster doesn't feel good."

"Ah, hon." She strokes his face, smooths an eyebrow.

"He's the sick one, not me." Teo holds Youngster up and
everyone stares, making diagnoses. Its pink nose quivers, fur
shiny and white, red eyes abulge.

"Fuchsia," Sylvan says, meaning not the eyes, Phyllis thinks,
but the cake in her hands. For several weeks now he's been
affecting a necklace made of a thin leather strap and two things
that look like nutshells but that he calls something weird, "feat
of consciousness." On anybody else they'd look hippie. She
even suspects him of being stoned all the time, the way he
laughs as if she did nothing but tell jokes. And with this new
haircut one side of his face turns out to look different from the
other. The left smiley, the right slept-on. Still—

"Not bad," he says, taking a fingerful of frosting.

Still, the way he licks his fingertip is—

"Are you going to let go, or am I going to have to wrestle it
away from you?"

"Oh, please." She hands him the cake and he starts toward
the table. "Hey." She can't wait, has to ask.

"Yeah?"

But Sam's close by, not exactly watching, just there. "What's
with your mustache?"

"Ran out of Nair."

"I don't believe in hair removal."

"I don't believe in hair." He wonders about her armpits,
yellow tufts or dark ones like his own. Maybe she thinks the
half-mustache is some kind of political statement. Whatever,
she is not through grilling him.

"Where's Santa?" The city policeman she usually hires

couldn't do it this year. Sylvan promised he knew someone for the job so she issued him the Santa suit and a blank money order for fifty dollars. "Kids are getting impatient."

Sylvan has learned that Phyllis sees her own emotional state reflected in the behavior of children, the way poets do in the weather. The way he himself does in the push and pull of the continents. The way Mom does in crosswords. The way Dad does in grapes, light, and soil. "Supple breeze," he says. Or "Soil's running a fever." Or he holds up a single grape and exclaims, "Shucks." Sylvan misses him, only a week till he's home for the holidays.

Phyllis pulls on her fingers, waiting for an explanation.

"Are you going home for Christmas?" he asks.

"Tulsa." She smiles and stops pulling. "My folks will already have the nativity scene set up on the lawn, life-size." Then she turns serious, resumes pulling fingers. "But I'm not going."

"Youngster sick?" Sylvan asks Sam, who's standing on a folding chair to tape some mistletoe to a roofbeam.

She shakes her head no. "The elephant seals are back."

When Teo misses his dad, the elephant seals are back. He has nightmares at home and is terrified of naptime at Tres Ojos, where he'll wake up sobbing and reaching for Youngster. In real life, elephant seals have floppy whiskered proboscises, a mouthful of canine teeth, rolling eyeballs, and they beach themselves to snort and fart and fuck. Forty percent of their body weight is blood; they can dive thousands of feet and stay down half an hour. Once they were nearly extinct, now there are thousands: Año Nuevo is teeming with them. Every winter they come up the coast (passing the gray whales headed south) to a rocky point just north of Santa Cruz, where they breed. It was an elephant seal, wildlife biologists speculate, that the great white mistook Salty Wilcox for.

"Poor—"

"Elephant seals, gray whales, monarch butterflies, what is it about Santa Cruz and breeding?'' Sam asks, eyes still on the mistletoe.

And banana slugs, Sylvan thinks. He has to smile. A group of Camp Fire girls and Blue Birds from the San Francisco Bay area is leading a campaign to make the banana slug California's official state mollusk. Just think, the squishy, hermaphroditic, large-penised, marathon-copulating university mascot elevated to even greater glory.

Santa Claus appears in a flood of light and butterflies, wearing hi-tops and dribbling a basketball. ''HO HO HO Hah ha ha . . . ,'' bellylaughing, scooping up children. Phyllis is all mouth. She has never seen a basketball Santa. ''Don't go looking for my reindeers, boys and girls, cause they invisible. Special deal today and today only. Be good for goodness' sake, and everybody get what they want.'' Maximus Loach winks at Sylvan, then pulls a can out of the rumpled red velvet suit and starts sprayflocking the room.

''Adonis! Stop licking the floor, Adonis!'' Adonis's father yells. His name is Isaac and he has skin as gray as a raw turkey's. A self-described communist, he now has Adonis sitting up and ''behaving'' while he complains that the honey in the hot cider was made by ''bee slaves.'' The poor child's eyes are wandering everywhere.

Sylvan's fault, Phyllis decides. He neglected to wipe up the spill. Everyone knows Adonis doesn't sugarbuzz normally; anything sweet turns him animal. ''I've got just the thing for you, amigo.'' She gets a slice of the cake the Joneses brought, puritanically natural, and offers him it. Adonis, vinyl bow tie clipped on, coarse black hair neatly parted, crams the cake into his mouth with the palm of his hand. Despite his normal body, Phyllis can't help picturing him as a miniature fat man. It started when his mother dropped him off last Halloween (the first and only time she appeared at Tres Ojos) with one pillow stuffed under the belly of his sweatshirt and another in the seat of his jeans, along with a straw hat and suspenders. Phyllis had sent home flyers cautioning parents that young children cannot distinguish between costume and the real thing. But as it turns out, the image stuck with *her*.

Humberto comes in wearing a plaid leisure suit, and advertising his new hobby with a swim mask and snorkel. On seeing all the decorations, the food and drink, and Astrid playing with the dreidel, he sticks his neck out, flaps his arms, and hiccups —his trademark gesture. Then he rushes over to her. It makes Phyllis feel better. She notices, across the room, Sylvan is smiling too. At her.

Wolfgang has just pushed Humberto into the Christmas tree and is about to club him with the dreidel.

"Words, Wolfgang, not weapons." Sylvan resists his first impulse: to grab the dreidel out of Wolfgang's hand, show him how it feels to be bullied. You have to make a child feel he's doing a thing on his own if you want it to work out. Sylvan learned this from Phyllis, who just now happens to be watching him from across the room with an expression on her face that says she's not getting enough exercise.

"I'm mad." Wolfgang has red hair that sticks up like Alabama's and a tight little mouth, lips bloodless and puckered as if to blow a trumpet. "I wanna play drable." He's gripping the dreidel in one hand, and in the other a He Man briefcase, which he brings to Tres Ojos every day but opens only for those he considers worthy. Sylvan has had the privilege of seeing inside: blond, tan, and supermuscley He Man; Skeletor; various weapons; a broken Gobot; and a couple of Hot Wheels. Wolfgang's favorite playground game is He Man of the giant rubber jungle gym: whoever gets to the top is Master of the Universe. He ringleads this game for hours every day. Inevitably kids get hurt. It gives Sylvan a headache.

"Humberto stoled the drable," Wolfgang complains. "He won't listen."

Often Wolfgang doesn't know when he's lying, and this trait, combined with the Tres Ojos textbook ability to state his feelings in I-message complete sentences, can make him a real charmer.

But the complete sentences are lost on Humberto and Astrid, who are constant companions, maybe because neither speaks English. It doesn't matter that Humberto speaks Portuguese, Astrid French. They understand each other.

"Gi mi drable palooga, you dumpster." Humberto stands bowlegged and pigeon-toed in his plaid leisure suit, steaming up his face mask. He's frightened by the playground so he stays indoors and reads books, making up his own jabberwocky narrative to go with the pictures. On good days he gets a circle of five or six kids and maybe a parent or two listening rapt. His favorite words in English are *blood, exactly,* and *cooperate,* and he does a pretty decent Dracula laugh. Now he looks up, eyes slightly crossed beneath the swim mask.

Astrid is looking expectantly at Sylvan also. He realizes he's their role model. He stands for things, and whatever he does is liable to show up in their behavior a few days down the line. At first he was uncomfortable with this; not knowing what is right himself, how can he ever guide anyone else's decisions? But after faking his way through dozens of early trials, he has figured out that the first trick of authority is just sounding like you have it.

"Wolfgang, did you ask if you could join them?"

"Yeah, I did ax them." Wolfgang nods to convince himself.

"Non." Humberto crosses his arms.

"I did."

Astrid bursts out with a stream of French and shakes her pigtails.

"I'll tell you how it looks to me." Sylvan pauses for gravity to build. "Humberto and Astrid were playing calmly before you took away the dreidel."

Wolfgang has a look of relief on his face, grateful to be told what's what. Phyllis says children need limits and limits need strict enforcing, otherwise nobody feels safe, or, in Wolfgang's case, knows where the truth lies. And not just children. Even people Sylvan's age. Searching for what his mom calls True Suchness.

Last spring, hoping for fresh perspective, Sylvan had the kids draw True Suchness. God, Yahweh, Jah, The Great Spirit, he called it. The Maker, Infinite Being. He opened his arms in a great sweep of the sky. Soul. Funny thing was, not one kid had a problem with this. They got right to work, scribbling and coloring with crayons and felt tips. Adonis's picture was all scratched through with black slashes. Heaven's was mostly blank except for a pale blue swirl in the upper right corner. Wolfgang said, "I don't believe in no dog spelled backwards" (this from a kid who hasn't learned yet how to spell) as he folded up his paper into a spaceship, the very one sticking now in the roofbeam. And Teo of course drew the inside of a shark, teeth.

Sylvan notices that Phyllis isn't really watching him at all, but studying the way he fingers the conch hanging on his neck, the one Simba gave him, and he feels caught in the act, judged. It occurs to him she's waiting for an answer.

"Cooperate." Humberto takes Wolfgang by the arm.

How can she be waiting for an answer when she never officially asked him? And if he's going to say no, why hasn't he already?

"Okay." Wolfgang hands over the dreidel.

Now she's wiping the cider area with a sponge for the third time. What does she think, that he can read her mind? And who's it going to be, her or Sam? Not that that should make any difference. But he sure wouldn't mind if Phyllis . . . if Phyllis what?

"Syl, my man!" Santa has him in a headlock. "Are you gonna tell me what you want?" He drags Sylvan across the room. "Or do I gotta pound it outta ya?" He suddenly plants a lip-smacking kiss on Sylvan's head. *"Mistletoe! Mistletoe!"* Then he grabs Heaven, wriggling and giggling, and smooches her loudly too.

"Set an example now." Santa Claus insists Sylvan sit on his knee. "For the childrens." Some of the kids have stopped what they're doing to watch. Teo is one of them, hanging back, observing. He really wants to sit on Santa's lap but he's at that age when it's no longer cool. "Not you," Santa growls to the delight of Heaven, who is trying to scramble onto his lap. "I already got you. Candy bars and a flying pony. *Him.*"

Sylvan finally agrees to sit on the chair arm, but not before snapping the velour spandex of Santa's suit. "Plush duds."

"Your boss got good taste," Santa says, thumbing the lapels. "A pair a legs on her too." He winks. "Real stocking stuffers. HO! HO!"

Sylvan sees Phyllis as Maximus Loach must. A nice piece. Athlete's legs. Broad shoulders and slender arms. The odd grace of being tall and light on her feet. And kind eyes that won't let you hide from yourself. Eyes that she suddenly turns on the two of them—catching them looking, maybe leering—and then away, but not before Sylvan sees the beginnings of a beautiful grin.

"Awrightie, whatcha want?"

Sylvan thinks. Rubs his half mustache. He wants things normal here at Tres Ojos, with Phyllis, everything simple again, but he doesn't know how to ask for that. He wants something else for his collection, a feather from a wing of one of those golden eagles. The pair nests nearby, but Sylvan hasn't yet discovered exactly where. He wants Emma never to have had a miscarriage. She told him over the phone there had been no warning, just cramps and a lot of blood. "True Suchness."

Just before Thanksgiving he repeated the True Suchness assignment, but he'd had to leave in the middle of it to check the Richter scale in Applied Sciences, which was picking up a series of minor quakes. He left the kids under the supervision of some untrained assistant named Shane who combs his hair every five minutes. Shane sat down and drew the pope with a long white beard. And all the kids begged him to draw them one, or tried to copy. It will take a couple of years for Tres Ojos to shake that image.

"True Suchness? What the hallelujah kinda gizmo that be?"

"It's no gizmo, silly Santa, it's like a soul," Heaven says, finally staking a claim on Santa's right knee.

"That I got plenty of."

Sylvan remembers how confused that word—soul—made him when he was a boy, conjuring images of a mushy fish fillet, the bottoms of tennis shoes, just-plowed soil, and the plastic breakaway heart his dad had brought home. And the other day, Alabama, explaining the boot heel nailed to his bedroom door, said, "Soul is plural for everybody's secret." A good one, whatever it means; Mom will get a kick out of it.

"I want to see my folks."

Heaven is confused and incredulous, unable to picture grown-ups with moms and dads. Some of the younger kids here are convinced that Sylvan and all the other teachers live at Tres Ojos.

"You're not the only one with a mom and dad, you know," he says, though she is one of the few kids with both.

"What else?" Santa Claus asks.

"Gloves, a Stumpjumper, a new set of rapidographs, socks and underwear, a lubristrip razor howabout, but no more deodorant please, and steak and onion rings."

The nap room is cool, quiet, a refuge, and Sylvan sits in a rocking chair with Teodoro on his lap. The kid seems low, cautious and distant; not saying why. In just four months he's grown less pudgy, stronger-faced. "Lazertag?"

"I don't know." Teo hands Youngster over to Sylvan and pulls the elf's cap down snug.

"Space Legos?" Sylvan asks. Youngster is such a mix of textures, quivering fur, scratchy feet, whiskers tickling his wrist. Littlest pounding heart.

"Unh-hunh."

"A new bike?"

Teo shrugs. A hint of desire there?

"Are you going to go sit on Santa's lap and tell him?"

A shake of the head no, both hands still pulling down the cap. "Do you like me?"

"You bet I like you."

Teo pulls away a little. "Mom says it's your job to like me."

What? Why would she tell him a thing like that? Unless she believes it. Would she turn Teo against him on purpose?

"It's my job to see that you learn Outdoors and to see that you're safe. And that goes for all the kids. But liking you is something I just can't help."

Teo shrugs again as if a chill ran through him, and he puts both hands on Sylvan's knee. "When are we going in the cave?"

Damn. Set himself up for that one. Sylvan suddenly feels caught in a chain of consequences that make it hard not to believe in fate. If only that shark had never attacked. Then Salty Wilcox would still be alive and he and Sam and Teo would be a family, and Phyllis, well, Phyllis, who knows, but she might very well have found somebody, a man maybe, it is possible, and Sylvan himself would be just another guest at the party, not the guy here in the center of everybody's plans. He did promise, though, and the cave is always there whether he thinks about it or not. Also, he doesn't like to admit it, but he suspects that some part of himself actually likes this tension, makes him feel important.

"The cave has to dry out. All that rain, you know. Ground's saturated."

Teo fixes him in a squint; one more clumsy adult. Avoidance tactics. Broken promises. Lies. "You always say later."

Sylvan decides to get to the point. "You miss your dad?"

"Mmmmm." Teo looks sideways out the window. Butter-flies dance absurdly through the empty swing set. He takes Youngster back, strokes protectively.

"How do you keep that hat on Youngster's head?" Sylvan asks.

"Velcro." He pulls away the hat, revealing a patch of Velcro taped to the crown of the rat's head.

"Velcro's a good thing."

"Mmmmm."

"Is he feeling any better?"

Teo pulls the rat closer to his body. "He's got a virus. Phyllis says he just gets sad when I'm sad. But I'm not sad. I'm nothing. Besides, look. His nose is chapped and he's always sleepy."

The rat does look a little sluggish, and its nose does have a flake or two. But who can know? It certainly doesn't look terminal. "Say ahhh, Youngster," says Sylvan.

Teo almost laughs. "I gave him some vitamins crushed up in yogurt. Maybe they'll work."

Just then Phyllis bursts in, needing Sylvan's help. He is, after all, clocked in. "Solomon and Wolfgang are going at it and I've got my hands full with this one." She's holding Faith, fat and pink and giggling, wrapped in a blanket. Phyllis's own cheeks look pink too, a sympathetic blush maybe, or a few glasses of cabernet.

Solomon is trying to buy He Man off Wolfgang with Hanukkah gelt—a stack of chocolate coins wrapped in gold foil. Wolfgang scoffs, offers a broken Gobot instead. This isn't fighting, this is negotiating.

"Let's go back to the nap room," Teo whines.

High-pitched girl screaming comes from across the room. Sylvan takes Teo's hand and walks over, counting on his tall-ness to quiet things down. But the girls, all with dolls, ignore him. More accurately, Chamunda ignores him and the other girls, as always, take their cue from her. Chamunda has long black hair that reaches to the backs of her knees. Her mother lets her wear mascara and eyeshadow, and today she has a red dot on her forehead, and bangle earrings. Her pierced ears are intensely envied.

"Mine's Ann!" she screeches, gesturing with her Barbie. The doll has long dark hair, a lot like Chamunda's own, and impossibly long legs.

"Is there a problem?" Sylvan asks, searching his voice for the power spot.

"We're playing Barbie," Huatlán says, slightly trilling the *r*. She speaks Spanish at home but she'll speak only English at Tres Ojos. Her parents are involved with Teatro Campesino over the hill in San Juan Bautista, and her mother is responsible for the tamales on the table, her father for the Silvio Rodriguez playing on the stereo. Huatlán knows strange things like how many petals in a tulip and the names of exotic cheeses. She says, "I named mine Ann first. Chamunda's copying."

"Nunh-hunh." Chamunda shakes her head so her earrings swing and sparkle.

Gaia is also playing. "I want mine to be Ann too." She was born in the last days of Rajneesh and is an open-faced smiley kid, undemanding of attention. Her Barbie is a half-size copy with real false eyelashes and dirt-smudged legs.

"No," both Huatlán and Chamunda tell her.

Chamunda turns her large brown eyes on Sylvan and flutters them coyly. She's five years old. Who taught her that? Maybe her mother is already preparing her for marriage. He remembers the time—the times—she asked him to unzip his pants, or tried to do it herself. "What's in there?" A dangerous curiosity in this era of child-abuse headlines.

"Hey," she says. "You have one side of a mustache."

The girls all giggle.

"Mine's Feelin Groovy." Chamunda holds up her Barbie. "And Huatlán's is International Peruvian. But Gaia only has Dawn." As she speaks, Huatlán stares at her earrings; Chamunda gives them an extra swing. "But I thought up Ann, so I get it!"

"No!" Huatlán's furious. "It's already a name. You can't think up of what already is."

Sylvan likes for kids to work out problems on their own. Who doesn't? But here he's really at a loss. No hunch, and no clue why a Chamunda, a Huatlán, and a Gaia would want a bland name like Ann.

"Why do you all want the name Ann?"

"Not us, silly," Chamunda says. "For our Barbies."

This is the difference between boys and girls. Boys become He Man and GI Joe, but girls never become Barbie. Boys toss their dolls off jungle gyms, bury them in BBQ coals, rescue them from the mouths of enemy dogs, while girls spend an hour naming them, an hour dressing them, and an hour thinking up relationships. A few weeks ago, at the beginning of the rainy spell, Chamunda came in with raincoats for all the Barbies, raincoats she had cut from the shower curtain at home. Her mother wasn't angry at all, but bragged, shrugging. Later that day Sylvan had had to break up a fight about which Barbie (one of six dressed in raincoats) was whose mother to somebody's sister's cousin.

Another thing altogether is Ken. Boys never buy Ken. And the only kid at Tres Ojos who owns Ken is of course Chamunda, and she shares him, passes him around, one Ken serving as "the date" for all six Barbies.

"Mine's the mom, so mine's Ann." Chamunda's trying a different tack. "Yours is Ann too, Gaia, since mothers and daughters can have the same name." Ganging up. Huatlán is about to cry. Even though doll play is different between boys and girls, in both the central concern is power.

Suddenly Youngster's loose, climbing onto Feelin Groovy Barbie, sniffing in her hair. Chamunda shrieks, bringing Phyllis over in a hurry.

"You do this," Sylvan says. "I can't deal."

Back up in the nap room, Teo says, "Why do they care so much about Barbie?"

"Beats me."

"They're fighting over her and she's not even real."

"I don't know about that, Teo. She may not be alive, but she's very real."

"Youngster's realer."

Sylvan wonders if this is true in a world where sixteen million Barbies are sold annually. Then he's struck by a realization: at Tres Ojos you have to be crying or fighting to get attention.

Sam comes in with Maximus Loach, who's beginning to look lopsided—the Santa suit sagging in the tummy and butt. He scowls at Teo's quiet stare.

"Whassamatta, boy? The look on your face freeze up the Salton Sea." He's dribbling. "Never saw an NBA all-star, didja now?" He moonwalks while spinning the ball on two fingers, "fakes once, pumps twice," executing an imaginary slamdunk that sends the defender into "the popcorn machine," and converting a "garbage play" to put the game in the "frigerator. Door closed, butter gettin hard."

Sam claps, expecting a pass that never comes.

"Basketball's a man's game, honey."

She frowns, puts her hands on her hips. "The Harlem Globetrotters have a woman player."

"Gotta admit," he says. "She a great ballhandler."

Sam looks self-satisfied, claps again. "So give it here."

"After she warms up," Maximus Loach says. "Even dribbles between her legs."

Sam finally gets it, sighs and shakes her head. "Ha. Ha. Ha."

"Now get over here." Santa waves an arm for Teo. His chest heaves from the effort of his performance, and the cottonball beard makes his cheek and nose look shiny and black. "And tell me what you want."

Teo stays where he is. "Are you really Santa Claus?"

"You got eyeballs in your head. Use 'em." He rolls the ball slowly with a spin so it curves over to Teo, who picks it up. "Now bring me that basketball and bring that rat a yours too."

"Do you—" Teo hesitates. "Do you still have that can of snow?"

"For me to know and you to find out."

"But—"

"No buts." Maximus Loach picks him up—"sacka potatoes" —and carries him out of the room, Teo giggling hysterically.

While Sylvan sits rocking, Sam, hands clasped behind her back, walks the perimeter of the room.

"Teo thinks the world of you."

What is she asking for? Nowadays she, Phyllis, and even Teo speak in codes; everybody third-eyeing each other. It's getting so you can't even have a normal conversation.

"Teo's a great kid. About the greatest. You did a great job with him." Sylvan keeps rocking the chair with his toes, flexing and unflexing his calves, and is ready to ask her what she told Teo about him when she comes near, gets on one knee, puts her face close, breathes his air.

"If you had a choice," she asks, placing a hand on the chair arm, stopping the rocking, "would you live forever, like a god, say, but not be able to have children? Or be mortal but able to have them?"

A question essentially about sex, as Sylvan sees it. "It would depend on my mood, I guess."

"Different versions of eternity, see? The funny thing is, last night I asked Phyllis and she chose living forever." She waits for some kind of response. "Don't you think that's funny?"

Sylvan realizes she's scared. He can see it in her eyes, extreme neediness. Fear of losing Phyllis. He's a rival Sam can't, for sheer biology, compete with. He wants to tell her she has nothing to worry about, that—

"I myself chose mortal."

Or maybe she's scared of getting older, of the years behind creeping up on the years ahead. Being scared makes her more beautiful.

She puts her hand on his arm, a sales pitch. So. It's come down to this. She's the one. Phyllis chose godhood and no longer wants to bear a child. Sam gets the call. And by the way she's trying to look into his eyes, it seems she has in mind the old-fashioned way of baby-making. This eye contact is a challenge. Sylvan's giving some of himself away with each blink.

"You're trembling." She rubs his arm, the touch unwanted but soothing. A pleasant tingle nowhere in particular. It feels wrong somehow, as if he's betraying Phyllis. Absurd. What allegiance does he presume to have with her that he can't go off with anybody he desires? Not that he even desires Sam. A pretty girl may be a public fantasy, but not Sylvan's private one.

"We'll lock the nap room door," she whispers loudly. Sylvan can hear the thud thud thud of "Jingle Bells" through the wall. Maximus Loach's muffled Ho, Ho, Ho. Sam rubs his shoulder more, and he has to shift his hips to make room in the crotch of his jeans, the buttons beginning to pull. Damn. "What do you say, Syl?"

It occurs to him that she and Phyllis might have stayed up late last night plotting this moment. Get it for free. Sylvan begins to feel used. "I'm supposed to be working."

Sam tempts him. But he doesn't trust her. Sam tempts him *because* he doesn't trust her. What will Alabama say? Any normal Joe would bang his head on a wall for this opportunity. Why not Sylvan? In the telling he can invent some kind of interruption—kids fighting, Maximus Loach barging in, an earthquake, four-six on the Richter. Funny how Alabama is becoming the one he tells his stories to. What does that say about things? Is that what you call friendship?

"Well?"

Maybe he'll allow a blow job. A blow job is a way of saying

no without losing a story. If she and Phyllis are going to use him, he'll use them first. Yes, that will be fine. Also, he hasn't had any sex in quite a while, it'll feel good, or great, or—but it isn't right of Phyllis to sic Sam on him. High-minded, pure-of-motive Phyllis. A woman he respects (respected?) so much he can hardly imagine her ever, say, giving a blow job. And he wonders now, Has she? Did she? Does she like it? And why is he even wondering this?

Sam already has a hand down his pants. She squeezes him, hard, yanking away his breath.

"Something you want to say?" she asks, tightening her grip on his balls. Taking revenge.

He all at once wants out of the bargain, feeling he's traded away something he's not prepared to part with for something he needs but doesn't really want. But he just shakes his head no, and keeps shaking it even after she loosens her hold and bends over his lap to do the acceptable.

The party is edging into late afternoon, the light sideways and orange, Charlie Brown music repeating itself, food ravaged (only the fruitcake remains untouched), kids falling asleep everywhere, when Phyllis decides to get a jump on cleaning up. But the pile of Barbies distracts her. Huatlán's brown one, Chamunda's with the long black hair, and Gaia's half-sizer. Figures that the girls would abandon them after fighting a full half hour over which got to be called Ann (Chamunda's, naturally). Phyllis also picks up the Ken doll, dressed for today's party in a black tux.

At home, she and Sam have been bickering, among other things, over names for the Child. Sam wants Gabrielle, which is kind of nice, or Gabriel.

Phyllis wants Sarah, though Sylvia is a possibility. Or Kurtis. Sam hates Kurtis, sort of likes Sarah, and has no comment on Sylvia. Which is a comment in itself. The last name, of course, will be Mentone, since Phyllis is the one getting pregnant. Although Sam has been doing some hinting. The other night, reading aloud from *The Pregnant Woman's Bodybook* about "the birthing experience," she got nostalgic and started in on Her Life. How Teo was worth the pain. How all this talk was making her want another. And earlier today during the Barbie squabble she even made a crack in poor taste about her and Phyllis "sharing the Ken." But it's just talk. Sam talks. Where is she anyway?

Phyllis examines the brown doll, Huatlán's. A Peruvian version of International Barbie. It has a slightly more oval head than the everyday blonde, and dark hair you can braid. But its body is distinctly Barbie's. A month ago a group of concerned parents approached Phyllis and cited a statistic from *Harper's*: if Barbie were life-size, her measurements would be 39-23-33. What little girl can possibly live up to that image? They suggested Barbie be banned. "The whole point of Barbie is that she owns things and buys things. What does that teach our kids?" There are worse images, Phyllis argued. Tammy Bakker dolls, or She Ra, Princess of Power, a eunuch He Man. Besides, children aren't so fragile. *"Our children are too fragile!"* they screamed, as if their five-year-olds were the dolls and they themselves were the children. Phyllis didn't tell them that she still has several of her own old Barbies, probably becoming valuable now.

In the How to Conceive chapter, which Phyllis waited until Sam fell asleep to read, there were pictures of penises. And positions. It said rear entry was the most effective way of achieving conception. Phyllis turns Feelin Groovy Barbie's back to Ken, bends her forward from the hips. It's also better if the woman doesn't have an orgasm, something about the chemistry of the vagina being less acidic that way, less hostile to sperm, which doesn't seem at all fair and which Phyllis wouldn't have believed except that the book was written by a women's health collective. Thrust, Ken, thrust. Barbie doll voodoo. It isn't a bad fantasy. Who knows? She wants that baby. And wanting changes a person.

This worries her. Though she denied it to Sam, she's having a hard time lately convincing herself she's not "using" Sylvan. Or "bullying" him. It's just that he's . . . the perfect candidate for the job.

"*Yo, Phyl baby!*" Santa bellows. "Get ova here and tell Santa what it is!" The hulking Maximus Loach, reeking of Brut, gives her a bear hug. "Sylvan tole me you throw a good party but this one be a smoker."

The compliment pleases her, and she's flattered that Sylvan talks about her in circles outside Tres Ojos. She lives in his imagination. That's a start. "I like a good party, Max, especially if you can call it a cultural event."

"Tres Ojos your brainstorm, Phyl baby?" He tries to sit her on his lap.

She resists. But then decides to relax and finally falls in. "Sure is, Max." They look around. People are having a good time. The Joneses are gathered around Humberto, who's reading. Adonis is picking at the fruitcake, while his father, Isaac, yuck, just tapped a cigarette ash into a tulip. Teo has finally loosened up and is playing with the other kids, Wolfgang and Solomon no less. A rare sight. They're making Youngster tread the basketball, which is Planet McPlanet, a good planet that he must save from Skeletor.

"Thanks for coming, Max."

"How'm I doin?"

"Flying colors." She surprises herself by telling him he's the best Santa ever. She's usually not so free with her compliments. Less is more. But 'tis the season and she's jolly and the party wouldn't be "a smoker" without him. He gets all the kids laughing, even the young ones who are normally terrified of Santa. And the way he wouldn't take no for an answer from Teo but picked him right up and sat him on his lap. Sometimes a child needs just that—especially Teo—the hard, arbitrary love that comes only from a man. Sam would kill her for saying it, but that's just the way it is.

"D'you work out, Phyl baby?" he asks. "Nice legs. I mean,

just that they strong, like." Giving up on explaining his way out of it.

"I run," she rescues him, her tone gift-giving. "I run around. And swim. Lotta exercise." Despite herself, she's pleased.

"I hear ya, Phyl baby." They pause to watch the boys. He Man is teaming up with Youngster, whom Teo has endowed with X-ray vision. He can read Skeletor's plan to blow up Planet McPlanet.

"Some kinda kid," Maximus Loach says. The superheroes subdue Skeletor with a blast of sprayflocking. "*Ho!* Okeydokey, Phyl baby, talk to me. Whatcha want?"

He's the first person to ask. It occurs to her that other people, Sam especially, may have good reasons not to. You don't like to hear it when a person wants what you cannot possibly give.

"Black suede pumps," she says. Ha!

"There ya go, girl. What else?"

"A new wet suit." Her old Body Glove is beginning to crumble. All at once she can think of lots of things. New rugby shorts, Lancôme rehydrating fluid, Grampa toys, glacier glasses, maybe a salad spinner, books on babies. It's easier to want little things, they don't steal your time. "New clothes for Teo." His old will be hand-me-downs.

"Generous soul, givin your gifts away like that. Bein good just plain for goodness' sake, there's peace of mind." Santa thoughtfully tugs on his beard. Cookie glitter in it. "Ain't no lie. He be one lucky kid. And Sam be one lucky momma." He looks Phyllis in the eye. "And Sylvan be one lucky dog."

"What?" No longer flattered, she feels exposed. Just how much has Sylvan revealed?

Santa ho ho hos. "Watch out you don't get what you want."

Phyllis has cleared off the entire table by the time Sylvan reappears. He's slouching behind a shoulder, fingering those shells on his neck, forcing back a guilty smile. Cleanup time and he cuts out. Irresponsible.

"Need a hand?" Sylvan asks. She's scrubbing the tabletop and won't answer. The nerve. After setting him up? Shame and regret make him hot behind the ears. Plus he's a little raw where Sam used her teeth. "Eternal life, huh?"

Phyllis looks up but continues scrubbing. The table is very clean. She's almost directly underneath the mistletoe. "I oughtta dock your pay."

"I oughtta double my price."

"Where were you?"

He's folding up chairs and nodding vigorously like he's got her number. So full of posture and at the same time so eager to please. Hard to take him seriously with that half mustache. In a rush of fondness she longs to put an arm around him, take him fishing, or to a ballgame, somewhere she's never gone. "Forget—"

"Where the fuck do you think?"

Angry. He's funny when he's angry.

"Are you stoned?" She asks him in a voice so quiet and gentle he doesn't know whether to take it as an insult or an invitation. So he ignores it.

"Don't you want to have a kid anymore?" he asks, the disappointment in his voice startling to himself.

She's practiced at staying calm, a job requirement at Tres Ojos, but the question tests her composure. His eyes, blue, all iris, test her composure. Was that a yes? Did he just say yes? She has purposely avoided the subject, not wanting to pressure him, letting the idea grow on him, every day dying to get a commitment out of him one way or the other, and now this. She has to look away, up, at . . . at the mistletoe. Wasted. An opportunity in ordinary circumstances. "Are we having the same conversation?" Her eyes are wide, her surprise genuine.

"You mean you and Sam didn't plan . . . anything?"

"Sam has nothing to do with this." She looks around, wondering where Sam is, what she's done. Both she and Sylvan, Phyllis suddenly realizes, were gone at the same time. What did she tell him? Frowning, she says, "It's my—me having the baby."

Sylvan laughs, a painful squeal. He was only being paranoid in there. But he fucked up hugely. Somebody has some explaining to do. "Phyllis, I—" He has a strong urge to confess, get it out now. "Hey, mistletoe!" he says instead, and chases her lips.

Phyllis is blinking. What's going on? She can't see through all this blushing.

Sylvan wants outdoors, and he's almost there when Teo calls him back.

"He won't wake up. Temper. Wrong. Crashed." Teo's chattering, words jarred loose from any meaning, and his hands are cold.

"Slow down, Teo." But he won't. Leaning forward at the chest as if straining against belts, Teo leads Sylvan back to the nap room. Inside is going dark, things no longer stick to their boundaries but move off into shadowy eddies.

"In there, though," Teo says, eyes dilated, pupils swallowing available light, it seems, in gulps. He holds on to Sylvan's hand as if it's something very fragile. Sylvan turns on the light.

A Star Wars lunch pail is open on the floor next to the rocking chair, its contents spilling out. Rolls of gauze, a bottle of aspirin, a tin of Band-Aids, the snakebite kit, grape suckers. Teo has gotten into the first-aid box.

"I tried to save him."

A thin loop of blood on the floorboards disappears behind the chair. It leads to Youngster. The rat lies belly down, white fur slightly matted with blood, the tip of the thermometer sticking out of its mouth. The red velvet elf's cap is still attached, slightly off kilter, a cruel joke.

"I was trying. I was saving." Teo convulses. "I was taking his temper but I pushed it in too far."

"Shhhhh. Okay. Shhhhhh." Sylvan sits Teo down and goes

to the rat. He grasps the thermometer between thumb and forefinger and pulls. It doesn't come out easily, and when it does, it makes an awful clicking sound. He wishes there were a way to close Youngster's eyes, but they just won't stay.

6 Parents as a State of Mind

Vow of Silence Man has skin that looks vulcanized, bulging eyes, and plugs of black nose hair; Sylvan wants to hug him. But he and Alabama have just intruded on a sacred moment. The Man demands a half hour alone in the den when tasting wine. Sylvan flashes him a peace sign, waits on the barest hint of a smile, and yanks Alabama out the door.

"That's Gyorgy. He must have the new Beaujolais in there," Sylvan says. Beaujolais is the only wine Napa Park produces that requires only a few months' aging. For the past three years the quality has been borderline and Dad has donated the rejected cases to charities and the San Francisco Giants (a home-run, double-play ball club, he likes that combo). Whether or not this year's yield turns out will depend on Vow of Silence Man's word at dinner, the Christmas Eve custom.

Alabama's looking backwards as they walk down the hallway.

"He never talks," Sylvan says. "But his work has brought Napa Park wines several dozen awards." Right now, he's in there stroking the glass with two fingers. In a moment, he will set it on the windowsill, turn his back on it, and hyperventilate for three or four minutes. Then he will sniff the wine, rub some on his wrists, sniff there, sip, and finally open his throat and gulp it down. Sylvan's not supposed to know all this, but once he spied. "He's got the gift like nobody."

"Saves his tongue for tasting, does he?" Alabama asks.

"Could be." It's what Dad always says, as if any analysis will jinx the power.

The kitchen smells like gingersnaps. Mom's at the stove, hasn't heard them yet. When she does, she spins, claps her hands, and rises on her tiptoes. "Boys! Alight and rest your saddles." She hugs Alabama first. Maybe it's the way he looks windblown and bloodshot. Then it's Sylvan's turn. He's so much taller that she has to stand back to take him in, approves of his new short haircut, and hugs and kisses him again.

"Coffee?"

Alabama has a look of extreme puzzlement on his face. It's his first Christmas away from Tennessee, and apparently the situation hasn't quite sunk in. His own mother had suddenly embarked on a fact-finding mission to Paris. "What kind of facts?" Sylvan asked. "Facts à la mode," Alabama said and explained how his father wasn't up to decking the halls and all, and needed to catch up on some Solar Parlor bookkeeping before the year expired, so the family decided to delay the festivities till New Year's. He tugs on an ear. "Beg pardon?"

"I said, 'Coffee?' " Mom says, getting some anyway.

"Oh sure thing, ma'am." Alabama nods profusely.

She pours coffee while Sylvan goes to the fridge for milk. Magnetic letters in bright colors stick to the door. Two messages: IS ITS OWN REWARD, and   IS IN THE EYE OF THE BEHOLDER. Even though Mom put them up, they more accurately reflect Dad's philosophy. Sylvan notices Alabama staring at things and he wonders how home looks through his eyes.

Practically everything is handmade. The mugs they're drinking from, thrown clay, lots of icy enamel. The table they're sitting at, wine corks under a glass pane. Even the redwood roofbeams are hand-planed. Dad did a lot of the work himself, with Gyorgy's help.

"Your parents must miss you," Mom says.

"Things came up. My dad had a fire—one of the Solar Parlors burnt down."

"I thought you said bookkeeping," Sylvan says.

"Essentially." Al mumbles something into his coffee. "He's got his fingers in a lot of pies."

Whenever he says this, he looks ashamed. It makes no sense to Sylvan.

"Well, we're glad to have you," Mom says, making duck lips and shrugging. "I sure miss having kids around the house."

Sylvan wonders if this means Emma's coming or not coming home. Mom's still a wreck about the miscarriage.

"Where's Dad?" He has been half expecting the hairy hand on his shoulder and to hear how good he looks.

"Downstairs exercising." Mom takes a seat. She looks young, her blue eyes haven't faded at all, and her hair is just a little peppered, one wave as if ironed in. She and Emma have the same smile, lots of teeth. Sylvan wishes Emma were here, wants to ask whether she's coming at all. But Mom's not mentioning it has made it unmentionable. "How's school, boys?"

"I have a professor who thinks so hard his forehead's callused," Alabama says, loosening up a little. He's referring to Egbert Wanamaker, the famous but unread poet on campus, old man with a bear-claw necklace, ancient friend of Robinson Jeffers and Harry Houdini, lecturer who rubs his forehead so hard the skin there has thickened. He likes Alabama's work but has warned him that he hasn't yet learned how to "transcend non sequitur" and that his stories "consist of gists."

"Sylvan tells me you're a writer," Mom says. She's the voracious speed-reader of the family, gobbling up classics and anything hardback. A few years ago she even veered off into

romance, spy thrillers, how-to, and self-help, exploring the ros-
ters of the Oakland *Tribune* best-seller lists. "I get all the books
free," was her excuse, though Sylvan always thought she secretly wanted to write one. On the whole, people pretty much
want that, he thinks, to put their own bible into each other's
hands.

"Well, ma'am." Alabama's laying the Southernese on thick.
"It's like, Sylvan's the earthquake and I'm the record of it."

The coffee scalds. Sylvan's sure Alabama's going to spill the
beans about something. About Phyllis and artificial insemination. Or even ask a stupid question about Emma, since Sylvan
already told him Mom has a bunch of baby clothes in the attic,
still boxed and tagged. This Christmas was supposed to be extra
special. "But what I want to know is, why doesn't Vow of—
Gyorgy talk?"

"He's on a spiritual quest," Mom says.

"Did something turn him mute?"

"He just decided one day that he didn't want to talk anymore," Sylvan says. Relieved to be out of the spotlight, he can
afford to be impatient.

"I feel like that some mornings myself."

They tell him the story of Gyorgy's last words back in '69: At
the corner of Haight and Ashbury he was holding a mirror up
to the faces in the windows of passing tour buses and shouting,
"Go visit yourselves!"

"Then what?"

"That's all."

"Show him the catalogs," Mom says, and pulls a couple off the
rack next to the cordless telephone wall mount. The *Psychic
Extra* and the *Berkeley Reader*, magazines of innerselfhood. Vow
of Silence Man is on the Council of Advisors for both. "Gyorgy
Welkman is a pioneer whose exploration of the limitlessness of
the human organism has yielded profound insights." It embar-

rasses Sylvan. It also embarrasses him that his parents are not only subscribers but "friends of," and that a part of himself believes some of this stuff to be at least marginally true.

The *Extra* offers news items on the current psychic-phenomena front—one headline is TOT READS TAROT: SURPRISES MOM—while the *Reader* is glossier and provides a list of educational programs. Course offerings include Brain Gym, How to Start and Finish a Conversation, Peak Experiences at Will?, Eurhythmy (here Alabama reads aloud the blurb, his voice preacherly, "Participants will be encouraged to develop a living relationship to space and nonphysical movement"), Homage to the Sun, and Psychology of the Chakras. There are also columns such as the Spiritual Marketplace, Déjà Vu Tours, and Nine Lives Pet Advice.

When Mom bends down to take a pie out of the oven, Alabama points out another item. The Wisdom and Folly of the Penis. He mouths a ha ha. " 'Conscious Sexuality,' " he whisper reads. " 'The focus is on integrating the timeless feminine mysteries and masculine virility into the context of the baffling sexual labyrinth presented by today's world.' "

"Okay. Enough."

"Why don't you boys go downstairs and tell your father there's decaf and pie?" Mom hasn't lost the old habit of telling you by asking.

"I'm drinking decaf?" Alabama asks. Decaf, to him, is—like diet candy bars, light beers, enriched white flour, plastic simulated woodgrain, and anything polyester—contemptible. He squints into his coffee, swishing it, no doubt ready to make some comment concerning integrity. "Delightful brew, Mrs. Park."

"Delightful brew?" Sylvan says on the way downstairs.

Alabama is grinning awshucksy. "Folkalities?"

The word's Sylvan's. It had slipped out on the drive up. Sylvan had to shout over the wind since they were cruising with the top down. "The Folkalities will be pleased we're early!" Alabama pinned his notepad against the dash and wrote it down one-handed. Sylvan felt a little strange about taking credit for a word he wasn't even aware, at first, of using. He and Emma originally made it up back in high school as a codeword when planning parties or scoring numes, short for numerous loads, as in numerous loads of sinsemilla. He hopes she comes. As a kid Emma was dark and delicate, claiming that aspirin gave her headaches, dandruff shampoo caused her scalp to flake, and ChapStick chapped her lips. She was the one who led Sylvan to a chest of toys hidden in the wine cellar—the incontrovertible proof that there was no such thing as Santa.

"Like personalities," Alabama says.

"Realities."

"Mentalities."

"Sexualities."

Alabama loves this. "Folkalities. Parents as a state of mind."

The living room is done up exactly like last year and the year before, and the year before that. The tree exudes resin and is loaded down with strands of tinsel that reflect blinking lights in wet-looking streaks. It's also got a smoke-detector ornament near the top; Dad insists, every year. Gifts are piled underneath in just two varieties of wrapping paper. A stocking-capped Charlie Brown, the Grinch, Rudolph, the nativity crowd, and Frosty the Styrofoam-man are all on display, and there's a porcelain Santa on the mantel. It's got a fairly realistic-looking face, some pain in it but also what Jesus is missing—jollity. Mom may not be religious but she likes icons.

"Men!" Dad's upside down, hanging from gravity boots, *exercising*. They're actually aluminum shackles, padded and with a hook for the chin-up bar. He puts out his hands, waves them in the air for Sylvan. "You look good!" His face is very red, cheeks like strawberry sherbet just scooped, bristly black eyebrows, and wiry hair, whiter than Sylvan remembers.

"Al," he says and awkwardly shakes hands. "Glad you could come. I've heard a lot about you, ninety-nine percent good." This is not exactly true. Sylvan described him as a redheaded Lit major from the South, a little strange and hyper, who had nowhere to go for the holidays. Now Alabama is cocking his head as if to compensate for a tilted picture. "Reverses the effects of gravity," Dad explains.

Dad believes the effects of gravity can be reversed.

"Mom says come have some decaf and pie." Mom believes in complete sentences and hot breakfasts.

"Rhubarb." Alabama nods. "Smelled absolutely delish." He has just made an excellent first impression. Rhubarb pie is Dad's favorite because, he says, it's slightly poisonous if you cook it wrong. He's proud of his special recipe, the one thing he cooks. Mom's only allowed to reheat.

"You like rhubarbs, son?"

"Love 'em," Alabama says, though Sylvan is fairly sure he doesn't mean the food kind. Alabama's looking around at the barbells, Biocycle, tumbling pad, and bar refrigerator.

Dad takes a huge breath, counts five, lets it out through puckered lips. He's worried about killer bees, "seriously." A hive has just been found in Fresno, moving northwest one mile per week, Napa-bound. The Parks know a family who knows a family whose son, while on a field study chronicling the nutritional habits of an Indian tribe in a Costa Rican jungle, got caught in a swarm. Unlike the honeybee, the killer stings more than once and the venom is extremely toxic. Hundreds stung the boy, kept stinging even after he ducked for cover in a crevice. Rescuers had to chip away the rock to remove the horribly swollen corpse.

"If they ever get to Napa," Dad says, so much concern nettling those eyebrows that Sylvan knows it's a put-on, "they'll make my vines unworkable."

A look of horror contorts Alabama's face, then pain, then something else. "Your vines?" he asks. "What about your person?"

"My person." Dad rubs his hairy arms. "Yes, my person. Well, I'm at that age, Al, where I don't buy green bananas anymore."

"How are ya, Silver?" Dad throws one of those hairy arms around his shoulder. Alabama has gone back upstairs, leaving father and son alone in the rec room. Sylvan can take this opportunity to tell him anything. But when there is nothing day-to-day to talk about, the choice becomes which major life event to bring up. Phyllis asking him to be a sperm daddy? The butterflies? Maximus Loach as Santa? Myth Golden State, Sam, or Teo overloving Youngster to death? When Sylvan told Alabama about Sam and the blow job, Al was wearing a T-shirt with birdshit stenciled on each shoulder and was taking all the money out of his wallet, writing his name on each dollar bill. "Grievous mistake," he said, not even bothering to look up. "Tantamount to putting a ring through your nose."

But instead of telling Dad any of this, Sylvan mentions how well he's doing in school. He will surely be granted Honors and invited to stay on as a Ph.D. candidate. "I went up in a helicopter," he says, and puts one of his arms around Dad's shoulder. Sylvan wonders suddenly if he were the father asking how he would want his son to respond. "Taking aerial photos of Año Nuevo."

"Some perspective, I'd imagine."

It was. Fissures crawling up hillsides like tiny wrinkles. The ocean sleepy and blue and smooth except for the stretchmark ripples where the currents met. And the elephant seals, hundreds, like turds washed up on the beach. "Sure was," he says, finally, to stop Dad's eager nodding.

"I'm going to clean up," Dad says, patting his face with a towel. "Meet you and your friend upstairs." He goes off whistling a tune. About seven notes in all, descending a minor scale, then back up. Like a bird call the way it comes off the tip of his tongue behind his front teeth. Very homey.

"Mom, is Emma coming?" Sylvan asks. Might as well get it out in the open. Besides, he misses her. "And Pete?" Pete's her husband. He hang-glides. They live in L.A., where Emma's doing pediatrics. Pete's got a job printing government documents.

"Maybe next week," Mom says, looking stricken. More fragile than Sylvan expected. "She's got so much work, a couple of critical patients, and, well, we'll see." If he were Emma, Sylvan would lose himself in work too rather than come home to be miserable with Mom.

Dad walks in carrying a duffelbag full of clacking things just as Alabama reaches to cut the pie. He's doing it wrong, making strips instead of wedges. Dad hates this. Once Mom applied the knife when the pie was still hot and it collapsed. Dad took it personally, slammed the door, went for a long walk. Now he's standing with one arm akimbo, gravity tugging at his cheeks while he watches Al jiggle long strips onto each plate.

"I love pie," Al says. Then again. "I love pie." As if he's the only one who ever really has.

"Syl, take a look at this." Dad puts his hand into the duffelbag and pulls out vital organs—kidneys, a liver, small intestines—all brightly colored plastic, and sets them on the table.

"Dad."

As he nears the far end of middle age he's becoming increasingly obsessed by the human body. "I've got all the organs now, and your sister's working on getting me a fiberglass skeleton with peel-away musculature. How about that?" He collects body parts the same way Sylvan collects fossils and artifacts. And now Emma being a doctor gives him vicarious purpose. It's disgusting the way he's assembling the yellow digestive tract next to the pie. But, cut in strips rather than the correct wedges, Sylvan knows, Dad won't eat his pie.

"Wait, son. You remember this." Out comes the old plastic heart. Something obscene about the way Dad handles it, rearranges its puzzle-part chunks. Sylvan thinks of the boot heel nailed to Alabama's door. Of Maximus Loach in the rumpled

Santa suit. Of Youngster's pulse, like a tic on his fingertip. Of Teo. And he wonders how a miscarriage feels, what it looks like.

"Larry," Mom says as if the name's sticking to a rear molar. Alabama eyeballs the blue aorta, burps. 'Tis the season, but the way faces around the table look just now, Sylvan would bet they're all imagining the feeling of hands working inside their own chests.

"Maximum splendiferosity." Alabama steps into the bay window of Sylvan's bedroom and looks out over the vineyards. In the spring they're green, ivylike with coiling tendrils, and in the fall they're weighed down with burstable purple grapes, the air smelling juicy and buzzing with insects. But now, in the winter, they hang like gray sticks from wires that run up the slope, every row converging on a single point where the hills begin to look like blue felt.

This view is as much a part of Sylvan as the stretchmarks on his knees. He grew into and up with it. An image never summoned but always popping up: when he talks with Mom on the phone, late at night after blinking off the desk light, as he shuts his eyes into the showerhead. So comforting in its spare beauty, its cyclical predictability. Makes school seem very far away just now, trivial.

Alabama is seeing too much, or nothing at all, standing in the window blocking the light. Sylvan's suddenly a little sorry he invited him; he doesn't feel like sharing.

Across the room Alabama flops bellyfirst on a beanbag and scans the walls. There are no posters. Sylvan is one of the few, one of the very, very few, who hardly ever listened to rock 'n' roll when he was growing up. So there are no posters of the Talking Heads, or U2, or Elvis Costello, or the Dead, or any like you see so many of at college. Instead, maps.

A NASA shot of planet Earth. A topographical of California upside down, with lettering right side up. Sylvan's idea; Pete had it printed. Reminds him of Emma's invention—the Spiral Calendar. Various circular layers—days, weeks, months—revolve around seasonal star charts. It never sold until Pete incorporated women's body parts. Then it had modest success in adult bookstores. Folkalities never heard this part of it.

"Ha!" Alabama says as if he knows the endings to all of Sylvan's stories.

"Why are you such a —"

"?" Alabama raises his impossibly red eyebrows.

"You're—" But then Sylvan stops out of guilt. It's Emma's husband he really doesn't like. Pete did time in the service, volunteered after Vietnam. Told Sylvan a story about a Philippines whorehouse: A naked teenage girl goes under the table during a poker game while the men toss out twenties betting on who's the one getting his dick sucked. That's Pete. Sylvan doubts Emma knows this story. Mom and Dad sure don't. Folkalities are majorly clueless.

"Groovy." Alabama's checking out the Buckminster Fuller globe, constructed out of one sheet of paper folded in a series of triangles. Dad thinks Bucky was a genius. Sylvan has doubts, ever since the old man made a big deal about not taking a drink of water during a three-hour speech in triple-digit weather. As if being thirsty were somehow a state of grace. The geodesic globe is something, though. You see a lot of dome houses around Napa nowadays.

Al feels at home. That much is obvious. He's whistling Dad's tune, and isn't aware he's doing it. Something about this strikes Sylvan as very sad.

Dad opens the cellar door, cool in here, electric torches giving off yellow light, shadowy pools. Sylvan remembers crouching in their umbras during Hide and Seek. Dad is beginning the tour, pointing out racks of Pinot noirs, cabernets. It was a cabernet that Sylvan secretly uncorked when he was ten, each swallow staining his teeth red, making his ears float a little higher till the light got syrupy and the shadows froze. The next morning Dad made him mop up the vomit. Doing it required great physical effort, his breath running haywire, panting one moment, sighing the next, and until then he'd had no idea that eyeballs can ache.

Dad's explaining climate control. "Unvarying temperature is paramount." And "quietude." The bottles must be turned a quarter revolution twice a week to keep the corks saturated. Before mechanization this used to be Sylvan's job, and he liked doing it. He'd bring his friends down for company, do numes, listen to each other's voices go fuzzy.

The wine "finishes up" in barrels made of American oak, "granted, they've not the charm of the French oak, but, I think, deeper promise." Dad's rambling, saying how wine is wine is wine. How wine, though, does have character. How character is all wine has, like a person. "It must be faithful to the qualities of the maternal soil and the paternal vine." His voice is taking on resonance against the stone walls, his eyesockets black and his teeth glistening. Sylvan listens carefully for new turns in this speech.

"At two years old"—he gathers a bottle off the rack—"the wine's just learning to stand on its feet." He gathers another bottle off the rack. "At twelve, it has innocence and purpose. You'll see what I mean, Al, tonight at dinner."

Alabama nods, cocks his head, trying to get a fix on Dad's tone. He doesn't want to miss the punchline. But Dad's not making jokes. He takes his time choosing the next bottle.

"A decent maturing process mellows the tannins and soothes excess acidity." He blows dust from a Pinot noir. "Given twenty years, the wine can finally, then, unmask a little of the mystery of its soil."

This is new.

Vow of Silence Man cannot sanction the Beaujolais. "It hasn't left the soil yet," he writes on a portable chalkboard, his PA system. Sylvan has always imagined, when reading the notes, the Man's voice to sound like the narrator's on a nature program, low and rich, hypothesizing, capable of making sex and violence sound utterly reasonable.

Everybody stares at his own glass. The candlelight shines through Sylvan's and makes a red heart flicker on the table linen. He wonders how Christmas Eve at Phyllis's is going. Teo's probably bouncing off walls. How Christmas is for a kid. Worth looking forward to again. If he said yes, his name wouldn't have to appear on the birth certificate. No one has to know, except Phyllis.

"Now hold on," Alabama says. He downs the wine, one shot, then sucks the insides of his cheeks. "I like it fine."

Mom goes into the kitchen for salad. Dad sniffs his glass and lets his focus go slack on the candle. "How about you, Silver?"

"Bouquet's decent," he says. "Hits the nose deep." He swirls it, the heart on the table explodes. No way he can live with a secret that big. No, if he does it at all, he will sign, the baby deserves that much. The Folkalities won't like the idea of being artificial grandparents, though. Thin redness rushes down the inside of the glass, doesn't hold yet, a sign of unfinished business. "Hasn't found its legs." He lets the wine wash over his tongue. Too sour, full of histamines. "But not bad," he says, because the room needs cheering up. "Not bad at all."

Mom comes back with a green salad and cheesy breadsticks. She offers them to Sylvan and, with the candlelight sparking her eyes, he can suddenly see her at twenty, see why Dad fell for her. He wants to tell her this, thank her for something more than the salad.

"What do you think, Hel?" Dad asks.

She sips the Beaujolais, wrinkles her nose, and says, "I like the noir."

So Dad proclaims that this batch, like last year's, and the year's before, will be donated away. Also, several cases will be shipped to the university for Sylvan's and Alabama's graduation.

It goes on like this, Dad presiding over the tasting of the prized bottles he brought up earlier, the fully fledged reds, including a delicious Pinot noir the same age as Sylvan. Alabama has got the hang of the lingo and entertains everyone by describing the cabernet as "juicy and ripe with a hint of marimba." Everybody's quite high when the prime rib comes. Mom makes the usual prayer of thanks, including thanks to the plants and animals that gave up their lives for the Park family. Then she asks an added blessing for Emma and "the unborn soul."

The roast is superb.

Looking at the steaming meat, Sylvan pictures the bull that chased him and Teo. El Toro, but now with a ring through its nose.

After dinner they all sit in front of the fire, except for Alabama, who goes outside to sneak a cigarette.

"I'd rather he smoke inside," Mom says, "than toss the butts in my rose garden."

When he rejoins the group there are several ashtrays out and a Scrabble game on the living room floor next to the Christmas tree. Gyorgy insists everybody play. Dad goes right ahead and lays down ORGASM on the R of Mom's FUTURE. "Double word score!" Mom says it's a sign of things to come, and Alabama complains that, if he'd've known, there were a number of low-ball moves he could have bolstered his score with. But it's Vow of Silence Man who laughs violently when Sylvan blurts, "I had SPERM before but no place to put it."

You have to destroy a made bed to get in, and it's one of Sylvan's favorite tasks. The sheets smell like a lawn and he's got quite a buzz on; the stream of pee in the toilet sounded like babbling Spanish; the moon over the vineyards is so full it looks about to drip.

He hits the remote control and the TV blips on. The pope waves from his popemobile to thousands of massgoers sitting in folding chairs next to ice chests at a Florida drive-in.

Alabama finally comes in after having been on the phone to Nashville or France for the last two hours. He undresses, hits his toe on the futon platform, and tells it "Fuck you."

On the news it's reported that a fifty-year-old woman has given birth to her grandson. A surrogate, she was implanted with the ovum of her twenty-five-year-old daughter, then inseminated artificially with her son-in-law's sperm. "It was an act of love," says the daughter, crying. It remains unclear legally whether she is now the sister to or mother of her own son. Three days old, the kid already has an agent and a contract for a television miniseries.

The newscast ends with the pope kissing sobbing people while credits float upscreen. The expression on his face suggests that the man has a direct line to God, and Sylvan wonders how such a thing would even be possible to fake. But, then, if you fake anything long enough it becomes true enough to be held against you.

"Do you think a person has to give himself permission to fall in love?" Sylvan asks.

Alabama doesn't answer, instead asks, "Is it possible to have an ironic orgasm?"

Weird question. Yeah. No. Like a compliment. If you give one that's ironic it turns into an insult. "Kind of an oxymoron, right?"

After a long silence, Alabama finally says, "I can see Tennessee." Must miss his family pretty bad. He's gazing at the ceiling made of soundproof paneling installed ten years ago when Sylvan took up trombone—a constellation of perforations. You can see whatever you want.

Sylvan opens his eyes as wide as they go. "I see, like, nakedness."

Sylvan has woken up lead-headed and coughing, and come downstairs for orange juice and aspirin. It's still night, the moon powdery now in a sky just turning green. He stands in the doorway and, instead of saying good morning to his parents in the living room, watches.

Mom's on the couch, pulling presents from a trash bag. She's wearing a V-neck flannel nightgown. Dad's in paisley boxer shorts. They're giggling, haggling over how to position gifts under the tree, when Dad puts a hand through the V of her gown. She grips his wrist, bites his hand, and reaches into the fly of his shorts. Sylvan's *mother*. Dad growls and lifts her half off the couch and pushes up her nightgown. Gifts tumble onto the floor. She's going flabby in the hips and buttocks and he's red-faced and hairy-jowly. The way they throw their heads back, slam into each other, and begin to moan suggests they're giving each other pain, though Sylvan knows of course this isn't so. He has to turn away.

In the kitchen he drinks a half carton of orange juice, swallows water from the tap, then finishes off the carton. He can't help taking another look.

Now Mom's straddling Dad, who's lying on his back next to the fireplace, her tiny breasts taking on a flush from the embers. Dad's oohing and squeezing them. Christmas tree lights blink dumbly. The scene Sylvan has never succeeded in imagining spooks him. Awful and hopeful. That lust went into making *him*. He barely gets to the toilet in time to throw up.

Back upstairs he dials Phyllis's number, hangs up before the first ring. Then he pulls the covers tight, feels thirsty again, and realizes he's forgotten the aspirin. No, not forgotten, decided against it. He can't remember ever feeling this lonely.

Sylvan can't pee. His stubborn morning erection won't subside. They'll be waiting for him downstairs, from where he can hear Muzak "Silver Bells" and smell bacon. Alabama has gone and left the futon made up, must be feeling contrite about something. Sylvan pulls on a cotton sweat suit, baggy enough to hide in, and picks up the telephone to tell Teo Merry Christmas, hoping some of that kid-zest rubs off.

At first Sylvan doesn't recognize the voice on the line, cigar-deepened, earnest: "His name's Charlie. I'd really like you to meet him." Then Alabama's voice comes through, "I don't want to meet him, Dad." Sylvan hangs up. Sounds like a problem. Alabama's dad's gay? A lot of fingers in a lot of pies. Whoa.

"Merry Christmas!" Mom's looking extra chipper this morning or Sylvan imagines it. The message on the fridge has been changed to MARBLIZE WHAT YOU TAKE FOR GRANITE. Ugh. All this good cheer. He's been here less than twenty-four hours and already Sylvan's nerves are shot. Mom pours him coffee and goes back to slicing pineapple.

Alabama enters the kitchen carrying a copy of the *Psychic Extra*. He has an angry-looking pimple right between the eyes.

" 'Dear Doctor,' " he reads aloud from the Nine Lives Pet Advice Column. " 'My pet cockatiel is a pest. She pecks my head when I am asleep. In addition, I used to enjoy taking her around on my shoulder, but now she squawks like the dickens and bites all my friends. What happened to destroy my lost communication?' " Alabama's voice is not his own, so monotone. And his face is rigid. "Any advice?"

"Sauté with butter and garlic," Mom says. Rare form this morning.

But Alabama doesn't even smile, poor guy. When he notices Sylvan looking quizzical he says, "It hurts"—and points to his pimple—"when I move my face."

Sylvan nods, sympathizing, and squirming on the hardwood seat. He really has to pee, especially after a few sips of coffee. But he's still got the burgeoning manhood problem, and nobody to tell or complain to.

Vow of Silence Man appears in the doorway, grins, his rubberized face imprinted with pillowcase lace. Everybody Merry Christmases him.

Alabama yawns, then puts two fingers on top of his head and grimaces. "Ow." He continues jawing and frowning. "When I open my mouth I get a pain here." He taps the crown of his head.

Vow of Silence Man puts a finger on his own forehead, between the eyes, and nods in commiseration. After pantomiming something nobody understands—a hula dance combined with football-referee semaphores—he resorts to chalking out a message instead.

Dad whistles in. "What's this?" He squints, holds the chalkboard at arm's length, and reads, " 'Blocked chakras to the max.' "

Everybody stops what they're doing to look at Alabama, feel sorry for him. The pimple glares like a bloodshot third eye.

"Looks like you've got a couple of crossed wires under the hood, son," Dad says.

Sylvan wonders about all those phone calls. What kind of a name is Charlie? Aren't gay lovers called names like Anton or Lance?

Mom's clattering the pots on the stove, wondering aloud what happened to "all" the orange juice.

Alabama continues reading. " 'Dear Troubled: You have moved the bird's attention and energy out of your body and aura. Also, you both had a past life together as birds in Africa. On a trance medium level, I see your mother and father clash in the birdic energy. You may want to get a healing on how to create a relationship with your cockatiel.' " Because of his flat affect, and because nobody laughs, he may as well be reading the morning news. "Birdic energy?"

Dad shrugs, asks Mom what's wrong with the men. "All we have to do today is be happy." He slaps her on the ass, which Sylvan has now seen bared, cellulite puckers and all, and kisses her. She pretends to fend him off. "I'm cooking here. Let me cook, Lair."

Vow of Silence Man has closed his eyes, and for a moment

Sylvan actually thinks he hears him whisper, "Phyllis." Impossible. When Gyorgy opens his eyes he's looking right at Sylvan. A slow smile splits his face. He'd make a fine uncle. They toast coffees.

After breakfast, Sylvan's hangover is gone. His erection isn't, however, and his lap feels like something warm has been spilled in it. He excuses himself and goes upstairs to the bathroom, where he jerks off. But he can't come, and in desperation takes a cold shower that just makes his headache return. He remembers having read somewhere or heard from someone about a condition in which an erection won't go away. Maybe that's what he's got. Nothing sexual about it. Too bad he can't remember the cause or the cure or how long he has to suffer. Finally, he goes back downstairs, wishing for somebody else's problems.

Everyone gets what they want in the Park household: Mom, sweaters and Chinese poetry; Dad, obscure French wine texts and a model eyeball; Vow of Silence Man, Apple computer software; Sylvan, a Stumpjumper mountainbike; and Alabama, an OED with a magnifying glass. Also things they don't want: Mom, another houseplant; Dad, another cute animal made of corks; Vow of Silence Man, a massage book; Sylvan, his seventh annual bottle of Ban Roll-on; and Alabama, hair tonic. The fire is roaring "for mood" even though it's sixty and sunshine outdoors, where hummingbirds are going at the red blossoms on the aloe vera.

Dad's getting the gift opening on the video camera, but Sylvan is still having a hard time "being happy." He fears bladder burst, and his dick aches, and he wonders who he can tell. Maybe Sam gave him some disease. Maybe there's some kind of medical hotline.

"Here ya go, pal." Alabama tosses Sylvan a gift wrapped in white tissue. It is impossible now to look at him without having your eyes drawn to that volcanic pimple. Like Chamunda's red dot, only a little lower.

"Thanks, buddy." Sylvan's pleased till he unwraps it. A black T-shirt silkscreened with dozens of white sperms. On the back, in splashy handwriting, SPERM DADDY.

"Ha!" Sylvan tries to look cheerful. After all, this is being videoed. Mom watches, perplexed. She wants to know what it means, and Sylvan has to interrupt Alabama, who's happily providing details. ". . . her name is Phyllis, she wants a baby but not a husband . . . "

"She's a nice person." Sylvan finds himself listing Phyllis's accomplishments. "Tres Ojos, she even designed the building, and wrote a textbook, and—" He can't think, Alabama's sticking the mike in his face, plus now he can see himself onscreen, is that really how he looks? Hyper and dumb, blushing, the bulge showing up in his sweats. Who is that person? Last night comes back to him, the appalling image, he suddenly realizes, of his own conception. He looks at himself, waits for that screen image to prompt him, or to show some particular feeling, so he can take its lead or just feel along. It won't. "I— I—" he stammers, and looks to Gyorgy for help. Vow of Silence Man holds his hands out like a conductor, silencing everybody, directing attention to the TV screen just as Sylvan says "—really really like her."

He blinks at his own image.

"There you have it, folks, live." Alabama moves on camera, occupying the screen like Ted Koppel with a bad perm, explaining, " . . . his sperm in a bell jar, then, using a turkey baster . . . "

When the pillow Sylvan hurls smacks Alabama's head, haw-haws come from offscreen, like on a sitcom laugh track. He picks up the pillow, appears to ponder it while rubbing his jaw, "just in from our Santa Cruz bureau," then throws it off camera, where there's more laughing, because the pillow has just caromed off Vow of Silence Man's head.

Then nobody's onscreen, just pillows flying. Dad has joined the melee; he and Gyorgy bob and weave behind sofa cushions.

"Stop!" Mom shouts. But nobody does, and she eventually joins in by tossing handfuls of tinsel.

Sylvan trips and when he's down Alabama clobbers him with a bolster. He keeps batting, knocking Sylvan's head into the coffee table.

"What's the matter with you?!!" Sylvan gets up, fierce, his lip bloody. Alabama has gone too far, taking cheap shots like that. Sylvan grabs him by the collar, yanks. But when he remembers this is being televised, he pretends to be bluffing, and breaks into a slow grin. When they play back the tape no one will be able to tell the fight is real.

But Sylvan's not through with him. "Charlie, Charlie, Charlie." He says it singsongy.

Alabama's face drops. Hit a nerve. Now Sylvan's gone too far, revealing Al's secret. But if Al can do it to him . . . No, that's bullshit. This is a bad Christmas.

Hotdogging falsely for levity, Sylvan throws a behind-the-back lob. But it's a direct hit, the pillow slams Alabama right between the eyes. His pimple erupts.

Vow of Silence Man follows Al upstairs, leaving Sylvan alone to explain the SPERM DADDY T-shirt and Phyllis to the Folkalities. If only Emma were here.

At least now that the camera is off he's more himself.

"Well," Mom says, making her duck lips again. "Would we still be grandparents?"

He feels like kissing her. He was expecting resistance, cautionary advice, mom-isms like "Children make us hostages to fortune."

"I don't know, Silverado," Dad says. "What's wrong with the old-fashioned way?"

"Dad, I'm not gay, if that's what you're asking."

"I miss having kids around the house," Mom says.

Sylvan realizes he can pee now. His boner is gone, thank God. Thank you, thank you.

"Your decision, son." Dad claps his back. "But, personally, that baster stuff gives me the heebeejeebees. Uh huh."

Later, as Sylvan walks out of the bathroom, relieved but afraid—what if this happens every morning?—he overhears Mom exclaim, "*Love*, Lair, that boy's knee deep."

7 This
Means
War

When the phone rings, Phyllis grabs it like a hat blowing away. It may be—anybody.

"Phyl, honey? Are you there?" Ma on the line. She has won one free phone call from collecting noodle-something boxtops. "You should feel honored, we can talk all day."

The thing is, Phyllis does feel honored, and would really like to talk. *Talk* with her mother for once. Tell her the good news: she's going to be a grandmother. Sylvan said yes, proving that sometimes in this world all you have to do is ask. But Ma's excited about beets. She's discovered beets. "They're nature's blood purifiers."

Teo comes into the room and mouths a question.

"Hold on, Ma." Phyllis cups the phone. Since they can talk all day free a moment's hold is no big deal.

"There's wind," Teo says. For the first time in weeks, he wants to go outdoors. The sun is strong, the breeze is kicking, and he wants to fly the kite she gave him for Christmas. About time. He's taking Youngster along "for the copilot."

Sam, horribly enough, had the dead rat stuffed. Then gave it (in Santa's name) to Teo on Christmas morning. Every weekend since he hasn't wanted to do anything but sleep in and watch nature programs on TV. Not that Phyllis can blame him. The taxidermist posed Youngster standing on hind legs like a little polar bear, and implanted pink glass eyeballs and nylon lashes. Sam provided a wardrobe that includes the elf's cap, three capes, and a tuxedo similar to the one Barbie's Ken wears. It's creepy, maybe even sick, but there it is. On top of the coffee table in formal wear.

Teo picks Youngster up, holding him upside down. "See ya."

Phyllis won't dare throw it out. Might confuse Teo even more. Plus when Sam returns from her convention in Houston she'll see through any lie. "How could you be so mean!" Phyllis had practically screamed when she finally got Sam alone in the kitchen on Christmas morning. Sam appeared deeply hurt, tears actually welled in her eyes, and she didn't answer for a long time. "It's not your place telling me how to raise my child."

"Remember, stay this side of the palm tree," Phyllis says. The official border for Teo's unsupervised play.

"I know already." He sighs like an old man and takes Grampa out the door with him.

"And keep an eye on Grampa!" she shouts. Princess, Jack Stark's Afghan, is in heat again. Then, into the phone, "Sorry, Ma."

"About those beets, honey, just boil them up," Ma says. Phyllis pictures home: Father sitting in the La-Z-Boy reading something Bible-related, or the *Wall Street Journal*, and munching on roasted peanuts. Mother with one hand on a wooden spoon over the kettle and the other gripping the phone. "Slip them clean out of their jackets."

Out the window Phyllis notices Teo trying, unsuccessfully, to send the rat up with the kite.

"You'll need a good apple cider vinegar for the marinade," Ma says.

"Mother," Phyllis interrupts. If only there were a way to talk about meaningful matters without getting preached to. Phyllis is almost thirty, for heaven's sake, and still they've never talked about sex, unless you count the time she had her first period and Ma said, "Congratulations, you are a woman," then taught her how to wash blood out of her underwear. "I'm going to get pregnant."

"Makeup?"

"Pregnant, Ma. P-R-E-G-N-A-N-T." Spelling it out feels very good. Like getting out of a car and stretching after a very long drive. Suddenly the call-waiting beeps. Irritating, but Sam insisted they get it.

"Hello?" Ma says, confused.

"And I'm very happy about it." Another beep. "Mother, I've got another call. Hold on." Phyllis clicks into the other line.

"Stark here. Your goddamn mutt is climbing my fence." Last time Jack Stark's Afghan was in heat, he spent hundreds of dollars on an eyesore of a chain-link fence to keep male dogs out. "If you don't get over here and pick his ass up immediately, I'll solve the problem my way."

Back on the line, Phyllis tells her mother she has to go, there's been an emergency, no, no, nothing to worry about, but sorry about not getting full use out of the free long-distance. Then, because she really is sorry, "God bless."

Jack Stark has total muscle control. He isolates a deltoid and flexes, then a single neck cord. Phyllis watches a pec jump under a tight T-shirt that says LIFE IS A BITCH. In honor of Princess probably, the lovely aloof creature who is panting uncharacteristically and pressing her rear up against the wire.

"You teach this dog how to scale fences?" he asks, pulling Grampa's choke chain tight. Grampa's got his tongue lolling, eyeballs straining after the Afghan. Lust is not a pretty sight, but irresistible.

"Well, it's got those squares big enough for his paws," Phyllis says, examining the steel mesh. He must have climbed his way to the top, then jumped. He can climb the cypress tree, even takes naps on the roof of her car. He also walks up the ladder, runs along the top of a cinder-block wall, and leaps up onto the roof, where he gets stuck and howls. Sam wants to sign him up to go on Stupid Pet Tricks.

Stark is impressed, but not overly. He arches his brow above an eye that looks as if it's aiming down the barrel of a rifle. "Where's the other?" He means Sam, who, since she's usually the one home on weekdays, has the duty of collecting and protecting Grampa from irate neighbors. Another chore to resent, and to resent Phyllis for. Especially lately; Grampa's been wild. And, what's worse, Sylvan said yes. As if Sam wasn't overjealous in the first place, now Phyllis can feel her eavesdropping on every phone call, and even simple questions like "How was work?" are packed with innuendo.

"Sam's at a convention," she says. Reminds her she's going to one herself in a few weeks. Be good to get away, even if it's only to Anaheim. "Out of town for a couple more days."

"How are things?" he asks. Stark isn't a bad neighbor. Wears his macho by not saying please, but at least you know where he stands. He'd be the first to call if anything suspicious was going on in the neighborhood.

"Great," she says, qualifying it with a shrug. Actually, she and Sam are on the outs, Teo's glum, and she can't talk to her mother. But Tres Ojos is good, and Sylvan's better than good. He said yes.

Grampa begins to yodel. "Behave."

"Glad to hear it," he says and flexes a trapezius. "But one more time, I'll have to razorwire the fence." He clicks his tongue and twirls a mustache tip. "In which case I can't guarantee your mutt won't self-fillet."

"It won't happen again," Phyllis says, trying to smile politely and sound stern at the same time. When Jack Stark turns to walk away, she notices the back of his T-shirt says THEN YOU MARRY ONE.

Grampa's literally running himself in circles, tangling his rope around the plaster Buddha. Every time he sits down, even for a moment, he gets a red pointy erection. It reminds Phyllis of when she was seven and her next-door neighbor ("Sticky") Vicki Langhorne used to jerk off her tomcat, Nitty, turning a mean-tempered thing into a slave of pleasure till it came all gooily, then five minutes later got mean again.

Teo is adjusting his kite while Youngster lies neglected in the grass. The tiniest hint of heat waves rises off the shingles. Spring's nearly here, already the trees are getting hard little buds.

"*Run, Teo!*" He almost has the kite up. "*Go go go!*" It catches a gust and takes off. When she reaches him, he's panting, neck stretched, chin aloft. The kite, a pyramid composed of smaller red and green pyramids, takes its place nicely in the sky.

"Good work," she says.

"Feel." He has her finger the line. A strong tug, her fingertips go white under the filament. Teo's giggling. Good to see him cheerful and having fun again like a normal kid. Relieves her of having to worry.

"Sylvan tole me the sky was a gas ocean."

The kite bucks and bobs. A streamer of geese goes by, a pair of sea gulls cross their path, while a huge blue heron, high, high up, battles the wind in still a third direction. In her mind, Sylvan is so vivid she can see the breeze ruffling his yellow hair. "The sky is full of creatures today."

"And a lizard now, too."

"Where?" She looks for a cloud lizard, but there are only a few cirrus horsetails.

"There." He points to his kite. "I taped on a bluebelly."

A cruel but unusual torture. "I don't think reptiles belong in the air."

"Youngster wouldn't lift off."

They both stare at the tuxedoed rat lying next to a tuft of grass, then back at the geodesic kite. "I think it might hurt," Phyllis says, though the lizard is probably dead by now of shock.

"Oh, then. I don't want it to hurt." He begins reeling in, singing "We Are the World." The kite lands softly, and the lizard, duct taped on, blinks slowly as Teo frees it. He holds the bluebelly in the palm of his hand, where it can take warmth. Gray except for the bright scales on its side, the lizard blinks again. "I caught him in the woodpile." Usually they don't show up for another month or two, but today the sun is hot enough to come out for.

"Okay, you can go." Teo sets the lizard down and it moves sluggishly for cover. He is waving good-bye when Phyllis suddenly doubts his innocence. It occurs to her that Teo wanted something at his mercy just so he could show some.

Phyllis is embarrassed when Sam catches her in front of the TV spooning Rum Raisin from the carton and watching a ball game. Fat and lazy, that's her. At least she isn't drinking beer, something she'd been considering.

"Hi," Sam says, but instead of a greeting the single syllable sounds like a mood probe. Sam drops her bags and sighs, then looks around as if checking to make sure the furniture hasn't been rearranged. On TV Magic Johnson alley-oops Worthy for a bucket, sparking the Forum into a landslide of clapping.

"How was Houston?"

"A Holiday Inn is a Holiday Inn is a Holiday Inn," Sam says. "But they had some good art on the walls, and there was some interesting new feminist theory bouncing around." She's got on a black dress, suede boots, and an army jacket—citiwear. Her hair french-braided to show off that perfect head. Going fishing? "How's Teo?"

"Fine," Phyllis says. "Sleeping. If we had known you were

coming home a day early we both would have waited up."
Sam sinks into an armchair without even offering Phyllis a hug
or kiss.

"Basketball?" Sam looks at the ice cream, Phyllis's thick
ankles, and the TV again. Larry Bird peers over his shoulder.
Phyllis likes him for being graceless and talented at the same
time. He sneers at thousands of enemy fans and mouths what
lipreads as *"Leave me alone!"* Sam decides to make tea.

In the kitchen Grampa is steaming up the window that faces
Stark's. He allows himself a moment's distraction for Sam, lets
her pet him and accepts the kisses Phyllis should have received.
Then he goes back to the window, a low growl sticking in his
throat like a motor that won't turn over.

"Oh, Goddammit!" Sam yells, picking up a piece of trash. But
it's not garbage. It's Youngster. Head chewed down, eyeballs
missing, tuxedo in tatters, and artificial sawdust trickling out.
Obviously Grampa's work.

"Bad dog!" She sticks the remains in Grampa's nose and
swats him. *"Bad!"*

"Please stop." Phyllis must be careful here. Sam's furious,
near tears, and Phyllis is now not only a slob, but also negli-
gent. Still, it gives her a secret thrill to see that hideous thing
destroyed. "It was my fault."

Grampa crouches under the blows. Phyllis grips Sam's wrist,
has to restrain her physically from swatting him with what's
left of the rat. "Stop."

Sam turns on her, hysteria in her face like a bad hallucina-
tion, and swings wildly. A blow catches Phyllis in the jaw, the
rat's claw scratching her cheek and lip.

Sam collapses and starts to cry. On her knees, she apologizes
for hitting Phyllis, for hitting Grampa, for getting the rat stuffed
in the first place, for "everything." The self-loathing comes out
in tears and sob-wracked sentence fragments as if she's choking
on her own beauty. "I'm so sorry," she says over and over,
deserving of more forgiveness than Phyllis can possibly grant.

Grampa has escaped—jumped out an open window and run off. Phyllis knows where to find him. She puts on a robe and rubber boots and goes out into the dew-drenched air. Even the stars seem to shiver. "Grampa," she calls softly, not wanting to wake up the neighbors. "Grampa."

The phone rings, waking her up. Only a dream. Rings again. For some reason she's sure it's her mother. As she reaches over Sam to pick up she sees it's four thirty.

"Jack Stark here. I haven't decided whether to kill your dog or just maim him."

"What?" Phyllis's blinks stick, and her voice is mostly air.

"Just get up here ASAP." Click.

As she gets out of bed, she thinks she hears Sam mumble in her sleep, "Either shut up or lie."

There are two director's chairs under a back porch light next to the dog pen. Jack Stark is sitting in one of the chairs and wearing a puffy orange down jacket that makes him look like a pumpkin. His mustache is drooping.

"Where's my dog?" Phyllis asks, feeling middle-of-the-night righteous and mean.

"Have a seat." He swigs a light beer, offers her a can from a six-pack.

"What is this, a joke?"

The whites of Jack Stark's eyeballs look sticky, like the backs of postage stamps, but with tiny distended veins. He shuts his eyes, swallows the last of his beer, burps, crumples the empty in his fist, tosses it over his shoulder, and opens them. "Yeah. I think you could call it that." He flips on a portable spotlight. "Motherfucker succeeded."

Grampa and the Afghan are side by side, two pairs of eyes gone iridescent in the whitewash of light. When the Afghan takes a step, Grampa whimpers. Jack Stark keeps the spotlight trained. Grampa wants right, Princess left, they cannot pull apart. Joined at the genitals, they move in an **L** for a shadowy corner.

"Shouldn't we call a vet?" Phyllis stands up, fidgets with the choke chain.

"It's natural," Jack Stark says. "Only way to separate them right now is with a knife. Which I already considered." He flips off the light and explains, in a voice that reminds Phyllis of two-by-fours and hardhats, how the dog's penis remains grossly enlarged after ejaculation, thus "keeping the territory occupied" and increasing the odds that his semen will do the trick. "The swelling can last for hours."

Phyllis decides she'll have a beer after all.

"Gotta respect that scragmutt," Jack Stark admits. "It's certain the bitch is knocked up. Yessirree." He strikes a match to a cigarette, the rough smell of sulphur and tobacco making the cold air sweet. In the east, a rosy sky. People there are already getting on with their days. "But you realize, of course," Jack Stark says. "This means war."

$$* \quad * \quad *$$

"What happened to your face?" Sylvan asks. A jagged ribbon of scab runs from Phyllis's cheekbone to her lip and, like another facial feature, involves itself in expressions. She stops smiling and it straightens out.

"Oh, you know." She unlocks his door and goes around to the other side of the car. "Scratched it."

"Phyllis?" Ever since that never-ending erection, he's been meaning to tell her about the nap room affair with Sam. He almost owned up the day it happened. But he couldn't, and now he's beginning to feel overwhelming guilt at certain times —when he can't sleep, and when he's with Teo. He wants to confess. It's an urge.

She takes her eyes off the road to look at him.

Not now. Not in the car.

He notices they're driving the route that goes by the Duke Kahanamoku Community Center. "Honk! Honk the horn!" She does while Sylvan sticks his head out the window and yells *"Simba!"* and waves at a skinny black man with a headful of beaded dreadlocks who's standing next to a bag lady who, at the last moment before Phyllis turns her eyes back to the road, crosses herself several times.

Oakland's future is bleak. So many buildings made of unreinforced masonry, Sylvan observes, that one good size temblor— a seven-fiver, for instance—will turn the city into a rubble-scape. He's been trained to think in terms of earthly destruction and now he sees the possibility everywhere.

Phyllis points to an extremely tall yellow-brick structure. "The lawyer's in there, we'll—" is all she can say before a gust takes her voice. Harsh winds are blowing off the bay, flinging sea gulls around, sending wrappers and scraps into airborne convulsions. A newspaper shudders, then swoops and pastes itself over Phyllis's face.

The photograph shows a woman holding a baby and the headline says: FAMILY FRONTIER: AMERICANS PUSH NORM. Phyllis and Sylvan duck into a stoop to hunch over the article. It quotes a *New England Journal of Medicine* study that puts the number of Americans conceived by artificial insemination at 450,000. And a Census Bureau report that 26 percent of U.S. families are headed by single parents. Benjamin Lamron, MD, and "family expert," reports, "There's no such thing as Destiny if you've got the right toolbox."

"Ha!" Sylvan has turned the page over. "Here's my mom's crossword!" The coincidence is reassuring. And so is Phyllis's taking his arm as they walk in the same wedge through the revolving door.

The lawyer waddles around a huge oak-slab desk and offers Sylvan a cold-fingered handshake. She's wearing a man's suit, except with stylized shoulder pads and a cranberry cravat, and her toes are squeezed into red pumps. A blond crew cut somehow accentuates her fat thighs. "Unfortunately, or fortunately, as the case may or may not be," she says, lighting an extralong beige cigarette, "there exists, as we speak, a scarcity of laws concerning the subject of artificial insemination."

She sticks her neck forward and clicks open an ostrich-skin briefcase, causing Sylvan to begin seeing her as a member of some bird species.

"*Alternative*," Phyllis says. Nothing artificial about it. She makes herself comfortable in the leather chair. May as well. She's paying for the luxury. The lawyer did not come cheap. "Alternative insemination."

"As you like," the lawyer says. She explains the current legal status of "alternative" insemination. Nothing is legal. By making a contract awarding and/or reserving parental rights, you can show intent, but so few cases have been tried that precedent has yet to be set. She launches into a series of hypothetical situations, and concludes, "The Baby M case notwithstanding, judges, especially here in California, look to the biological facts when ruling." She mumbles that the New Jersey Supreme Court ruled the Baby M contract unenforceable, invalid, and possibly criminal, then crushes out her cigarette half-smoked.

"Possibly criminal?" Sylvan asks.

"The contract, not the act. And California is much more freeform. Indeed, Oakland is, as a matter of fact, quickly becoming, so to speak, a surrogate and sperm-donorship mecca."

"So in other words," Phyllis says, "contracts are no guarantee?"

The lawyer does not answer the question, instead talks of "uncharted legal waters." Then, giving the impression that she's doing them a great favor by revealing privileged information, she describes a few cases. "Recently, for instance, a client of mine asked medical authorities whether she could be artif—ush, alternatively inseminated with sperm from her father, who suffers Alzheimer's disease. She wanted to abort the resulting fetus so that its brain tissue—you see, fetal tissue apparently helps cure certain nervous diseases—could be transplanted into her father's brain."

Sylvan does not like this self-satisfied lawyer—with her Berkeley and Stanford diplomas on the wall, and her nifty view of San Francisco flickering across the bay—making science fiction out of other people's problems. "What's in the contract?"

She hesitates, eyeballs his every feature, lights another beige cigarette, and slides a pile of documents across the desk. They're typeset on quality stock. Phyllis must be footing a major bill.

They settle on one that grants all rights and responsibilities to Phyllis. Sylvan is not liable for any needs, emotional or financial or miscellaneous, of said offspring. But he also waives all visiting and guardianship privileges. And "Father's Name Withheld" will appear on the birth certificate, thus preventing any legal claims or paternity suits.

The lawyer advises that they take blood tests, "to ensure blood-type compatibility and to prevent the communication of AIDS or any other STDs," then folds her hands and smiles.

The whole process feels ugly and shady, even more so after Phyllis excuses herself for a moment and leaves Sylvan and the lawyer alone.

"Just the nectar," the lawyer says, making a show of stabbing out another half-smoked cigarette.

"Pardon?" Sylvan asks, though he heard her well enough.

"Just the nectar," she overenunciates. "No diapers or doctor bills."

"Pardon?"

"You're lucky she wants a baby badly enough to agree to your male fantasy," the lawyer says and leans back in her chair.

Sylvan has to blow his nose. But there are no Kleenexes in sight. Just vulviform paperweights, Georgia O'Keeffe on the wall, a calendar with the dates up through yesterday's crossed off, and a Martin Luther King I-Have-a-Dream petermax cartoon bubble poster. He settles for his sleeve. "Aren't we paying you for your professional opinion?"

"Quote me." She scratches an overplucked eyebrow. Stretching the seams of her suit, and with that blond crew cut, she looks like a little boy picked last in a sandlot game. Sylvan wants to ask if it's ever occurred to her that he is giving up total say in this child's future. His child's future.

"You're explaining why my dreams are bad so your comfort is good," he says, hating himself for stealing a mom-ism, and then getting it wrong. Before he stands up to leave he wipes his cuff on the armchair.

"Forget it." Sylvan buckles his seat belt. "I'm not signing."

"It protects you." Phyllis refuses to start the car. At first she wanted to protect herself, retaining total custody, complete say-so concerning Father's Visitations. But lately she's been entertaining the idea of more involvement on his part. Maybe foolishly.

"Yeah?" he asks, shaking his head and emitting short bursts of air. Only the second time she's seen him angry; it amuses her. "Protects me from who? Ostrich lady? Judges? My own child? Who?"

"The law."

"Law pshaw," he says, watching things ride the wind—a shopping bag, tentacles of cassette tape, purple mylar. "You heard her. It's possibly criminal. There are no laws."

Phyllis will do anything at this point, desperate to keep the project in the works. "Look," she says. But he won't, keeps his eyes on the skyline instead. "It's for your own good."

Because brick is inflexible, Sylvan thinks, buildings crack and fall. The one he was just in is almost certain to collapse within his lifetime. Half the city jumped eighteen feet north in 1906, another eighteen feet is due any day. Why do people build elaborate structures on faultlines? "No lawyers," he says, suddenly facing her. "And no contracts."

Under the weight of eye contact, she agrees. His irises, whole, blue, intransigent; people are so unpindownable. She realizes she's sort of in love with him. A complication she'll just have to deal with. "What about the birth certificate?"

"We'll cross that bridge."

Sam is happy, "really," and wants details. Phyllis tells about the lawyer, Sylvan's balking at the contracts. "Then he said, 'Having a baby is not a business transaction.' "

"How romantic," Sam says, intending no irony. Ever since the blowup they've settled into a kind of truce. Sam no longer wants in on the sperm-daddy partnership, which suits Phyllis fine. Now content thinking of herself as Aunt, Sam asks questions but doesn't offer advice. "When's the big day?"

"Two weeks looks like," Phyllis says, leafing through her cycle charts. She'll try four or five days straight, Sylvan willing. "Oh, no."

"What?"

"Damn damn damn." She has the Listening to Children Convention in L.A. to go to. Maybe she can persuade Sylvan to come along. Hotel sex and room service champagne. Forget it. That's not what she wants anyway.

"Invite Sylvan to come with you," Sam says, either sympathetic or contrite, Phyllis can't figure which. She stops herself from running a finger along the few dots of scab left on her cheek. They look at each other a long time, but in Sam's face Phyllis can only see a mirror of her own suppositions.

Teo slams the door open. "Jack Stark's gonna kill Grampa!"

They all rush outside in time to see Grampa scurrying home. Stark has a rifle aimed. Bastard. It makes a pop and Grampa yips, his hindquarters taking a midair hop.

"What the hell do you think you're doing?!!" Phyllis yells, and hugs Grampa tight.

Stark has already razorwired the top of his dog pen. Now guns? He marches toward them, holding the barrel down. His handlebar mustache is extra starched.

"Berries," he says, showing a handful. The air rifle is loaded with the tiny red berries that grow on the monster hedge between their houses. "Harmless." Then he growls at Grampa, who ignores him and licks Phyllis's kneecaps. "Your scragmutt trashed my front yard." He explains how Grampa ripped open the garbage bags and strewed their contents all over his lawn. "Something has to be done," he says.

"I'll clean it up," Phyllis says.

"That's not what I mean."

*   *   *

A preschool teacher is generally one of those people who hang out with the only child at a cocktail party. So you can imagine a whole convention of them. Earlier today, during Phyllis's lecture on Process Listening ("as if your lives depended . . ."), a roomful of total strangers, consisting mostly of pudgy women and wispy men, granted her the absolute authority that Sam and Teo, and Sylvan, question endlessly. Say anything and these people soak it up. As if their lives depended.

Phyllis lets herself into her room, plops down on the bed, kicks off her heels, and determines to relax an hour before the closing reception. There are two double beds in here, the unused one a squandered resource. She jumps to rumple it up too. If Sylvan and Teo were here, the three of them could go to Disneyland.

But they're not here, neither is Sam (demoted to third place as an object of her affection? No, not true), home taking care of the house, of Grampa. Phyllis closes her eyes and lays her hands flat on her stomach. If biofeedback enthusiasts can run electric trains with wired brain hookups, why can't she feel herself ovulating? Sam says she gets hornier those few days.

But Phyllis just feels hungry, frustrated, older. Another microscopic crater on her ovary. None of us lives forever and the room smells like spray-can roses. She even offered Sylvan plane fare. But he said he had to monitor an experiment.

"This is more important than some experiment," she said. "Who are you?" he replied. "Cancel your convention." She would have too, if she hadn't been a featured guest.

She touches her bellybutton, runs a finger lower. No use. Something's the matter with everybody.

If she won one free phone call, whose number would she dial? She rings the desk. "Any messages?"

Several: Congratulatory notes on her presentation. Addresses of new friends and impressed colleagues. And call Sam.

Either something's wrong or she wants a favor. Sam would not have called just to say hi. Or maybe she's checking in to see if Sylvan made it after all. Whatever, it will have to wait.

Phyllis decides to take a nap. Looking for qualities you don't like in your friends and colleagues and lovers makes you sick and tired of yourself.

Home smells good, dry wood and pillows. Phyllis is happy to be back, exuberant even. There are no unsolvable problems, and when she sees Sam at the kitchen sink, she stops whistling to kiss her once on the cheek.

"Oooh," Sam says, and pulls away. "Tickles."

Teo is trying to catch the moment between flipping the switch and seeing the light, which strikes Phyllis as a worthwhile pursuit. She hugs and kisses him several times. "Wait—" He brushes her off. "I'm discovering something."

Under the strobing light, Phyllis admires the freesias Sam has displayed on the table. Unlike her. They're orange and smell like fruit punch.

"Another pregnant lady was attacked," Sam says, clattering dishes. There has been a rash of assaults committed by a man described as "homeless looking." They happen on the local bus just as it's making a stop—he punches a pregnant lady in the belly, jumps off, and runs away in the night.

Phyllis wants to kick his face in. But, then, that may be exactly his problem—abused as a child, abused all his life. A product of civilization, like nuclear waste. What can you do? She feels sorry for him. For the women he punched. Most of all for the kids who are born into the fucked-up world that has produced this "homeless looking" man. Phyllis wonders if Sam is obliquely warning her. "Was she hurt badly?"

"Lost the child."

This is truly atrocious.

"A group of vigilantes who call themselves 'trollbusters' has been beating up the bums that hang out at the Kahanamoku Center," Sam says. Phyllis remembers Sylvan's friend with the dreadlocks and the lady who crossed herself. "Also—" Sam breaks off, concentrates on wiping dry a pitcher.

"Also what?" Phyllis slouches in her chair. Already shadows are creeping into her sunny disposition.

"There is something I have to tell you," Sam says, glancing at Teo, who is occupying himself with a game that involves spinning, chanting "Open your eyes, turn round clockwise, shut them tight, speed of light," then falling down and giggling. Sam takes a seat, reaches across the table for Phyllis's hand, her own still warm and sudsy.

Phyllis's first thought is, Who died?

"Don't hate me," Sam says.

Her second thought is, What have you done, and does it involve Sylvan?

"Grampa," Sam says.

Phyllis looks under the table, quickly scans the room. "Where is he?"

"I had to get him fixed."

A car horn goes off inside Phyllis's head, gets stuck. "Where is he?"

"Resting in the bedroom."

Phyllis refuses to believe anything until she sees the sutured incision. A groggy Grampa lifts his head, whimpers a greeting, thumps his tail once, licks her palm, then seems to remember he's been doctored, and sniffs the wound, applies his tongue, a look on his face like he's anxious to remember what it is he's missing.

"How could you?" A gross violation has been committed. To her own person; she feels that horrible.

"I had no choice," Sam says, her eyebrows curving up in a show of compassion. She explains: Grampa dug under the fence, ruining some very expensive orchids, to be with Stark's Afghan. Stark came at him with a rake, but Grampa lunged underneath it and bit him right in the balls, "drawing blood, he said." Stark went to the emergency room, Grampa went to the ASPCA for rabies tests, lawyers were summoned, suits involving huge sums of money were threatened, and a few reporters even called. Turned out Stark had only superficial injuries, and it was decided all charges would be dropped if Grampa was simply neutered.

There had to be another solution. Phyllis watches Sam closely. Is it possible she used the situation to get revenge? For Youngster? For Sylvan saying yes?

Yes.

"You never returned my calls," Sam says, shrugging. Phyllis remembers only one call, but it's true she didn't return that one. "Meanwhile, his Afghan is pregnant, due in a month, and will bear a litter of Grampa's puppies."

Phyllis pets Grampa. No more fucking and fighting. His main interests, gone. She'll keep one of the pups, arrange that with Stark, the asshole. In the balls. Ha! Grampa purrs, but in his eyes she can see the truth of what it is she's thinking. He's less dog.

8 Trapped Animals

The great white shark, eyes black and rubbery like drain plugs, ignores the hunks of horsemeat a trainer has lowered into the water. It just swims in circles, suddenly spooking right or left as if to catch its boundaries by surprise and find a way out.

"Why isn't it hungry?" Teo asks. He's holding on to the rail with both hands.

"Won't eat in captivity," Sylvan says. *Carcharadon carcharias* cannot survive in a tank. At least it hasn't happened yet. This eleven-footer is Cannery Row Aquarium's second attempt. The first, a sixteen-footer, bit the glass walls till it concussed and had to be set free.

When a white shark attacks, the eyes roll back, the jaws thrust out, and, momentarily blind, it's guided by sense organs called Ampullae of Lorenzini. The ampullae are tiny sensors, like pores, all over the snout, receptive to electromagnetic fields, including the kind given off by warm-blooded mammals. Biologists discovered that the glass panels of the old tank (these ones are plastic) carried a small ionic charge, and the shark couldn't help biting. Reflex, "like a human knee jerk."

Teo looks at his knees, then back at the shark.

"In the wild it will eat anything," Sylvan goes on. He knows these things. "Hubcaps, scrap metal, Styrofoam pontoons, boat propellers, old scuba tanks."

A family approaches the rail. "This here is a man-eater," the father, a skinny and chinless man, says. Sylvan guesses Texas; the accent. His wife is fat, like ice cream melting.

"We can read, Norm." She and Norm wear matching gift-shop visors. The plaque says that the shark is a viviparous animal—it carries live, mobile young inside its body—and has no memory. Imagine.

Two teenage daughters squeal and hide behind each other while a young son, Teo's age, puts two fingers in his mouth and stares.

"I'll tell ya," Norm says to Sylvan, and pulls at his chinlessness without saying anything more. Sylvan nods politely. The daughters are wearing short skirts and you can see in their pubescent asses, now shapely, the fate they will share with their mother—pear-shaped womanhood and waddling. They giggle, flirting, and the mother puts herself between them and Sylvan.

"It hates us," the young son says. He's got a large head and glasses, and Sylvan immediately likes him.

"No," Teo says and points with his arm. "The shark is not proud." In an odd way, that makes sense. Goes along without any memory, the foundation for every emotion. A life of never waking up from a dream.

The boy seems to understand this, or at least to be comforted by it. He regards Teo, then looks back at the shark, which appears to be chewing, gills pumping water, mouth a jumble of impossibly sharp teeth.

"They have to put up nets in Australia," Norm says, and sighs, as if talking were climbing stairs. "Big shark problem there."

You don't have to go to the antipodes for sharks, Sylvan doesn't say. Signs are posted here in California, just two hours up the road at Point Reyes, warning bathers that beach waters are shark-infested. And five miles south of here Salty Wilcox got bit. *Five miles.* Teo's *dad.* They're going to visit the grave after. Phyllis insisted.

"If they can do it in *Jaws*," the wife says, snapping off a licorice stick, "why can't they keep doing it—rid the beaches of the likes of these monsters?"

Sylvan wants to tell her her life is too safe. So safe, in fact, that she has the luxury of obesity. Self-imprisonment as a means of survival. Like the soldier who wounds with his shield.

"Huh, Norm? Answer me that."

Norm throws up his hands. Sylvan dubs them the Family Norm, and vows that his own will never be like them. His and Phyllis's. Whoa.

"If time were a tape measure," Teo says to the boy while everyone else eavesdrops, "the shark has lived on planet Earth seventy-five feet and human beans only two and a half inches."

Sylvan loves Teo just then, for saying that, for—

"Quite a son you got there," Norm says.

* * *

Sam's spreading peanut butter on a toasted English muffin with such an innocence of purpose—eyebrows tensed, tip of the tongue showing through the lips—that Phyllis hesitates. She doesn't want to barge into the moment.

"Sam?"

Sam looks up. With her free hand she's scratching Grampa's head. Ever since the castration, Phyllis has to admit, things have been better. No more trouble with Stark. And even Grampa seems somehow both spry and mellowed, nothing to prove anymore, like an old man or a child.

"Nice to have the whole afternoon off. Just you and me,"

Sam says, licking her thumb. "But are you sure Sylvan taking Teo to Salty's grave is a good thing?"

Phyllis takes a seat, carefully, as if the air is full of precarious, breakable things. "There's a cave in a clearing about a mile from Tres Ojos and Teo thinks Salty's departed spirit went there after he—" Ever since Youngster got stuffed, death is a tender issue. Phyllis goes on, slowly. "Apparently there are fossils, seashells, and bones. Salty's, Teo thinks."

"Salty's departed spirit? Bones?"

"That's what he told Sylvan."

"Absurd," Sam says, as if she means Sylvan.

"It was Teo's secret." Phyllis edges the conversation back on her own terms. "He didn't want to make you sad." Already, the breakable things are rattling and she hasn't even begun to bring up the oral sex. She wasn't angry when Sylvan told her. A part of her expected it. The infidelity isn't so much the cause of conflict as it is a consequence. A symptom of deeper problems between herself and Sam. Still, it has to be dealt with.

Right now they're fighting through Teo. Turning him into a symbol of their differences. Each of them wants to mother him, insisting her way is best, making the other feel the guilt of possible inadequacy. Phyllis knows what she's doing and yet she can't stop. Like, she supposes, Sam in the nap room with Sylvan.

Sam wipes the knife and wipes it again, till it reflects the red of her sweatshirt, then plunges it into the jam. "Why didn't Sylvan just explain it to him? Isn't that his job?"

"He didn't want to go down into the cave," Phyllis says. "So I suggested he take Teo to the cemetery instead." She hesitates. "After the aquarium."

"The aquarium?" Another rattle of the breakable things. "But don't they have a great white?"

Phyllis nods, tightens her shoulders, anticipating a crash. But the crash doesn't come. Instead, Sam looks at the ceiling while grape jelly drips from the knife onto the floor, where Grampa diligently licks it up.

* * *

Outdoors is unseasonably hot, breaking records. Sylvan can't help wondering if it's a sign of the greenhouse effect—a buildup of carbon dioxide in the atmosphere keeping the heat in. It worries him. So does the enormous hole in the ozone layer over Antarctica. In fact, lots of things worry him: the gigantic mutant sea sponges discovered growing on the steel barrels containing nuclear waste dumped off the Farallon Islands, new viruses, exercise videos and liposuction, radioactive cheese, unidentifiable fungi afflicting southern California beachgoers, garbage and prison barges, the confused doe turning up last week at the end of the wharf, and then jumping off when the ASPCA got there. Now that he's going to have a child of his own, Sylvan can no longer just tell himself I told you so. Human beings are consuming planet Earth like slime mold an apple scrap.

"Why are you squeezing your teeth?" Teo asks. He's munching on a hot dog, not allowed at home.

It can be a cheap trick, buying a kid's affection by pitting him against the rules of his parent like that. But okay, Sylvan decides, as long as you know you're doing it. You are a child until you have one of your own. A mom-ism. "Why am I squeezing my teeth?"

Teo nods, chewing.

"Why choose white shoes?"

Teo kicks the heels of his tiny Nikes together and, squashing the hot dog in both hands, asks himself the question aloud, keeps asking long after the words no longer make sense.

The gorilla has coarse white hair, translucent like acrylic fibers. His face is pressed against the glass, skin pink and fleshy, eyes blue with red pupils, ennui robbing them of expression.

"He's albino!" Teo says, remembering Youngster.

They should give it company. Or a computer or crayons. It's so bored. The price, Sylvan guesses, you pay living in a cage. When you can remember better times. The price the shark won't, or can't, pay.

The Family Norm approaches. It's clear they have the same tourist day plan as Sylvan and Teo. Norm nods hello. The teenage girls cannot control their giggles of disgust, "gross me out," as they stare at the gorilla fingering his semihard penis. The mother, lipless and arms akimbo, grimaces. Norm is stroking his Adam's apple. The little boy goes and stands next to Teo—they're the only ones not embarrassed. Sylvan can feel himself willing the ape to stop it. Wouldn't be so painful except the gorilla is so human. Like watching the worst part of yourself live out some nightmare fantasy.

Sylvan has to look away. The sky is like too many blankets. And only April. Norm and his wife are bickering quietly. Sounds like, "You think feeding animals in a zoo is an expression of love?" Sylvan goes to buy Teo another root beer.

When he returns, Teo is making faces at the gorilla, and so is the little boy. But the gorilla does not acknowledge them, or anything else. Norm is leafing through brochures, the teenage girls are practicing cheerleading routines, and the mother's "corn is acting up."

Suddenly the boys shriek. The gorilla is baring its teeth and pounding the glass. Just as abruptly, it stops, resumes its slouch, then defecates into its hand, sniffs, and smears yellow shit all over the glass.

Teo will want an explanation. Only your enemies can help you. Murder would be an act of mercy. Loneliness is the root of insanity.

"Apeshit," one of the teenagers says.

*   *   *

"Sam, I have to ask you," Phyllis begins. The breakable things creak, might fall. Let them. That they are there in the first place is a danger sign. "Did you and Sylvan, did you do anything?"

Sam stops chewing her sandwich, frowns. "What are you asking me?"

Phyllis realizes she's not prepared if Sam lies. What if Sam lies? "Did you and Sylvan have any kind of affair?" Euphemisms, God.

"I don't know what you're talking about." Sam's chewing again, now vigorously.

"No?" Phyllis asks. What if Sylvan lied? Would Sylvan lie? No. He may be flaky, but he's honest. He would never make wild allegations. Sam, on the other hand, could and would forget to mention anything self-incriminating. "Are you telling me no?"

"*No!*" Sam practically screams. The breakable things rattle. "That's absurd."

Sam's lying. Phyllis watches carefully. Wants to see how Sam lies. Measure it against her memories. Judge the relationship's past and future both by what happens now.

"Never." Sam takes another bite, chewing, chewing, not taking her eyes off Phyllis. A bold liar. "I can't believe you're even asking me that." Verbal bomb shelters. She's got herself convinced, if not Phyllis. The righteous accused.

"You can tell me," Phyllis says. It's a habit from Tres Ojos, giving permission. Besides, if Sam doesn't tell the truth now, there will never have been anything between them.

"Did he tell you something?" Sam asks. "What did he say?" Sam's eyes are trapped animals. Pacing the far wall. Holding fear tight, all the fear in the world. "I wouldn't go near that scrawny weasel if you paid me." She takes a bite of her sandwich, washes it down with a drink of milk from Teo's Mickey Mouse glass.

"Sam, you can tell me. I won't be angry." Phyllis is using a voice she usually reserves for two-year-olds. Not singsong, but hushed, soothing. She wants to foster the mood, that's her field. Where she's a pro.

Sam shrugs. "I didn't do anything." Calm now, as though the charges were too ridiculous to merit an answer. At first this performance might have convinced, but now it's just a further conviction.

"I know what happened."

"What happened?" Sam makes a Jesus face with a Mona Lisa smile. "The jerk told you a lie. I can't believe you'd believe him over me."

"I'm not picking on you."

"And then you let that asshole take my kid," Sam says. "What gives you the right? Like what is this, confront your fears day? Who are you anyway, the bride of Freud?" Neither of them is capable of laughing so Sam begins to cry. "Do I have to oppose you to make sure I exist?" The skin on her chin is trembling. Phyllis is moved, reaches for Sam's hand, but can't, and picks wax drips off the candle instead. "I didn't do it, Phyllis," Sam says, solemnly, tearfully. The famous pout. "It's not true. What he told you, I mean. I did nothing."

The lie is bald and gross. It makes Phyllis feel old, wasting her life. Profound distrust. She can't live like this. The sad thing is, if Sam stopped now, stopped this bullshit and just admitted it, they could go on. Somehow. Not that there wouldn't be problems. But problems can be solved. Phyllis understands the sex. Sylvan is a very attractive man to start with, and Sam, well, Sam has had men before. And it's her way to seduce for what she wants. Control. A way back in. In any threesome, one person is bound to be left out. Having already lost a husband, she's not about to let go of Phyllis. Phyllis feels a little guilty about this and guilt makes it easier to forgive the unfaithfulness. It's the lying that's loathsome.

"What do you want me to do?" Sam is looking around. As if the walls or the window or the hanging lamp might give her the answer. The air is now empty of the breakable things. They're smashed, invisible shards lie everywhere.

"I—"

"I think I better get out."

* * *

Old Priest Grade Road, the sign says, is STEEP AND NARROW. Full of hairpins and blind spots. At the top of the hill Sylvan can smell the grass turning from green to brown, and garlic. Gilroy is the garlic capital of the world. Garlic wine, garlic macramé, garlicburgers, and garlic dolls can all be purchased at roadstands along the main strip. Salty Wilcox is buried ten minutes outside the city limits.

Eucalypti border the cemetery, and a few cypresses. Both are imported species, and they clash with the coyote bush and creosote growing outside the fence. A sprinkler shoots water into the air, making ersatz rainbows. Sylvan has never seen a dead person.

Teo grabs his daybag and hops out of the car. He's been here before and knows the layout by heart.

Crabgrass sprouts at the edge of the grave, and red and yellow plastic flowers, last visit's offerings, have melted into a gooey pool on the headstone.

SALTY WILCOX

FATHER AND HUSBAND

YOU WERE LOVED

1958–1987

Sylvan tries to swallow back cottonmouth. There are so many dead people. Not to have seen one is so . . . American. Whose life is safe? Not just the fat lady's.

Teo has alms: Youngster's old capes, a copy of *Surfer* magazine, a spool of thread, and something else he puts quickly back into his pocket.

"What was that?"

"Daddy's not really here."

Great. Not this again. Change the subject quick. "What'd you put back?"

"You told Phyllis about the cave." There is no other information in his voice, and he's fingerpainting in the melted plastic flowers.

"Did she tell you that?"

He shakes his head no. "I just think so."

"Yes."

If Teo can't trust him to keep a secret, at least he can be sure Sylvan won't lie. Now he's making red handprints all over the marble. He stops to hold up a leather pouch. "My baby teeth."

"What about them?"

"What I put back. I changed my mind. He's not here."

Teo doesn't want to go home yet. Not that Sylvan can blame him. Phyllis will have "had a talk" with Sam about that regrettable nap room affair. Sickening now when he thinks about it. Using sex for power (Sam) or revenge (Sylvan). At least Phyllis seemed to understand. Hardly even got upset.

"Let's go shoot some hoop."

"Why?" Teo asks. The seat belt's too big on him and his feet don't reach the floor. An hour of daylight left, the Pacific's glare-streaked.

"Because it'll be fun."

"Why?"

"They're nice guys. You'll like them."

"Why?"

"What do you mean, why?"

"Why why."

Sylvan pulls up at the Duke Kahanamoku. "Why not?" The basketball court is deserted and the rims have been bent down, rendered nonfunctional. The La-Z-Boy is gone and the lawn chairs are toppled. Something's not right. The park is never this empty of people. No litter even. Just a small crowd under the magnolia tree, commotion and jeering. Trouble, looks like.

When they get out of the car, Sylvan can make out red-and-green-beaded dreadlocks: Simba's head. It's snapping back and forth. Somebody's pushing him around. Somebody wearing a 49ers cap. The guy with the boiled-looking face who started the fracas last fall at the Myth Golden State Parade. He's surrounded by his buddies, about six of them, all wearing TROLL-BUSTERS T-shirts. So they're the ones beating up bums.

A group of vigilantes has been "cleaning up the streets" ever since some madman started assaulting pregnant ladies. Sylvan has read about these guys in the newspaper. Or maybe these guys read the same series of articles and decided vigilantism was something they wanted to get involved with. It pisses him off. No reason on earth to pick a fight with Simba, who's even crippled for chrissakes.

"I'll—" Sylvan notices Teo is looking at him, and there is something new in his gaze. Sylvan can see the day when they'll be equals, and Teo's suddenly an intrusion. A rival even. Or an ally. The way men relate as they hit middle age. Teo pushes out his chest and tummy even more than usual as they march.

The Trollbusters encircle Simba and the bag lady who's always crossing herself. The boiled-face guy gives Simba a shove across the circle toward another guy who pushes Simba away toward still another. Simba does not resist, and his face is expressionless, not a trace of fear or anger, both of which Sylvan is twitching with. The bag lady is cowering and the terror on her face is like a car wreck, something you can't stand the sight of but can't help looking at.

"Don't worry, lady," Boiled Face says. "You stink so bad I ain't gonna touch you with a ten-foot pole."

They laugh. All of them are white, passably clean-cut, maybe even "wholesome."

"Hey, man, ease up," Sylvan says to the guy nearest him, the only one without a mustache. His eyes don't answer Sylvan's; instead they flicker to the boiled-face guy. The leader.

"Get outta here," he tells Sylvan while looking at Teo. He's got Simba's arm twisted up behind his back, and Sylvan makes eye contact through the beads. Simba just shakes his head no. Boiled Face says, "You got no business here." His 49ers cap is expertly crested, a proud jock.

"Leave him alone." Sylvan takes a step forward, but two men grab his arms. He shakes free and three more jump on him. Total strangers, closer to him, physically, than he ever gets to most of his friends. Being restrained makes him feel unrestrainable. Violence's strange intimacy.

"Coolify," Simba says loudly, addressing Sylvan. "The one who take the blows the one energizin the fight."

"We got us a charismatic," Boiled Face grins. He has Simba and the bag lady face to face. Her expression reflects Simba's now, stoic, except her skin is chafed and there are pimples on her eyelids. "Any more words of constellation for the homeless?"

Brilliant by mistake.

"Ain't homeless," Simba says, looking straight into the eyes of the bag lady. "Planet our home."

"Oh, isn't that sweet. Guys?" They all nod and moan warmly, except for the one without the mustache, who seems to be wrestling with his conscience. "Show us, Mr. Planet, about love. Kiss your honey for us." Boiled Face pushes Simba and the bag lady closer together. Only inches apart, yet their eyes remain locked.

Sylvan can't stand this. He thrashes. They tighten their grips, make him watch. He gives the guy without a mustache a look. The only one capable of feeling guilt, he's going to have to feel it for them all. Then, using a t'ai chi trick learned in his air-pillow grammar school days, Sylvan goes limp, and when they let up, he blasts free.

They subdue him quickly enough. But he has destroyed their fun. Boiled Face gruffly releases Simba and walks over to Sylvan. "Why you wanna get involved with this?"

"They're my friends."

"Friends, huh?" More than just his voice is angry. There are spider veins all over the bridge of his nose and his breath smells like tomatoes. "Okay, friend, get involved."

They bring Sylvan struggling face to face with the bag lady. She's got cracked lips and a drifting eye, a face like a long way home. And she does stink, bleu cheese. They push his head from behind. He flexes the back of his neck, wonders if there's some chance Maximus Loach might come squealing around the corner right now in the lime-green Cougar. Nope. Same thing as hoping for divine intervention. A bad substitute for fists. Sylvan throws an elbow backward and feels it crack something wet. As he turns he thrusts his knee upward, catching a chin, then sees the 49ers cap go flying. Boiled Face collapses on the grass and cups a split lip.

"Get outta here," Sylvan says, though in a way he wants them to resist. Test his strength, lay them all flat. But their collective power is broken, and they retreat. A couple of them help Boiled Face to his feet.

"You think I'm gonna forget this?" he rants. "You think so?"

"I see men as trees," the bag lady says. Everybody stares at her. "Walking."

Then they all go off grumbling, pile into GMC pickup trucks, and drive away. The bag lady is brushing her sleeves. She has on several layers, though the day's still hot. Simba is looking at the place on Sylvan's neck where the conch shell should be.

"I lost it."

Simba takes the words another way, meaning temper. "Preciate good intentions. But why invite shame on yourself like that?"

Shame? Who was the one groveling? Sylvan *saved* them. How about a thank-you? "What do you mean?"

"Eye for 'n eye, tooth for a tooth, hand for a hand, foot for a foot, it go on eternal. Hatreds never cease by hatred."

It's true. The Trollbusters will be back, they know where to find Simba. But Sylvan? He'll be up on the hill, at college, safe, snug, on his way to becoming a professional. Still—

"What am I gonna do? Sit back and watch?"

"You fightin thy own causes, not mine." Simba is rolling a joint. Aggravatingly unconcerned. The bag lady is crossing herself again.

"I did the right thing," Sylvan says, only half convincing himself.

On the drive home, Teo insists Sylvan make a muscle so he can feel it.

At Phyllis's house, Sam has got several trash bags set out on the front porch. When she sees Sylvan pull in, she hustles over, takes Teo by the hand, kisses him three or four times, and tells him to "wash up before we go to Granddad's." They disappear inside, leaving Sylvan alone on the porch with the Heftys containing clothes, tennis rackets, toys. A long trip, looks like it's gonna be.

Grampa ambles out on the porch and thumps his tail against the white clapboard. Phyllis complained for weeks after Sam got him "fixed." Poor guy. Almost worse than having a disease.

Sam slams open the screen door. She's carrying a painting of apple trees, and her skin seems extra smooth, as if anger soothes it, gives it suppleness. Every ugly emotion becomes her, Sylvan thinks, as they regard each other in silence. Finally he says, "Need any help?"

Her laugh sounds like spitting. "We're more alike than you think." She starts to load things into her car. Sylvan picks up two bags, then decides not to carry them for her, and puts them back down. He won't miss Sam. Teo comes out of the house, hands full of jelly beans. Apparently he has no idea that it's not just another visit to his grandparents.

They finish loading the car, then get in and drive off. Teo

turns and waves all the way down the driveway. Sylvan has the feeling they won't be seeing each other for a long time.

Phyllis appears in the open door. Her blondish hair is pulled back, leaving her neck exposed, the skin there so white a few blue veins show through. There is a moment of anticipation as to whether they'll hug, and that moment defines their relationship.

9 *Homestretch*

Phyllis is wearing the ikat woven dress she usually reserves for seeking money. The State Capital look—hip, feminine, designed to cut through red tape and get what she wants. But it's the end of the day. The eyeliner is beginning to smudge, the mascara to crumble, and she's done something to her hair; a sweep and a stalk sprout from a black velvet barrette. She looks better without all this; nonetheless Sylvan's flattered. Also a little scared.

"You can still say no," she says. She's scared too, he can see, but he's not sure whether this should make him feel any better.

"I'm ready."

"Feel this?" Humberto calls. It's how he pronounces her name. He wants to know when his mother is coming. Phyllis tells him any minute, and hopes it will be. As soon as he goes, she and Sylvan can start. Her cycle charts say *today*; she's about to ovulate, and they've planned four attempts over the three-day weekend.

"Mamá, mamá!" Humberto runs to the door. His mother, a

heavy woman who wears extremely large, dangling earrings—
Phyllis wonders if they occupy some part of her consciousness,
jiggling and tinkling every moment—is "very" sorry for being
late, and "very" grateful for Phyllis's patience. "You look very
pretty today." The compliment stings. She doesn't want to
stand out. Besides, is she not pretty other days? Phyllis actually
locks the door behind them.

Sylvan is sitting on the couch, eyes on his tapping feet, a
hostage. It makes Phyllis nervous. She's not sure he isn't.

"Why don't you put on some music?" She walks around
latching windows and pulling curtains. Feels subversive, but,
then, what she's doing is just that. Here on school property,
there is a need for secrecy. People can do worse than tongue-
cluck. If she were discovered, there would be hearings. Sexual
harassment is a perpetual California legal issue. And Sylvan is,
after all, her employee. Many things could be said. It could be
said, for instance, that Sylvan's on the payroll for reasons other
than teaching. And there is some truth in that statement. Or
that the only way he kept his job was by granting sexual favors.
Not altogether false. She remembers the day she hired him, the
impulse, and she'd be lying if she said her motives were pure.

Only two people can hurt her. Sylvan, who won't, and Sam,
who already has. In the last month Sam has moved out, got an
apartment of her own on the other side of town, made a threat
or two, and withdrawn Teo from Tres Ojos.

"Can't we just get along as friends?" Phyllis asked a week
ago over the phone. She was calling to suggest Sam keep Teo
enrolled. Ever since she pulled him, he's been calling here,
sometimes not knowing what he wants to say, sometimes asking for Sylvan. It's bad to disrupt a kid's life like that. Home-
wrecking. A child needs routine.

"Is that what a friend does? Turns you out of your house?"

"I didn't turn you out, Sam." Long pause. "I think Teodoro
needs to continue school. Everybody misses him. Plus, a kid
needs to know he's safe, to have—"

"Phyllis knows best," Sam said, bitter. "I wish you wouldn't call here anymore."

"But Sam—" Too late. She had hung up.

"Puff the Magic Dragon," sung by Peter, Paul and Mary, is playing on the stereo. Sylvan has chosen this. It makes trouble seem impossible.

She unlocks the cupboard and takes out her special AI Kit: a leather mailbag full of the things they'll need. Red wine for one.

Tension tightens muscles, turns mucous acid. Sperm can live in the vagina only eight hours if conditions are prime. Four days if they get past the cervix. It may be true that alcohol can complicate pregnancy, but it simplifies conception.

"My dad would be pleased," Sylvan says when he sees the Napa Park label on the cabernet. It was expensive, but she doesn't mention that. "What's in the bag?"

She pulls out a beeswax candle and strikes a match to it. The orangish light makes Tres Ojos a different place. "Puff" on the stereo, miniature furniture, kids' art everywhere, romance does good business here. They toast "Baby."

"What else?"

Phyllis pulls out a tall Mickey Mouse glass. "Container. I didn't know how big—"

"There's not that much."

"I know." She smiles and runs a finger through her hair, tucking it behind an ear, then takes another sip of cabernet. "I just wasn't sure what else to use. Maybe these?" Packets of condoms.

Sylvan's alarmed. She's grinning, and her lips and teeth are stained red, making her look, with her bleary makeup, like an ogress.

"Don't worry." She touches his shoulder. "I'm not going to. They're . . ." To explain, she pulls out a syringe. Fiendish. "Receptacles."

The syringe (without the needle, of course) will easily fit in the rubber to draw up the semen. That's a twist, using a birth-control device to achieve rather than prevent pregnancy. Still, the whole process, whether it's a Mickey Mouse glass or a rubber, feels kind of sloppy.

"Hey, Phyllis?" He takes a gulp of wine.

"Yes?"

"Why don't we just—" No. Her eyes are pushing him away. He won't insist. He's not even sure he wants to. It would imply . . . all sorts of things.

What is it? Phyllis wonders. Could he be about to ask what she thinks he's about to ask? The world is not a bad place. At all. But she'll say no if he asks. Maybe if they were stranded on a desert island, but not here, not in Santa Cruz, where tomorrow crowds you.

"What else is in the bag?"

She's a little relieved, but mildly disappointed, and sips some more wine. "It's very good." Not just the taste. The buzz is superfine, like no buzz at all. Just a clarity. A lack of pretense in things, in herself.

"The bag?" Sylvan gestures. Now "I'm Being Eaten by a Boa Constrictor" is playing. He likes this song, the kids go crazy on it.

"I'm embarrassed." She smiles. "Here, you." She hands him the bag, and he takes out a couple of magazines. Erotica. Photos and text. "I wasn't sure if, of what"—her hands make a motion as if spooling out thread—"you might need to—"

"Thanks, Phyl. Considerate of you." He thumbs through, skimming. Naked women sucking pearl necklaces. Men and women, women and women, men and men. " 'Oh heck, it's up to my neck . . . ' " Porn in the day-care center. And syringes. And condoms. And Phyllis brought them. Little does she know it's not getting it up he's worried about, but getting it back down—a relapse of the endless hard-on, his Christmas condition. Are the two of them being weird? Perverts? Sylvan tries to feel like one, but can't. "Really, thanks, but I think this would have the opposite effect."

Sylvan comes out of the bathroom (the kid-size toilets fraught with silly meaning) with a blotchy flush all over his neck, and a dumb grin. He hands over the used condom, slightly disgusting, but Phyllis seems eager for it, and disappears into the nap room with the syringe. A moment later she comes back for her wine. "I'll have to lie down for fifteen minutes after. Get gravity working on my side. You can go if you want." She closes the door.

He plunks himself down on the couch. It doesn't feel so good, this businesslike quality they've been striving for. Behind-closed-doors facial expressions. Bisolitude. Cold and impersonal, like a reverse one-night stand. Yes, Alabama, it is possible to have an ironic orgasm.

He gets up and kicks around a Nerf ball, then puts on another record. "William's Doll," sung by Marlo Thomas and Alan Alda. It's about a little boy who wants a doll, but whose insensitive father says no. Truth of it is, Sylvan wouldn't want his son playing Barbie either. Well, it depends. If the kid made it do things, turned it into a thrillseeker, or invented dramatic situations, something like a play, okay. But dressing her up and bickering, like Chamunda does with hers, forget it. Mom says, though, that if you don't let a kid do something, he never passes through that stage and gets fixated. So by not letting him play Barbie you could turn him queer. He'd rather his kid not be homosexual, even less a faggot. Two different things altogether. No offense, Alan and Marlo, but sometimes professing an open mind seems worse than admitting your prejudices.

Basically, he decides, he'd want his son to be just like Teo. A kid you can respect. Too bad Sam yanked him from Tres Ojos.

The telephone rings. Shrill and creepy, a brutal intrusion. Again. Tres Ojos closed two hours ago; nobody should be calling now. Again. Makes him feel spied on. He answers. "Hello?"

The line is open, but no one speaks.

"Hello?" Sylvan says again. It clicks dead.

Phyllis hurries out, not wearing shoes or stockings now. "Who was it?"

"They hung up." He wonders why she looks so careworn. It's not that big a deal. They're two consenting adults.

But she's packing up her stuff, preparing to leave, already asking if he needs a ride home.

* * *

Day two has been reserved for a scuba-diving trip. By mid-morning a thick mist is still sapping the world of colors. Trees are dripping gray, and the wild roses growing along the highways refuse to open. Neither he nor Phyllis has said a word since Moss Landing, the only sound the hum of the car.

Last night Alabama wanted to know all about it. "Grab a dab" is what he called Phyllis's "reverse birth control method" of taking her temperature and checking her mucus to determine fertility. Then he complained about the small size of his own dick and claimed that's why Monica "left" him. All this stupid, but amusing. Then he started really getting on Sylvan's nerves when he began singing "Wedding Bells," and insisted he be the best man.

"Only two rules you have to know," Phyllis says, interrupting Sylvan's mental replay. Without wanting to, he suddenly imagines her in a wedding dress, white. "First, buddy breathing, which I'll show you when we suit up, and, second, when you're ascending, don't go up any faster than your bubbles, and never, never hold your breath. Gas expands." Since he's not certified, what they're doing is slightly illegal. But she's giving him a fairly thorough brief lesson, which she ends by explaining air embolism, literally when lungs explode, to scare him a little. He has a tendency not to follow instructions. "Your brain gets spritzed and pink foam comes out of your mouth and ears."

Sylvan's unimpressed. He's a better than good swimmer.

Mishaps can be avoided. It's the possibility of sharks that worries him. Now that he's seen one up close. "They had to release that great white at Cannery. It wouldn't eat."

"Don't worry," she says, then cites probabilities. Car wrecks, getting struck by lightning, and slipping critically in the bathtub are all more likely. So is winning the lottery. "Still, you don't want to tempt fate. But the elephant seals are long gone, and, of course, I'm not menstruating." Supposedly it's the same thing with grizzly bears, they'll smell the blood and come hunting. Sylvan has heard stories. And surfers at Steamer's Lane crack nervous, bad jokes, wondering aloud if the few women who go there are "chumming" the waters. "I've gone diving hundreds of times here and not once have I seen a great white."

"Salty Wilcox saw only one." It is a cheap thing to say.

At Point Lobos several ecosystems overlap. The fog is beginning to lift, revealing sunlight that smells of tide pools and pine trees. Monterey cypress grow on the rocky outlooks that plunge into an ocean so tourmaline the breaking waves look ultrawhite. You get the feeling something's going to happen.

They drive past the parking lot full of Winnebagos and Jamborees and brushed aluminum Airstreams. A family of tourists who has set out a picnic spread alongside the road flags them down. They're Germans, extremely polite, good posture, blond and smiley, straight out of a fifties catalog. The father says, "Hello, I'm a nice day." Then he points to a pamphlet and asks for a translation.

Phyllis tells them it says "be a nice day, and don't kill anything." They all gather around the car and smile, insisting she take one of the brochures and some chocolate bars.

At the remote parking lot by Whaler's Cove, Sylvan gets out of the car and stretches before unloading scuba gear from the trunk. Compared to Phyllis's hydrodynamic yellow aqualung, his own rented and dented steel tank looks extremely low-budget. "Yeah, it's pretty dated," she says. "Usually when they're this banged up, they get stress fractures."

"Thanks for the high-risk equipment."

"Don't worry, they do tests. It's safe."

Besides the tanks and the wet suits and the buoyancy compensators and the masks and snorkels, there's a lunch packed in an ice chest and the special AI Kit for after.

Offshore, kelp beds mottle the surface. Beyond them, Sylvan knows, the ocean floor suddenly drops miles: the Monterey Bay Undersea Canyon, several times larger than the Grand Canyon. It starts here and sucks down the volumes of sand that migrate south along the California shore. Deepwater upswells bring cold Pacific water and fresh nutrients for the plankton, the single-celled animals at the beginning of the food chain. Whales come here often, even humpbacks. Overlapping ecosystems.

"Sir Francis Drake landed here on his voyage to discover the New World," Phyllis reads from the brochure. Not a bad place for a first impression. Point Lobos never loses its newness. She hands Sylvan a mesh bag full of equipment, and takes one for herself. The only bad thing about scuba diving is the scuba. Terribly cumbersome, but, like a spacesuit in outer space, necessary.

Sylvan looks like sausages in his neoprene. She shows him his gauges, how the regulator works, how to buddy breathe, and then how to keep his mask from fogging by crumbling a cigarette into it, spitting, and rubbing the mixture around. A trick she learned in Baja.

Whaler's Cove is flat, no waves to fight. Sylvan goes backwards into what feels like crushed ice, till he's deep enough to use the snorkel. Breathing in through your mouth takes getting used to, and so does that huffing sound, loud and internal. The bottom is covered with polished stones, round and smooth and colored like Easter eggs. Skinny silver fish and tiny sculpins swim away scared. Phyllis appears alongside and they look at each other. Everything is slightly magnified, and the way the mask presses in makes her face look goofy. So does the way her lips wrap around the snorkel mouthpiece. Reminds him of Humberto's wardrobe at Tres Ojos.

The kelp bed's border is rigid, like row planting, bull kelp growing thick, translucent ocher, with vinyllike streamers for leaves and carbon dioxide–filled bulbs that float. Sylvan squeezes one until it pops. Satisfying, like snapping air-node packing.

Phyllis points below. Here's where they switch to scuba.

He spirals down headfirst. Bubbles spill out of the regulator on the exhale and tickle his cheeks. Pressure builds in different places inside his skull. He squeezes his nose shut and blows out, unpleasant sensation, to equalize his ears. Thirty feet under. It feels like, not flying, not swimming, but like forgetting your dreams when you first wake up.

Phyllis is a different animal down here. The suit is snug on her, and shows off her body. Well put together. Very lithe, kicking, letting out a stream of bubbles. He's suddenly grateful, the gratitude you feel towards a guide who has just shown you something you've never seen, therefore something new in yourself.

Bright orange garibaldi flock around them. Starfish cling to the rock at the roots of the bull kelp. He remembers the ecosystem he created at Tres Ojos—the kids role-playing these very creatures, all connected by string. Where do he and Phyllis fit in?

Actual shafts of light scintillate, illuminating a fold in the rock, the iridescence of a couple of squid (they're rare now because El Niño, the freak warm current sweeping alongshore, keeps them away), and the water itself, like a blue and gold mosaic in his peripheral vision. Suddenly a school of angelfish swallows him up. They're purple with yellow faces. He rolls his head, sticks out his arms while they float lazily by, accommodating him, moving one at a time and in a group, giving him a pleasant vertigo, until a large fusiform shape appears at his side and he bolts, causing the school of fish to explode soundlessly.

Something takes hold of his ankle and panic scalds the back of his throat. He thrashes free and turns and there's, goddamn it, only Phyllis. Goddamn.

He shakes his head and moves his hands in front of him as if he's rattling a fence. Pissed off and no way of expressing it, except in his eyes, which can't even blink straight in this tight rubber mask. Now he knows how Vow of Silence Man must feel, trying to get things across.

No, he shakes his head. Don't do that.

She shrugs, Sorry, and takes his hand, leading him through the subaqueous forest, stalks as thick as wrists. The rock falls away in a shelf of grottoes. Here fish are abundant, and purple sponges, and abalones camouflaged with a thin layer of green silt. Phyllis points at a lobster, its antennae sticking out of a crevice next to a moray eel that has a head like a burnt stump, eyes like a fish's, and teeth like a dog's. On the surface, fifty feet up, Sylvan can make out the silhouettes of two sea otters. A group of his bubbles rise towards them. Why isn't everybody doing this?

Ice water surges over him, seeps into his wetsuit. He peers over the last shelf: the Undersea Canyon. Big, cold blue. No bottom, no sides, no fish, nothing but blue. Like a cloudless alpine sky.

He swims slowly into it, away from the grotto. Phyllis is waving him back. He makes the A-OK sign, then a small pinch meaning just a sec. Now he's thirty, maybe forty feet from the rock, and his wrist meter says he's facing south at a depth of seventy feet. He goes even farther, until Phyllis is barely visible, blending in with the dim outline of the rocks. Then even that outline fades, and the blue opens. Like spacewalking.

This is aloneness. Self-contained. And the thing is, he's never felt less lonely.

Some large body appears, Phyllis scaring him again. But it's not her. As it comes near, like a photograph just emerging in a darkroom tray, its body acquires more detail. Shark. Holy . . .

The gill slots, the chewing of water, the dorsal fin and the two pectoral fins, all triangles. Like the teeth. The black rubbery eyes. A great white.

Phyllis's fault. No, that's crazy, but she promised no sharks. Has she seen it? Better not come out here looking. The rocks are safe, you can get tight against them so the shark can't make a pass. That's where he has to go. Beyond them, the kelp bed, total safety. He must not panic. Predators thrive on fear. Eat it up. He checks his wrist, moves N toward the cliff, toward Phyllis. Don't panic don't panic don't panic don't . . .

When he finally remembers to breathe, sending out a stream of shimmering air blobs, the shark's eyes move. It flicks its tail and veers to investigate.

God, it's huge.

He swims slowly, against all instinct, no panicky vibes. Things come back into view. He can see Phyllis now, backed against the rock. She waves, gestures toward a hollow where there's protection. Only thirty feet.

But the shark's getting agitated, more flickering movements of its tail and fins, sudden changes of direction. Sylvan abandons caution and sprints, burning adrenaline, keeping his eyes on Phyllis, who's shaking her arms. He's close enough to see her eyes now. They're terrified, focusing beyond him, and—

He's hit. A blast of screaming metal. The impact knocks him forward in a rush of bubbles, a crush of water. When will the pain come?

Phyllis is here. She's got him, and they crouch against the rocks. Puts a regulator in his mouth but he's hiccuping and can't get a breath. Finally his lungs stop jumping long enough to inhale, and he fumbles to clear his mask. More breaths. No sign of the shark. Nothing out there, just blue, and thin streamers of bubbles rising from nowhere, like carbonation. He manages almost to catch his breath before Phyllis takes back the regulator. It's hers, he suddenly realizes. His is gone.

The pain comes. Somewhere on his back, stinging, and when he arches around for a look, he sees his tank is gone. The fucking shark ate his goddamn tank.

Back onshore, after a long nauseating swim, Sylvan can barely stand. His knees feel like raw eggs and his teeth are chattering even though he's boiling. Where the shark bit him on the ass stings and burns.

Phyllis rips off her mask and laughs as if she's gone mad. "It exploded!"

He somehow cannot picture the shark exploding without him.

"It bit your tank and blew up!" Phyllis is talking hysterically. "It must've punctured a stress fracture!" Jubilation. She describes the speed of the attack, the jaws opening, the eyes rolling back, then the explosion of compressed air inside the shark's mouth, sending it into convulsions, swimming upside down, down into the canyon. Jubilation. Tears now. "But don't you ever," she cries, "go off on your own like that again."

Sylvan shivers. Refuses to feel guilty for his own shark attack. He puts his arm around her, tries to get her to stop crying. Shouldn't she be comforting him? He's the one in pain.

"Let's take a look at that urchin wound," she says, sobs subsiding.

"Urchin wound?"

Three purple spines are sticking out of his wet suit. He must have leaned against a sea urchin when she brought him into that rocky hollow. The shark didn't get him at all. In a war story kind of way he's disappointed.

"There were millions. You got off easy."

That doesn't stop the pain. Actually, it's beginning to hurt worse.

She takes his pulse and checks him for signs of shock. There are none. "In about ten minutes, when the adrenaline wears off, you may start feeling strange."

They walk back to the car, where she gets a scissors and pliers from a toolkit, and a couple of codeines from her purse.

He swallows them with an icy Coke from the chest, then wants another, suddenly parched. She cuts away his wet suit. The sun and breeze feel ridiculously good on his bare skin. A cormorant skims the waves, the sky still ordinary blue. Trees green. Nothing's changed, except the otters are gone.

Still no sign of shock. If anything, a dreamlike quality, as if it never happened. Maybe he should report the attack. It won't be real until he reports it. Other divers and surfers should be warned. But he'd have to go in front of the TV cameras. Become famous. Forget that.

Phyllis takes up the pliers and tells him to picture something nice. He imagines Teo eating pineapple. What will Teo say? First his father, now his—

"Ow!"

She has extracted a three-inch spine from his right buttock. "Urchins release a toxin, that's why it hurts so much." Like being stabbed with burning sparklers.

"Ahh!" Another, this one smaller.

"Ammonia breaks down the toxin. You don't want these things getting infected."

"Yeah!"

"Unfortunately, I don't have any ammonia, the hospital's an hour from here, and—"

"No hospitals," Sylvan says, eyes shut tight as clams against the pain. Doesn't want anything to do with a hospital. *"Ouch!"*

"—peeing on it works just as well." She puts down the pliers, finished.

He looks at the three punctures on his butt, welting up, dark purple. Then at Phyllis. Salt has dried along her eyebrows and upper lip, and her hair hangs in wet locks on her neck.

"Peeing on it?"

"Huh? Oh, yeah. Kills the pain same as ammonia. Some say even better. Detoxifies too. Urine's sterile, you know."

"Are you serious?"

"I don't know myself."

He needs more codeine. Drugs. If he could stop his pulse, the throb would go away. Pain all out of proportion. And Phyllis is standing there smiling. Beaming even. Yes, you could call that expression beaming.

"Won't . . . can't . . ." He cranes for another look. The punctures are puckering before his very eyes, the skin there brown and yellow and green and purple, thin trickles of blood. "Reach." He gingerly wraps a towel around his waist.

She takes a long sip of his Coke. "I'll do it."

They go into the bushes, even though modesty seems unnecessary at this point. But Phyllis insists. She's in a skirt now, over a snug one-piece, and her nipples are erect. They're nice breasts, on the small side, upturned, the kind that would look good in a strapless wedding dress. It's the toxin making him think like this. Psychoactive.

"Here looks fine," she says. They duck under a cypress, where the earth is cushy with fallen boughs. He lies flat on his stomach and drops his towel. Embarrassing, the way it used to be getting his temperature taken. But . . . anything to stop the pain.

"Don't look," Phyllis says. It amuses him, this new bashfulness. She plants her feet on either side of him and lifts her skirt. Sylvan waits for, then feels, the warm trickle between his shoulder blades.

"Whoops! Aiming problem."

A splash over his back and down between his buttocks, where it tickles. When it hits the wounds the sting intensifies for a half second, followed by a feeling of extreme satisfaction, like an insatiable itch being scratched.

The tree rustles and between the branches faces appear. The German family. They all smile and wave. "Hello, I'm a nice day," the father says. The mother is carrying a bouquet of poison oak. It is, after all, at its most beautiful this time of year, the leaves red and oil-lacquered. Tomorrow her vacation will turn into a bad trip, if it affects her like it affected Rusty—the swollen head and the oozing pus. Sylvan points and says, "You don't want to be touching that."

She smiles and nods and buries her nose in it, sniffing.
"Phyllis?" Urine is still trickling down his butt.
"I can't stop midstream." By her tone of voice he can tell she's forcing a smile. He smiles too, as if biting down on a dental X-ray, causing the whole family to renew their smiles. Everybody's nodding and smiling and nodding. The pain is gone.

* * *

The smell of a house reveals something about its occupant. His subconscious maybe, or a hidden self. Chocolate and oranges in Sylvan's case. But he also has a roommate, who, Phyllis has been assured, will be out all afternoon. She looks around the apartment, guessing who belongs to what.

The bobcat skeleton, either grinning or snarling, is posed in a cat crouch, ready to spring from the top of a huge console television. Definitely Sylvan's, but the twinkling lights strung through it probably the roommate's. The huge amplifier the roommate's, along with the record collection: extensive blues, Elvis, Led Zeppelin, Kansas, Lynyrd Skynyrd, Boston, and the Beatles; very seventies. A rumpled box of throat lozenges on the coffee table, along with empty beer, Seven-Up, and orange juice containers. A stack of old newspapers. Textbooks. Paperbacks. *Lolita, One Hundred Years of Solitude,* and Homer's *Odyssey.* On the windowsill an antique tin can full of crispy flower petals. Definitely a woman's touch. Has to be. Men don't value flower petals. She wonders if Sylvan has women after him. There's so much she still doesn't know.

"Sylvan?" She yells through the closed bedroom door. Something in there falls and crashes.

"Tell them I'm not here."

He thinks the phone's ringing again. All morning newspapers have been calling him. Word's out about yesterday, either from Student Health (who gave him antibiotic ointment and a codeine prescription) or from the scuba-rental shop (who took a whopping deposit on the wrecked equipment). The TV news has been reporting the shark attack and referring to Sylvan, who won't grant a single interview, as the Mystery Survivor. But worst of all, yesterday the two of them didn't even get a chance to do an insemination. So today Phyllis is eager, ants, as her mother would say, in her pants.

She turns to the other bedroom. A boot heel is nailed to its door. She considers taking a look inside, a quick rummage around. Other people's homes have always interested her. Viewing the intimate details of another life, the secrets they don't know they have. But she resists the bedroom and goes instead to the kitchen, opening the refrigerator. This, she decides, can be the psychological equivalent of dark, unmet appetites. Beer. Lots and lots of it. She didn't even know they made thirty-packs. Tortillas. A five-pound can of refried beans half-eaten. Sprouts. A cheese crust. A dozen or so individually wrapped pats of butter in the egg tray. Withered carrots. A jar of bee pollen. Has to be Sylvan's.

She opens a few kitchen drawers. Forks and knives and spoons all mixed together with chopsticks and pink Sweet 'n Low packets, thick blue rubberbands, a Swiss army knife, a compass, and toy soldiers. What's taking him?

The bathroom is very male. Toilet seat up, pubic hairs sticking to the rim, dark ones Sylvan's, red ones obviously the roommate's. For reading material, ha! the erotic magazines she brought Sylvan, but now they look thumbed through. Disposable razors and Barbasol shaving cream and Ivory soap and a few worn-out frizz-bristled toothbrushes cluttering the sink. Head & Shoulders shampoo in the shower; which one has dandruff? The roommate. In the medicine cabinet there's aspirin, Nuprin, Tylenol, vitamins B and C—hangover remedies, she supposes—along with combs, eyedrops, mousse, several bottles of deodorant, and Encare spermicide. Whose?

Feeling like a snoop, she goes and sits on the couch, leafs through the Oakland *Tribune*—Sylvan's mother's crossword halfway completed—*Sports Illustrated*, and an opened letter addressed to Sylvan Park, frilly handwriting, a girl's, no name on the return address at UCLA. She looks at the tin of flower petals, then back at the letter, wonders again about the Encare, is just starting to extract the letter when the front door opens and five red-haired people walk in, all plopping luggage in a pile on the floor.

"Hi there," one of them says. He's got the reddest hair of all, unruly eyebrows, ears that stick out, and he's carrying a dictionary. "I'm Alabama—"

"*Tho*burn," the only girl among the five says. She's over-freckled and has copper-colored eyeshadow. "Tell the truth."

"My real name's Thoburn," he concedes. "Thoburn Whitaker. But you can call me Alabama." He holds out his free hand. "You must be Phyllis. Sylvan sure talks about you." As they shake, he winks. "Shamelessly." Already she dislikes him. Smug bastard, disrupting their—uh oh, Sylvan's still in the bedroom hard at it. "I'd like you to meet my—"

"This wall shoulda been a door," one of the other boys interrupts. "And that hallway's all wrong." He knocks on the living room wall. "At least it's plaster"—makes marks on it with a pencil, and opens a tape measure. "But you got a whole lotta *misemployed* space."

"I'd like you to meet my family," Alabama repeats, loudly. "This is—"

"Charlie," Charlie interrupts again. He looks different from the others. His hair darker, caramel-colored, and his skin pale, smooth except for a few whiskers poking through at the chin and several coarse black hairs growing out of a mole under his nose. Must be hell passing a razor over that. Since his right hand is full with the tape measure, a pencil, and another gadget, he offers Phyllis his left hand. It doesn't match up with her right. They fumble and squeeze fingers in a way that feels too intimate. "Y'all the one fought off that shark?"

"Yes," she says. "I mean no. We were lucky."

The Whitaker family wants to hear the story, but first they line up, all of them, single file, to be introduced. Mackenzie, in

addition to copper eyelids, has copper lips and copper fingernails, and red hair encrusted with glittered hairspray. It gives
her a metallic look. Riveting. She's twenty-five, a lingerie buyer
for Busby's Department Stores.

Next comes Charlie, the odd one, who, on second appraisal,
looks to Phyllis a lot like Alabama. Both are wearing starched,
creased, flare-leg jeans. They have the same ears and chin, and
though Charlie's hair is darker than Alabama's, it's got a simi-
larly explosive texture. He's twenty-three, same as Alabama,
and working construction. Fraternal twins? That would explain it.

Then there's Overton, majoring in Poli Sci at SMU, a very
large head and bony knuckles, keeps licking his lips.

And, finally, E. Graydon, "Cubby," who's just seventeen and
can't stop smiling.

They're all alike in the eyes and eyebrows and they all say
"Pleasure," with a soft *r* as they shake her hand. Such nice
manners, every one. Their mother must be proud, or an animal
trainer. Alabama asks if Phyllis would like a beer, but Charlie
has beaten him to it and is already passing out Coors. They
take seats around her and beam, like flowers facing the sun,
the attention overwhelming, intoxicating.

"How big?" Charlie's got his tape measure out. "Bigger 'n
this?"

Phyllis pictures the shark and nods. "Bigger."

"Bigger 'n this?" He extends the tape another two feet.

She nods.

"Say when." He increases the length, slowly, teasingly.

She waits till it looks about right, then a bit longer. "When."

"Eleven-and-a-half-footer. Mercy!"

She begins to tell them the story. Why not? It's a good way
to buy Sylvan more time. But they already know the story,
and, like kids, sit politely through all the description waiting
for the good part, the action. They want to hear over and over
again how the shark exploded.

"Did it really blow up?"

"There were so many bubbles."

"So did it die?"

"Looked critical." She tells them how it went into spasms and swam away upside down. They like this.

"How'd Sylvan's face look at the exact moment?" Alabama wants to know.

She has to think about it. "It looked like, well, it was hard to see behind the face mask." Where is he, anyway? They're making enough noise out here that he must have heard them. She's given him plenty of time to finish up, or cover up, whatever it is he's doing.

The Whitakers surround her and are waiting to hear how Sylvan's face looked. She doesn't want to disappoint them, or lose their attention, so she replays the scene in her mind, trying to freeze-frame that moment. Now she sees: openmouthed, wide-eyed, panic-shot—he lost control of his face.

Suddenly they're all laughing and she realizes why. She's been making an expression to correspond to the one in her imagination. They all try mimicking it.

"Speaking of Syl, where is the Mystery Survivor?" Alabama slaps both his thighs and stands up.

"He's"—she considers lying, buying him even more time, but decides against it—"in the bedroom."

"Hey, Syl!" Alabama yells. Everybody marches to the bedroom door. Pounding. Making faces. "Dudesworth! Open up. Want you to meet my people."

Sylvan opens the door smiling. He's got that splotchy flush on his neck and his eyes are moist. "Aren't you guys early? Graduation's not till next month."

"Family never needs a *reason* to visit," Alabama says.

As Sylvan goes through a round of introductions, Phyllis tries to get a look into the room behind him. Did he finish? Is it in there? Yes, there's a condom on the bed, barely visible in the rumpled sheets. Every minute that sperm stays outside of her, chances decrease. Several thousand are dying every second, the weak ones, she hopes. The strong will survive. The quintessential competitive act, all those little sperm squiggling desperately to become a person. Imagine, her baby might be in there.

Sylvan's frowning. "I thought you only had two brothers."

"I thought so too," Alabama says. "But I was wrong."

Sylvan takes a sip of beer. When he sets it down a bubble rises on the mouth of the bottle, gets large, then pops. Cubby thinks that's funny and giggles.

"Charlie here is my half brother." Alabama and Charlie look at each other, then back at Sylvan, who is still frowning. "*Charlie*," Alabama repeats, as if the name itself is explanation. But Sylvan is still puzzled. "Remember, at your Folkalities?"

Sylvan finally nods and closes his eyes. "Crossed wires under the hood?"

Now Alabama is confused, screwing up one side of his face. "Huh?" Then a crooked grin. "Oh, yeah." He points to a spot between his eyes.

"A lot of fingers in a lot of pies," Sylvan sighs.

Alabama nods.

Phyllis is starting to feel uncomfortable. Does her presence require that they speak this inside language? Or does Charlie's? He's got his back turned, and is now passing a hand over the living room wall, as if he were reading its aura, unaware that both Sylvan and Alabama are staring at him like he's fireworks.

"Studs," Charlie announces, turning toward them.

Both Alabama and Sylvan face him expectantly. Charlie opens his hand, revealing a magnetic stud-detecting device. "You got studs every two feet. It's well framed, I'll say that much." He goes back to reading the wall, making pencil marks. "But look at that." He jabs the pencil towards the highest part of the slanted ceiling. "Don't get me wrong, I love open space. Nobody likes living in a box. But that space"—he shakes his head sadly at the air—"is misemployed. Frankly, I find it offensive."

Nobody says a word. Sylvan is gazing intently at the misemployed space. Phyllis begins to fidget. Cubby is smiling at her.

"Aw, hell," Alabama finally says, taking Charlie by the arm. "I'm not ashamed." He turns to Phyllis. "Born two days apart. Me, then him."

Phyllis imagines the birth, must have been very painful. The poor mother.

"See, twenty-some-odd years ago my father had a child," Alabama continues, "not by my mother, and he never told anybody."

"Me." Charlie points to himself and smiles. He's got Alabama's grin, the same overlapping front teeth. But the mole makes it almost sinister. "Dad was cards in the mail."

"Finally owned up. Him and Ma are in therapy, and, well, now Charlie's one of us." Alabama slaps him on the back, rubs his shoulder. "Glasnost. You know, open-ness. New family policy."

"Except my mom's still, like, Afghanistan." Charlie smirks.

"Get lost." Alabama gently shoves him. "Gorby's pulling out." They horseplay, then make faces.

Phyllis is impatient to get into the bedroom, close the door, and—can she get away with twenty minutes alone in Sylvan's room? Too asocial? Or will they think she's his girlfriend? And why won't they stop grinning at her, as if competing for her attention? Maybe she's imagining it.

"Are we keeping you from something?" Charlie asks. "You look restless, your face."

Phyllis resists touching her cheeks. She's been trying to hold on to this polite, amused expression so long it feels jelled. And now the family doesn't seem so much nice as just weird. Their eerie cheeriness.

"No, it's just—" What can she give as an excuse? Headache? Cramps? That's not bad, mildly related even if untrue. She looks to Sylvan for help, but he's ignoring her, the dummy, marveling at the half brothers. "I've got to go lie down for a few minutes."

"Do you feel okay?" Alabama asks.

"How about some tea?" Charlie grabs the kettle.

"Ah, honey." Mackenzie stands up and pouts. "Let me get you."

"No no no no no." Phyllis waves them all away. She wishes she could. Not getting what she wants burns her fuse. "Really, I'm fine." She directs this comment toward Sylvan, and motions with an eyebrow to come with her.

"Can you believe that?" he asks, after she closes the bedroom door behind them. "Talk about double lives."

Phyllis falls backward onto the bed. "They seem to be handling it okay." Maps cover the walls of his room, all topographicals. Also three posters of planet Earth and one of the Milky Way. Protractors and mechanical pencils set out next to some kind of scope on a drafting table. Two open windows, their white muslin curtains blowing. Shirts on hangers blowing too, on doorknobs, on bookshelves, and several pairs of pants, splayed out on the floor.

"Do you feel ill?" Sylvan says, voice unsympathetic, almost accusing.

"Sorry," she says. "I'm a spoiled brat." She feels as if she's becoming a person she hates. One half of a possessive couple, the kind who whisper in front of friends, or hold soft, single-syllable conversations in public, or lock themselves in the bathroom together at parties, or exert their claim on each other in a thousand tiny ways. Like just now, henpecking. "I only wanted to, to touch base with you before I go ahead and do it."

"That's okay. Don't worry about it." He's looking over his shoulder, feeling a tug from the living room.

"Who gave you that tin of flower petals?" She begins to pull things out of her leather mail pouch: a foil-packaged syringe, a Mayan fertility doll, and the poem that goes along with it.

"Huh?" Sylvan wrinkles his forehead. "Oh, that. My sister."

She's relieved. A sister is safe. "Listen," she says, "a Mayan fertility chant:

"There is so little time
All we want, all we want is
Not to die
All I want, all I want is
To live, is to live
So I may see my baby
See me die."

"Nice," he says, distracted. "But I like when poems rhyme."
Through the thin walls she hears someone say, "She's his girlfriend?"

"Go," she says, jerking a thumb toward the door. "I'll be out
in twenty minutes." When she pulls back the bed covers, the
sheets smell like chocolate and oranges.

* * *

Sylvan never uses the brakes, hates to waste gravity. Plus, now
that he didn't die, he's got *guts*. "Getting attacked was one of
the best things that ever happened to me," he told Alabama.
"Cleared my life of bullshit." As if a sleeping part of him has
woken up, the novocaine worn off. Now he has guts. And a
new philosophy: Even the very hairs on his head are numbered. Recklessness begets invulnerability. So by the time he
turns his bike off East Cliff onto a long dirt driveway, he's going
so fast the air's loud. A fat dog suddenly escapes its leash and
runs at the tires. "Ahh!" He jerks the bike left and goes toppling
into the bushes.

"What the—!" yells the dog's master, out of breath from the
short run over. Sylvan's okay. The bushes broke his fall and
the dog, an Afghan, is playfully yipping and sniffing his feet.
The Stumpjumper is lying sideways on top of the shrubs, the
rear wheel still spinning.

"Who do you think you are?" The man stands over him,
threatening. He's got a handlebar mustache that challenges you

not to stare at it, and tiny deep-set eyes. "Racing around gaga like your head's screwed on backward!"

Sylvan blinks a few times. The dog darted in front of him, it was either run over it or crash. Can't the man see that? "Do you live in one of these bungalows?"

"Depends on who's asking."

"I'm here to see Phyllis Mentone." Today's the last session of AI this month.

Suddenly the man smiles and offers a hand. "Stark."

Sylvan takes it, and wonders what that's supposed to mean, as the man jerks him out of the bushes and keeps pumping his hand. A remarkably dexterous grip for someone so burly. "Jack Stark."

"Sylvan Park." It rhymes. Sylvan pets the dog to show there are no hard feelings. An extremely pregnant Afghan, not fat at all.

"Phyllis?" Jack Stark asks. "You're here to see her?"

Sylvan looks around. What's so unbelievable about that?

"You're not her brother?"

"Look, where—?"

"Awright," Stark claps his back. "None a my biz, I know. Just that you can't be too careful nowadays." A reference to the recent "climate of crime"—the pregnant-lady puncher whose unstoppable attacks spawned several vigilante groups, Trollbusters among the worst. For a while the city was getting national headlines, and the Guardian Angels even made a showing. They stood on streetcorners in their red berets, glowering at bums, insisting on escorting young ladies, some pregnant, some not, across streets and through the main downtown municipal bus station. Pissed people off, even the cops, who wanted them gone. "We're here to raise public awareness," a lead Angel reported. "Everybody's already aware," the police chief responded.

Stark is grinning and licking his mustache, a lascivious gesture. "Young man like you, that's what I like to see, some normality in this neighborhood."

No more romance, Phyllis scrubs her face, no more makeup. She's got the AI Kit laid out like a tray of surgical tools next to her bed, and purposeful jazz playing on the stereo. Today is it, last attempt, unless—she doesn't even want to think about unless. Failure would mean another month, and the last few days have been a series of minor fiascos. Banish all negative thoughts. Think positive. Visualize. Visualize what? She sees sperms trying to penetrate a happy face.

All morning she's been looking for signs. The fog, bad. The toaster working, good. Sylvan calling on time, very good. She knows these are just silly superstitions, but you can't deny the power of luck. On the other hand, what they're doing is basic science, and science never—

There's an animal leaping on the roof. A big one, the whole house booms under each jump. But this old wooden house is so wobbly it shudders even when a bus drives over the train tracks a block away. Possum? Raccoon? Feels bigger. Human?

Earthquake.

She runs outdoors.

"Here, Phyllis!" Jack Stark shouts. He's standing next to Sylvan, who's trying to hold his bouncing bike and looking at the sky (an earth scientist and he looks up?). The dog, Princess, is yawning back barks and sticking out her tongue as if the air tasted bad.

The quaking stops. For a moment everybody looks around, at trees, at the house, at dirt, waiting. Nothing happens. When they look at each other, they laugh. Earthquakes, like other freaks of nature, make people able to see each other.

"Thank our stars it wasn't the Big One," Stark says.

"Was that a good omen or a bad omen?" Phyllis asks. But she's already decided. Like a falling star, it's not the meteor but the wish that counts.

"Only four and a half, I'd say." Sylvan pictures the seismograph zigzags, anticipating aftershocks.

"Been awhile," Phyllis says. The last earthquake happened when she was at Tres Ojos. It was bigger than this one, and when Legos and books started tumbling off the shelves, the kids hushed up ominously. Shane, one of the TA's, planted himself under the doorframe, blocking it, keeping everybody else indoors. Selfish bastard. No women-and-children-first ethic in him.

"Well, gotta walk the royalty," Stark says, nodding at Princess, who has almost regained her regal bearing. "Ten miles on Sundays."

At the end of every exhale the dog still trembles faintly. One of Sylvan's professors thinks dogs and cats can sense impending natural disasters. Maybe hokum, maybe not; in experiments, they've proved as accurate as any other forecasting method. That is, not very. Sylvan can't help noticing Princess's nostrils are wide open. And what about that shark the other day? (Already seems like weeks ago.) Maybe a kind of reflex, those Ampullae of Lorenzini picking up on minute underwater seismic waves, causing—

"Don't want to keep you kids from your date." He winks and heads off.

"What'd you tell him?" Phyllis wants to know. May as well broadcast it to the whole city.

"I asked if you lived here and he started giving me a lecture on coyotes," Sylvan says. "They're monogamous."

She offers him a beer and they sit down to watch some basketball, Lakers versus the Celtics. Good sign—he puts his legs up on the table, twists open the bottle, and flicks the cap, comfortable, wearing a thin velour shirt and baggy pants. She asked him not to wear anything tight, or take hot baths, both of which supposedly raise the temperature of the testicles and lower the sperm count.

"Imagine a parallel basketball league," he says, gulping a third of his beer, thirsty from the bike ride. He waits for her to finish clearing papers from the table and look at him. Her hair, pulled back in a stringy ponytail, reveals a nice jawline. But he can see where she'll have a double chin in another ten years. "Where all the players are women."

She looks at the TV. Larry Bird is shooting free throws. Sam used to give her a hard time about watching sports. "Another female flying the flag for jockdom." He sinks them both. Phyllis hates to admit it, but she kind of has a crush on Larry Bird. He's a little like Sylvan, the tall, gangly, blondish look. Sylvan, thankfully, is handsomer. "Sure," she says. "And beauty contests for men."

"Sam would like that." Ainge has just missed a shot and thinks he's been fouled. Sylvan doesn't like the guy's face, grimacing at the ref as usual. None of those Celtics ever smile. And every time they're quoted in the press it's either bragging or complaining. Too bad they're so good.

Take Magic Johnson, though; there's a smile. That's why he's so watchable. He loves the game, he shares the game, passing off and leading the league in assists, which is not a sign of unselfishness so much as a way of playing that brings out the best in your teammates. Maximus Loach must understand this better than anyone. Sylvan can't help thinking of the Duke Kahanamoku—adobe and earthquakes don't mix.

"I told Teo we were gonna have a baby," Phyllis says.

"I know. He asked me to explain elbow insemination."

"Did you?"

"Told him to ask you."

At halftime, the Lakers take a five-point lead to the lockers.

Phyllis points to her bedroom.

"Awright, awright," he says, crumpling a newspaper into a ball and throwing her a no-looker. Of course she misses it, clapping her hands a second too late and blinking wildly, like one of those uncoordinated moms trying to catch a ball at Tres Ojos. "Sure you don't want to join me?"

The blatant flirting catches her off guard. Maybe sports does this to him. He's had only two beers, but now he's looking at her legs. They're so pale they almost look blue. She's pleased. Her thick ankles don't even bother her. Feeling good feels good.

"You've got thick ankles," he says. "I never noticed."

"Asshole." She throws the ball at him.

Phyllis's bedspreads are frilly and a bookshelf takes up one entire wall. It's filled with a set of encyclopedias, hardback texts on early childhood education, and an amazing children's book collection. There's also a TV on a cart stacked with *Time* magazine, *TV Guide*, and Playskool Toy catalogs. Kids' drawings and cutouts are taped to the mirror of the vanity, which also contains a shelf of tiny jars filled with colored liquids. Perfumes and lotions and potions, and a jewelry box. The femininity is striking. He was expecting wallpaper, oil paintings, neutrality.

He jumps onto the bed. It's hard. There's a crib on the other side. A *crib*. Cards are inside, and dried flowers, and half-knitted baby booties. Also that gruesome plump Mayan fertility doll that looks about to sprout. And a tray set with a sterile-wrapped syringe, gauze, a tube of something, and condoms in light blue wrappers, "For the Feeling of Feeling in Love."

It hits him. They're going to have a baby. And for the first time he can remember, Sylvan actually prays. Now that he has the guts, he prays that he'll have the guts.

"Let's do it again," Phyllis says. Grinning.

"It's only been an hour."

"If you're up to it."

Sylvan makes a face that says, Oh, all right.

"Can't you at least pretend it's not a chore?" Angry, she brushes her hair back, then tugs at her fingers.

Sylvan takes a step toward the front door. He can walk

straight out. She has no right to get hostile when he's doing her such a favor. But maybe she's doing him a favor; he wants that baby too. Besides, he wasn't making a face because it was such a chore, just the opposite in fact. It's no chore at all, except in relation to what it could be. "This is getting confusing."

Now he's hungry, flipping through the channels (he missed the end of the game, which Magic won on a crazy bank shot in the last second) and waiting for Phyllis to finish so they can eat. Thirty-something channels and nothing to watch. Fat lumpy men arguing politics on a talk-show set. Weather maps. Championship wrestling. Where is she? He needs food. A lead guitarist in an expensive hairdo leaps through dry-ice fog, before a studio audience of boyish girls and girlish boys. A tractor with a high-gloss paint job and four enormous chrome engines runs over and crumples seven old Dodges. He leaves it here, the crunching metal suits his mood.

Suddenly the earth quakes. Again. "Phyllis!"

The hanging lamp becomes the focus of the room, as if it's still and everything else is revolving. Cassette tapes go clacking off the shelves and the windows bend, creating glare spots. Empty beer bottles clatter on the coffee table. The walls groan, a chunk of plaster cracks off, and Grampa begins to howl. Sylvan can't make it down the hall because it's lurching, like the fuselage of an airliner in turbulence. He keeps his hands in fists, elbows out, and reaches the door to Phyllis's bedroom just as she swings it open. Doorframes, they both know, are safest, but now that they've gotten here, the shaking comes to a stop in what feels like a giant, terrestrial sigh.

They are grabbing each other's wrists.

Sylvan clears his throat tentatively. Phyllis says she needs a Kleenex and giggles, high-pitched, wild, as if the sounds are squirting out of her.

News anchors Chuck and Sue, who two nights ago reported the shark attack and coined the phrase "the Mystery Survivor," interrupt the program for a newsflash. The first quake of the day was only four point one. Not in itself such a big deal, Sylvan knows. Just that in these old wooden houses, you feel every slight vibration. The same flexibility that makes a small quake seem big will make a big quake seem small. He's getting anxious to check in at the lab, examine the machines, and bounce around theories. The animal correlation, for instance. The prof who studies the cats and dogs says vets report huge increases in pets afflicted with bladder crystals in the two-week period preceding moderate quakes. Makes them nasty. Bladder crystals, yikes, the kind of thing that would probably drive a shark to attack.

But the second quake of the day, say Chuck and Sue, registered seven point two on the Richter scale, and was epicentered eight miles east of Santa Cruz on the San Andreas. Plate tectonics. Moderate damage reported, including the possibility of casualties. The screen shows the Duke Kahanamoku, half crumbled. Then a close-up of the destroyed mural. The defaced kid has toppled over and large pieces of the other figures are gone. Casualties? What casualties?

The phone rings. At least they work; no lines down. Phyllis answers.

"Phyllis?" A breathy voice, female.

"Who is this, please?"

"Phyllis, this is Benita." Line hanging open. Phyllis can't summon a face to go with that name. Draws a blank. "Remember? Third wigwam from the top?"

"Oh, yeah." The corn and flowers at the bottom of campus, the pumpkins with bumper stickers, the tie-dyed tanktop and peace-sign necklace, the soil-caked toenails. Benita. "Hi."

"Did I wake you up?" As if the earthquake wouldn't have.

"Oh, no, no, no," Phyllis says, shrugging at Sylvan, who's curious. Is she calling for a date? Eight months is a long time getting up the nerve. "How are you?"

"Oh, I've got my feelers out, you know. These rifts in the ground. Someone's trying to tell us something." It occurs to Phyllis that she never gave away her phone number. How did this person get her phone number? Who is this person? "But the reason I'm calling is, Teo."

"Yes?"

"He's here."

"Where?" Alarmed.

"Well, not here. He's back up at my wigwam. I'm at the pay phone at the campus entrance." Bizarre. Why on earth? "Don't worry, he's safe." Benita explains how Teo rode the bus cross-town, but it being a Sunday ("I had to ask somebody, I never know myself what day it is"), Tres Ojos was closed, and when the earthquake hit, "he got scared and ran all the way here." He didn't know his new phone number, only this one. "But he's safe with us." Us?

"I'll be right there." Phyllis motions to Sylvan, but he has sensed something's wrong and is already lacing up his hi-tops as she dials Sam. A machine. Her recorded voice vaguely belligerent. "You know what to do." Go to hell. "At the beep."

"Sam. I've got Teo. Call me immediately."

"Where is he?" Sylvan asks, already halfway out the door.

"Third wigwam from the top."

Phyllis drives fast, jerkily, either gassing or braking, as if the car were a wild animal she must tame, till they get downtown, where the roads are crammed with rubberneckers and she has to slow up. "Damn."

"Can you turn up High Street?" Sylvan risks asking. Phyllis is liable to snap, but he's worried about Maximus Loach and Simba too, and wants reassurance that they're safe. Neighbors are clustered in each other's front yards, shaking their heads and pointing at the sky.

"No." The forbidden word in her philosophy. So much for Process Listening.

"We're not in that much of a hurry," he says, looking down the side street. He can barely make out the Duke Kahanamoku. A slow jam of cars and flashing police lights, another twinge of adrenaline. "Fifteen extra minutes is all it will take."

Phyllis wheels around and her gaze ices him. "No."

One of the limestone and wood ranch houses at the campus entrance has collapsed. The donkey cart has fallen apart and produce is scattered. Gathered at the scene are university police in blue cars, firefighters in green trucks, and students with easels and cameras, recording. Definitely an event, this earthquake. One people will talk about, judge their achievements by and regrets against, be nostalgic about. How will Sylvan remember it? The weekend of the great white? Kind of apocalyptic. The day he became a sperm daddy? You can romanticize anything. And exactly what position was Phyllis in when it hit?

To get to the wigwams, they have to pull onto a dirt road that curves up a pasture and stops at a cattleguard in front of a locked gate, where they get out and climb over a stile. A barn is visible from here, housing another donkey cart and hay and tools. Next to it is an animal pen. Blue-eyed geese with orange beaks run cackling toward them and snap at their heels, and pigs squeal, and white goats stand on their hind legs. Hundreds of smells competing with the sun and air.

The Farm and Garden is officially part of the University, but a kind of sidekick program. A special application is required for enrollment, but you don't have to meet any academic requirements. Once accepted, you get housing in a tepee, or wigwam, for one harvest season, ten months, living almost totally off the land. After that, supposedly, you know French-Intensive techniques of organic farming and Integrated Pest Management— warding off bugs with plants they hate or other bugs. To judge by the produce in local markets, the Farm and Garden is successful. Organic farms have in fact become popular all over northern California. Their fruits and vegetables, the best Sylvan has ever tasted, come cheap and have even found their way into the chains, like the Albertson's downtown. Farming is the most noble calling, Mom always says.

A large barefoot woman wanders out of the apple orchard. She's wearing overalls and has a mass of random braids. "Welcome!" she says, arms out for a hug. But Phyllis hesitates and offers a hand instead, so the girl ends up kind of hugging it. Partially to break free, Sylvan's sure, Phyllis introduces him.

They touch fingers. Hers are warm and dry. Dusty. She's pretty in a physical, healthy way, very smooth-skinned and pale, uncomfortably light eyes. "Magic out, no?"

Sylvan nods. "You mean the earthquakes?"

"I'm not sure what they mean." She looks at the rows of artichokes, the baby sunflowers, the sprawling lavender bushes, as if they do. "But our donkeys ran away."

"How's Teo?" Phyllis asks. She looks out of context here, square-jointed, needlessly uptight, like a disgruntled parent.

"What a beautiful child," Benita says, staring at her. "Don't worry, he's safe. Follow me." She walks toward the tepees. They look different close up, not alike at all. Some deluxe with nylon sailcloth and zippers and aluminum support poles, some of hide with pins and pegs held up by sticks. "He asked me, does 'I can't stand it' mean you like it or hate it. And I'm like, wow, this kid's a thinker. You know, I told him it depends."

"Beets," Phyllis says. Complimenting Teo worked, drove the worry right out of her face, now she's even smiling. "I can't stand beets."

"But say somebody's tickling you," Sylvan says, actually thinking more along the lines of sex. Specifically, the blow job Sam gave him. "You like it at first, then you can't stand it."

Benita grins. Her breasts are almost hanging out the sides of her overall panel. There is always sex between people. Always. Even if it's the farthest thing from your mind. She looks away as if she's reading his thoughts and is embarrassed by them.

"Or if somebody's telling you very funny jokes," Phyllis says.

"Or the *day* is just so . . . beautiful." Benita gazes at the day with those bleached-blue eyes. The bay is lazy and the sky clear, neither showing any evidence of the recent shark attack or earthquakes. "You just . . . can't stand it."

The third wigwam from the top, Benita's, has wooden support posts wrapped in heavy white canvas. A furry flap is open at the front into a kind of sun-porch vestibule. "Hello, it's me!" Benita sings as she disappears inside. Phyllis follows, then Sylvan.

Dark here, hushed. And large. At least twenty feet in diameter. Around its perimeter, the floor is packed earth, outfitted with woolen spreads and thatched mats. Three figures sit cross-legged and hold hands in the half light. "Hi." "Howdy." "Ho." A woman and two men.

"Hi, everyone, this is Phyllis and Sullivan."

"Hi, everyone," they say. Totems are everywhere. Bird-feather macramé and herb-stalk weavings. Seashell mobiles with rosebuds. Fired blobs of clay. Ropes, candles, water jugs. Benita gestures for them to sit on a mat next to a stack of books. *Seven Arrows, Black Elk Speaks, Green Bananas,* and *The Way to Rainy Mountain.* It smells kind of like sex in here, an odor between a saddle and a swimming pool. The three figures are holding hands in the dark. Sylvan wonders about those rumors —strange harvest rituals, solstice celebrations, orgies.

"Where's Teo?" Phyllis asks.

"He was right here," Benita says.

One of the three emits a sound that's friendly but all snort. He's wearing only shorts, his chest pale and shrunken in contrast to a heavy beard and long hair. "Funny little guy . . . telling us some weird things . . . how can we live without clocks? . . . or a television?" he says, voice trailing up at every pause, the way some poets recite their work at campus readings.

"A lot of yang in him," the girl says. She's blond, all-American gone to seed, wrapped only in a Navajo blanket, shoulders and feet sticking out.

"He left about fifteen minutes ago," the third guy says. Flannel-clad lumberjack type, something mean in the eyes. He rubs the blond girl's hand possessively, though the bearded man has hold of her other.

"You guys." Three syllables. "I told you to watch him." Benita's words are at odds with her tone, which seems to be commending them for a job well done.

"We're not going to put him on a leash," the blond girl says.

"A kid's a person . . . " says the bearded man, a line of poetry.

"We're not his boss," the lumberjack says.

"A kid has a way . . . of dealing . . . "

Everyone nods in agreement. Farming may be the most noble calling, but these three reek of a deep-seeded creepiness.

"He mentioned a cave . . . says his father will—"

Sylvan's gone before he can hear the rest of it. The cave. Swallow him right up in an earthquake. If El Toro doesn't get him first.

The fields are green, poppy-spangled at the height of spring, hopping with red-winged blackbirds and crawling with snakes. One of which Phyllis steps on, trying to keep up. It's blue and long with yellow eyes and it whips back and hisses, releasing an oily odor. She actually apologizes to it and keeps running, almost faster than Sylvan. They cut through a ravine, shadow-darkened by huge redwoods and a sheer limestone cliff. Hundreds of squirrels' skulls are piled at the base. Hundreds. They seem to be grinning and frowning and going soundlessly hysterical. Sylvan stops to examine. Feels sacred, like a burial ground, or cemetery, too sacrosanct to collect for his Museum of Natural History in a wine crate.

"Do they come here to die?" Phyllis asks, panting.

Sylvan bends down to pick up a feather. A long wingtip, perfect condition. He scans the face of the cliff. "Eagles." No sign of the nest, but he's sure the golden eagles he's been watching are here. "Nest up there; they eat, then toss out the bones." Hundreds of skulls, like empties now, brains picked clean. The feather, though, he'll keep for his museum.

"Come on," Phyllis says. Bad sign, these.

They leap over a spring, the third of Los Tres Ojos, the one he's never been able to find, and cut straight up a steep hillside, feet disappearing to the ankles in three-leaf clover. They finally arrive at the edge of the pasture. "I don't see him."

"Do you think he went down?"

Phyllis just swallows.

No cows and no bull. They run straight to the limestone outcrop and climb up. While they catch their breath, Phyllis frowns at the seashells.

"Tropical bay three million years ago," Sylvan explains, out of breath. "Right here. Acapulco like."

Phyllis points to Teo's tennis shoes set neatly at the mouth of the cave.

"Oh no."

Phyllis cups her mouth and yells down. "Teodoro?"

"Give me your keys."

She fishes them from her pocket. "Why?"

"Flashlight. Wait here."

When Sylvan, breathless and sweat-soaked, finally arrives at Tres Ojos, Teo is sitting barefoot on the front steps, building what looks like a colosseum out of sticks and stones. He smiles briefly. "Oh. Hi, Sylvan." Turns back to his play, and begins humming to himself.

In the driveway a bunch of ten-year-olds are riding bikes in circles. "*Suicide!*" they all yell, and one of them, a dark-haired rough-looking kid in a denim jacket, speeds right at the wall, fast, then lays down his bike at the last second, sliding to a stop in the dirt inches from impact. The other kids boo and hiss. "That's no suicide, you didn't even touch." What goes on at Tres Ojos when school's out. Suicide.

"Teo—" Sylvan starts, determined to make the child feel guilty for wandering off, being lost, being alone when the earthquake hit, causing Sylvan to worry like a helpless adult with the illusion of having the capacity, and maybe even the urge, to rescue. You are a kid until you have one of your own. As Mom says. And Dad with that molded, blue-and-yellow-veined plastic heart on the kitchen table. What you have to look forward to in life. Where you go when you grow up. All somehow just now Teo's fault. "Let's go home."

Teo scatters the sticks.

"No gloves in suicide!!" The ten-year-olds are yelling. Apparently one kid has brought gloves and kneepads to the game, changing its nature.

"I don't want to go home, yet," Teo says.

"You don't want to go home, yet," Sylvan says, Process Listening. There is all the time in the world.

The kid with the gloves succumbs to peer pressure and peels them off. Then the kneepads. He speeds toward the wall, screaming *"Suicide!"* His voice is cut off as he smacks into it and starts to cry. Meanwhile the others are clapping for him. Does that mean he won?

"Shoes are bad for you," Teo says, and wiggles his toes. They're so dirty they're almost black. It's a long way here—through the sculpture garden, under the gate, and across the highway—from the tepees. Especially barefoot. "That's what the farmy lady tole me."

"Phyllis found yours at the cave. Come on, we'll go get her."

"No home," Teo says like a much younger kid or a foreigner. "I can't stand how Mommy is now."

"How?"

Teo turns and looks at the school door. "Those tepee people," he says quietly, "stare."

Sylvan insists on driving home, that way Phyllis can sit Teodoro on her lap and cheer him up, while they swing by what's left of the Duke Kahanamoku, which is sectioned off with yellow POLICE LINE DO NOT CROSS tape. Sylvan scans the crowd of bystanders, official types, neighbors, black teenagers drinking soda from plastic liter bottles, aging hippie wearing the same robes as always but holding, not playing, his guitar for once, then, yeah, who he's looking for. Honking, Sylvan sticks his head out the window. "Max! Simba! Over here!"

"Hah!"

"Yo!" Maximus Loach walks over, dribbling the basketball, and Simba follows, gimp and dainty. Maximus Loach insists on sticking his huge head and neck, gold ropes dangling, through the window and hugging everybody. "Phyl, baby. Good to see ya. Ho, Teo my man, you look shook."

Teo shrinks. "Who are you?"

"You remember Max," Sylvan says, then remembers he knows him only as Santa, the hulking man who, in his mind, brought him Youngster for Christmas, stuffed. "Or maybe you've never met."

"Don't matter none." Maximus Loach glowers, both frowning and grinning, hair shellacked with gerricurl. "You think you're bad?"

Teo shakes his head no. Everybody laughs.

"God, I was worried about you guys." Sylvan shakes Simba's hand. He's grinning, yellowish eyes barely visible behind dreadlocks coiled in copper today.

"There will be famines and earthquakes in various places," Simba says, tapping the tiny Old Testament that dangles from his necklace. "All these are the beginning of birth pains."

Phyllis and Sylvan exchange a private eyebrow raising.

"We be shooting hoop when the shaking start," Maximus Loach says. The basketball posts have been renovated with springloaded rims and thin, stealproof chain nets, since the Trollbusters hassle. For the past few weeks the vigilante groups have remained largely invisible, even though (or maybe because) the pregnant-lady puncher was never apprehended. "I be thinking somebody drop the bomb, Simba here get on his knees and pray, everybody looking at each other like judgment —you know what I'm saying?—the company you die with."

"Then the bricks shoot out the building," Simba says. Teo's entranced by the shiny copper, the clinking necklace, the Caribbean lilt. "And the Kahanamoku go boom, echo feel it inna bones, adobe dust inna mouth."

It goes on like this for too long, everybody politely waiting for each other to finish, then trying to outdo descriptions, until Teo whines that he's hungry.

"Anybody else?" Sylvan asks. "You guys hungry?"

"Whatchyou got in mind?" Maximus Loach asks, a leer on his face that suggests he's remembering the picnic they made of Sam's lunchmeat dress.

"Hop in."

"Don't want to put you out," Simba, always the gracious one, says to Phyllis.

Reaching back to unlock the rear door, she says, "Don't be absurd."

The radio is blasting gospel and everybody is singing along and rocking as the car pulls into the long dirt driveway off East Cliff. Two patrol cars are parked diagonally in front of Phyllis's bungalow, and three policemen are standing on the porch next to the front door, their hands hanging nervously at their holsters. Jack Stark is there too, fingering the bill of his Caterpillar cap. He points out Sylvan and Phyllis, identifying them.

"Somebody in trouble," Simba says.

Sylvan cuts the music, slows way down.

"I gotta rescue yous from the cops again?" Maximus Loach asks. "Mr. Beau-jo-lais?"

"Probably Grampa," Phyllis says, "committed some new heinous act with Stark's dog."

Another patrol car zooms up, blocking the driveway behind them.

"Holy." Sylvan opens the door to a policeman who looks like a middle-aged boy with a crew cut growing all the way down the back of his neck. His cheeks are shiny, his uniform a size too small. The name on the badge is REASONS.

"Step away from the car," he says, eyes jumping around. Other cops are yanking out Simba and Maximus Loach, roughly, then hustling them behind the car. Teo crouches down and hides half under the front seat. "Hands against the wall, pardner."

"Why?" Sylvan asks, feeling stupid. Reasons frisks him, taking his wallet and ID.

"Suspected kidnapping. You have the right to remain silent . . . " He drones on, making the words meaningless, just phrases to get through, how it used to be in grade school saying the Pledge of Allegiance. Steel handcuffs knock against his wrist bones. Handcuffs?

"Sir? I'm sure there's been a mistake," Phyllis says. Reasons tells her she's under arrest, reads her her rights, then pats her down, though she's already been frisked once and cuffed.

"Aw, heck, I ain't done nothin . . . " Maximus Loach is saying. They take a small blue gun from his pants pocket.

Police 48 specials are drawn.

Oh, no. Sylvan's been hanging around a guy who carries a gun. Just what you do when you're the baddest dude in a bad neighborhood? Or something worse? He and Alabama could've been shot just for taking Max's parking place. Oh, no. This is the Santa he recommended for a preschool? They cuff him. And Simba too, who, thank God, is not carrying any concealed weapons or pot. But no ID either, which makes them mad.

Just then the car door creaks all the way open, and Teo crawls out. He's looking into a gun barrel. Reasons sighs, exasperated, then holsters it. "You're Teodoro."

Teo sucks his lower lip and nods, awestruck. Holster and Gun and Badge. A real man with a real job, not like Sylvan or Phyllis. This cop is realer than anything.

"Come with me, son. We'll get you home soon."

"I don't wanna go."

Reasons ignores him. After lining everybody up on the front porch, he makes a call to headquarters. Apparently, they have to wait for a paddy wagon. In an attempt to be polite and normal that comes off sounding absurd in this situation, Phyllis invites them inside.

"I never would have thought." Jack Stark shakes his head and winks, flexing his muscles and blocking the doorway.

"Move," she orders him.

"Fine." Stark sighs. "It's your life."

Sylvan understands why when they go inside. A mistake. Beer bottles everywhere, scattered cassette tapes, upset shelves, crumpled newspaper basketballs, and drag racing following that hot-rod tractor pull on television. And a mistake on a tray: syringes and condom wrappers and KY jelly in the living room. Reasons points with his billy club, then looks at them as if they really were criminals; as if up till now he hadn't really thought so.

"It isn't what it looks like," Phyllis says. "No drugs. Let me explain."

But Reasons helps himself to the syringe, picking it up for a sniff. Sylvan cringes, expecting the cop to taste it the way they do little drug packets on TV, but luckily he only frowns, and sets it carefully back down. Then he cocks an eye at them and shakes his head to let them know he knows what perverts they are.

"Son, did they . . . *do* anything to you?" Reasons asks Teo, who's shaking his head no and looking around the house. His old house. A shambles. Though Teo couldn't recognize the equipment on the tray, Sylvan winces when he sees the child look at it. Like himself watching his own parents fucking, only different. Much different.

"First you was caught with your pants down, but this be the whole nine yards," Maximus Loach says. "Don't worry, though, Mr. Beaujolais, kinky don't mean illegal."

"Can it." A cop shoves him unnecessarily hard.

Maximus Loach, hands cuffed behind his back, stumbles face first into a wall. Powerlessness does not become him. First time Sylvan has seen him without a basketball. And it's all his fault. "This was an invite for eats!"

Grampa comes out from the bedroom, licking his gums as he does when he first wakes up, thumping everybody with his tail, and sticks his nose in Phyllis's sticky, moist crotch. At least she and Sylvan got a couple of tries in. She can't even push Grampa's nose away. Humiliating.

Jack Stark studies Simba, the only innocent one, though perhaps the most criminal-looking, who has wisely used his Miranda rights, not a peep, then Maximus Loach, then (after a wink for Sylvan) tells Phyllis, "I gotta pup for you. Or had one. But by the looka this I'm not sure the Humane Society would approve." Ha ha.

Phyllis is strangely calm, not even breathing fast. She has foreseen this moment. Ever since the day she asked Sylvan to be the father of her child. Sam's behind this. Those veiled threats. But if it weren't Sam, it would be somebody else. It's the price you pay if you choose to live a life the law hasn't caught up with. She's embarrassed and wrong now; they'll be embarrassed and wrong later—450,000 people in this country have been conceived artificially. Alternatively. And that's just a start.

Teo is looking at Sylvan's manacles. Sylvan the Criminal; he tries not to slink. An image like this sticks. Oh, Teo, he wants to say. Just—Oh. But he has to look away because he's sort of crying, no, not sort of. Damn. No hands even to wipe his face. Teo, Teo. Who else would run away from home and go to school? Tres Ojos, Phyllis's, the only school a kid would run away to go to.

Out the window, Sylvan sees an unmarked car arrive. Sam jumps out, brisk, full of herself. It's safe to say he's never hated any human being in his life until right now. Kidnapping, the nerve. Arresting them for rescuing her son, who doesn't want to go home anyway. Explain that.

When she comes in, she's crying too, almost sobbing. An act. "Teodoro!"

He reaches his arms out and runs over. "Mommy! Mommy!"

They hug and hug and hug. If you didn't know better, you'd think he was just now rescued. Everybody watches, pretending not to, granting that illusion of privacy.

Then Sam looks up, at Sylvan, eyes tight with disgust, next at Phyllis, cuffed and therefore guilty. On the floor between them are the condom wrappers, syringes, and KY jelly. "What have you done to him?!!"

Phyllis opens her mouth but doesn't say anything.

Sylvan does. "We found him." The found comes out sounding like an unnatural act.

"I'll kill you." She slaps him. When he's cuffed, figures. 'Cause he'd slap back otherwise. He really would.

"Mommy, stop," Teo whimpers.

Reasons is beginning to look very concerned, very bright in the cheeks, and puts his middle-aged, boyish bulk between them.

"I was walking to school," Teo says. He has stopped crying, but looks wilted. "I disobeyed."

Sam turns to him, puzzled.

"You said I could go back to school, so I went."

Phyllis takes it up from here, explaining the rest. "I tried calling you, but only got a machine. Didn't you get my message?"

Sam looks devastated. "Officer, please set these people free."
Her voice like air escaping. Finally. Even so, it's barely consolation. They've already been made to feel worse than criminals.
Full-fledged deviates. Engaging in venal squalor and debauch-
ery. "There's been a terrible mistake," Sam explains. She
stepped out only for a moment, she says, to the store, and
when she came back and found Teo missing, she got worried
and drove all around looking for him. "I knew he'd probably
go to Tres Ojos. It's all he ever talks about." This for Phyllis's
sake, a concession. "I told him he could go back." But when
she didn't find him there or along the way, she notified the
police. They took her out in a cruiser for an extended search.
When he still didn't turn up, now missing three and a half
hours, the earthquake hit and she really freaked. They went
back to her house, where "the whole posse" listened to the
message on the machine. "Your voice sounded so . . . desperate." Sam's crying again. Teo too. Poor kid. At the center of
this mess. "*They're* the ones who thought it was a kidnapping,
and I, I, *they* put the idea—" More tears and noseblowing, then
the famous pout. All the cops are spellbound. "I was insane
with worry."

Phyllis looks down, as if refusing. Obviously Sam was getting
revenge. Sam the liar. Sam the stunning, utterly sincere, emotionally wrecked liar. Phyllis tries but cannot forgive her,
though she makes herself nod and even smile a little, accepting
Sam's implied apology, sort of.

"So, Officer," Sam says, "please let's just forget this."

"Can't do that, ma'am," Reasons says. "Found a concealed
weapon on this man—"

"Aw, c'mon man, it's registered," Maximus Loach says before the cop slaps him.

"—and this"—he points to the tray—"needs explaining."

"I can explain that, Officer," Phyllis says. Can she?

"You'll get your chance. Downtown."

When the van arrives, it has ominous grillwork on its windows. The cops load Simba and Maximus Loach and Phyllis

and Sylvan—all still cuffed—pushing down each of their heads as they step in, ostensibly to prevent injury, but actually more to shame. Then a cop shuts the door and locks it twice.

As the van turns down the long dirt driveway, Jack Stark restrains Grampa, who is howling vowelically. Sam screams, "I'm so so so so so sorry." Teo just waves, bunching and un-bunching his little hand.

10 *True Suchness*

From now on there's no tomorrow," Alabama says, keeping his eye on the doorframe and his hands out as if to sense any more movement. Too late, the fortieth tremor of the day has already passed.

Three days after Sylvan was arrested and released without being booked, a subtropical air mass, having been sucked in by a low over the San Joaquin, coalesced. Clouds opened up like blue waterfalls in a yellow sky. Raindrops big as eggs splatted on the streets. That's when the "earthquake system" started.

Tens of thousands of smallish quakes have hit central California since that day at Phyllis's about a month ago. Seismologists are flying in from all over the world to study them as "living organisms." MONO CRATERS MAY ERUPT, headlines warn. And the other day, news anchors Chuck and Sue, issuing the tsunami alert, got mixed up, called each other Suck and Chew. Longtime residents began packing for early vacations east, while disaster enthusiasts searched the shore on tiptoe for the tidal wave, which rolled in at fifteen feet, a disappointment to everyone but surfers. The Big One, it seems, is imminent.

"Liquefaction," Sylvan is explaining. Alabama has been extremely freaked out, and wants "information." He's trying to be brave. Not only for himself. The last earthquake frightened Monica and Dawn so much they forfeited their pride and asked him to "sleep over." Though only, they made it clear, "as a next-door neighbor." As long as he didn't have to sleep on the floor, he said. Monica gave him her bed, while she herself shared Dawn's. "But check this out, in the middle of the night I woke up and found this gigantor cockroach tickling my stomach. Scared me spitless. And I flicked it on the ground, but it just stayed there, like, looking up at me. So I dropped my Webster's on it."

"Finally got some real use out of that thing," Sylvan said, not surprised. Alabama even sleeps with the dictionary.

"Wanna see the stain?" Afterwards, Alabama felt guilty, "not really," because the cockroach, he's since decided, was trying to warn him: a four-fiver hit less than fifteen minutes later. A just big enough deal that he got to spend the rest of the night with Monica. "Rockin and rollin . . . Sure do feel bad about that roach, though."

"I'm pleased," Sylvan said, "to see you finally showing some interspecies sensitivity." In a way he meant it.

"Stinks," Alabama says, interrupting Sylvan's seismology lecture to open a window.

"Yeah, really smells." As if the earthquakes weren't enough, in the last few days, billions of dead anchovies have washed ashore to rot in the early summer heat. You can smell them all over the county.

"Aw, man, nasty. So, go on. What do you mean, 'waves'?" Alabama returns to his position under the doorway.

"Earthquakes hit in waves," Sylvan resumes. He's the expert, and will stay on at UC to become even more of one. They invited him back to study for his Ph.D., promising large sums of grant money. Basically a case of good timing. Earth sciences are, understandably, the current fad. Plus, being in Santa Cruz, he'll get to spend more time with Phyllis, keep at it. "The waves pass through bedrock, then amplify in valleys, getting so large and choppy that houses, buildings even, pop off their foundations, the ground under them giving way like water. If the quake's big enough, solids behave as liquids. That's what happened at San Francisco Airport." Built on landfill, which is tantamount to quicksand, it had to be closed down briefly last month after two runways buckled.

"Tell me again what good is standing under a goddamn doorjamb gonna do me during liquification?" Alabama asks.

"Lique*fac*tion. As in fact."

The day is blazing and Sylvan's shift in the lab doesn't begin until nine this evening. Nothing to do but sunbathe, now that there's no more schoolwork and the press has finally stopped hounding him for Mystery Survivor stories. He and Phyllis have planned another four days' worth of AI attempts starting tomorrow, finishing before graduation next week. Emma and the Folkalities will be here for the ceremony, along with Vow of Silence Man and reject Beaujolais, but only for two days since a few killer bees were recently discovered in Napa. (Dad's seriously freaking.) They all want to meet Phyllis. And she doesn't even seem nervous about it. He would be, and is.

On the fireroad through the pasture, millions of ladybugs bead the ferns growing at the shoulders. A bluebelly skittles across the dust for a strike, sending the beetles up in a cloud. The red swarm rises and floats, palpitating like an airborne heart. Summertime, and the living's . . . busy. He'll invite Maximus Loach to graduation, and Simba too (if he comes back; nobody seems to know where he's disappeared to). Of course the cops hadn't been able to hold the four of them on anything, and, after publishing their humiliation all over town by driving the long way to the police station, they had been set free. Only

Maximus Loach had been booked. The snubnose was registered, otherwise the judge would have set a four-figure bail. As
it was, Sylvan had to cash in some bonds to post, and he did it
gladly. After all, it was his fault. Max has got a court date next
month. He expects complete acquittal. "Cake."

A meadowlark sings out, the pair of golden eagles rides the
thermals, and no sign of the bull El Toro. All in all, a gorgeous
afternoon. Except the air stinks of fish.

El Niño, the freak warm current, just won't leave (scientists
are trying vainly to connect it to the earthquake system, like
Sylvan did with the shark; if you have a ball of string and an
imagination, you can interconnect anything). As a result, no
fresh squid for the Calamari Festival; they'll have to be imported from Indonesia. Worse, the generation of anchovies that
died and washed up all over the beaches is clogging the yacht
harbor and bringing in slow tornadoes of sea gulls. Nature, it
seems, is going haywire.

Sylvan spreads his towel next to a pile of limestone, then lies
there picturing everybody together: the Folkalities, Emma,
Gyorgy, Max and Simba and Alabama, all of Al's people (even
his father's supposedly coming), and Phyllis and Teodoro. But
not Sam. He doesn't care if he ever—

A shadow falls across his eyelids, holy—El Toro? No, it's
Teo's upside-down face, one fingertip pugging the nose, the
other dimpling a cheek. He grins and giggles when Sylvan
jumps.

"C'mon, Teo." Sylvan shakes his head and covers himself
with a pair of shorts. "Show some consideration."

"I scared you," Teo says, marveling at that power. He has
literally grown up, elongated, these last six months, cheeks
hollowing out, eyes showing new levels of understanding and
a capacity for subtle expression. How is it possible to love the
child so much, yet dislike the mother?

Sylvan does, though. Despite Sam's showing signs of repen-
tance. (She's reenrolled Teo at Tres Ojos.) And despite her re-

laying an apology through Phyllis. Sam and Phyllis are apparently on speaking terms again. Sylvan wonders what, other than Teo, they talk about.

Phyllis appears, blondish hair bobbing above the limestone outcrop as she climbs to the top. Sylvan tries not to be obvious as he notices the definition of her thighs. More than definition. The other night they actually went to a movie together. You could call it a "date." He even got nervous about putting his arm around her. Like teenagers going steady. Imagine, openly sharing bodily fluids but being tentative about sitting arm in arm.

"Sylvan?!! What a surprise!" She comes down from the boulders and kneels next to him. "Nice spot to get a sunburn." She pulls off a daypack, winks.

"Sure stinks."

"Whew. Bad."

"Like . . . "

"A huge decomposing Caesar salad."

"Phyllis! Here it is!" Teo yells from the rocks. "The cave! The cave!"

Sylvan, forgetting the trunks are draped over but not on him, stands up and they fall to the ground. He bends down to grab them, practically jumping into them, but catches his foot in the legging and loses his balance. Just as he's falling, both ankles tangled up, Phyllis is there, supporting him.

"Hmmmm," she says, raising an eyebrow at his privates.

"Cave?" is all he can manage to say.

Tree roots twist along the mouth of the cave, splitting the limestone, which tends to crack in straight lines. The proper Earth Science term for this shadowy area is the *twilight zone*. Fitting, Sylvan thinks. Tendrils droop and dangle, while spider-webs catch red and green dots of light. A bright yellow banana slug squeezes itself into a moist crevice.

The governor vetoed the bill designating the banana slug as California's official state mollusk. A staffer must have enlightened him about their wild sex lives. The Camp Fire girls and Blue Birds are disappointed, but may rally for an appeal.

"I'm six," Teo says.

"I know," Sylvan says. "Happy —"

"Phyllis is taking me down." Teo gazes into the twilight zone, hypnotized.

"Help me with the lifeline?" she asks Sylvan as if there's no question he will join them. Right after Tres Ojos, she says, they walked up here because she promised. She promised?

"I know my dad's really not down there," he says.

"Wait," Sylvan says. "Go down? Me?" Scary.

"Wait for what?" Teo asks.

"Oh, what the jalapeño," he says, trying to assume light-heartedness. To remember that he has guts now. Recklessness begets invulnerability. Still, to leave a sunny day for a dank hole—only for these two.

The lifelines are simply two balls of string. The same ones Sylvan used with the kids to make an ecosystem. He fastens both lines to a tree root. One will be his, the other Phyllis's. She in turn will tie herself to Teo. She issues Sylvan a flashlight and keeps one for herself. Then she takes off her clothes. Underneath she's wearing a bikini.

"Relax," she says. "Nothing's going to bite you down there."

The three of them sit cross-legged. "Just breathe," Phyllis says. It's some kind of prayer. She's on a kick. Being in tune and totally healthy for the baby. "Breathe deep, feel it like a sunbaked stone just below your navel." She takes a deep breath and holds it three counts. Teo does the same, blowing out through puffy cheeks. They all sit there breathing, and, yes, Sylvan begins to feel some kind of energy, hot as a sunbaked rock at least, though slightly lower than where Phyllis said he should feel it. Not wanting so obvious a display, and fearing one of those persistent boners he sometimes gets, he imagines ice cubes. Then a refrigerator. And then, of all things, Rice Krispies. Snap, crackle, pop.

"Don't fight it," she whispers, squeezing his hand. "Breathe."

Okay, but breathing gets weird when you think about it. Like thinking about what your tongue is doing every moment of the day. Vow of Silence Man should be here. He likes doing things like breathing. Sylvan doesn't. Meditation flunk-out.

He opens his eyes. A slight breeze stirs the grass. The pair of eagles is circling above the row of tepees. The roller coaster is still in action, despite the earthquake system. Waves break like zippers across the bay, and a gray whale breaches, startling a flock of pelicans that churn up the water taking flight. All those anchovies. When there's death in the air, anything you choose to do with your life seems okay.

A squeeze of the hand tells him it's time to rise and the three of them stand, a little wobbly.

"Hey-ho, hey-ho, a-spelunking we will go," Phyllis sings, to the delight of Teo, who goes wild with all the different ways to pronounce *spelunking*.

Amazing how fast Teo disappears, his spry wiry body swallowed up in the dark. Next goes Phyllis. Then Sylvan, lowering himself into the cave, where the air is moist and cool, like opening a freezer full of Popsicles on a very hot day.

The leash keeps Teo from getting too far ahead. He seems to have an instinct for maneuvering the tunnels and crabwalking the diagonal shafts without any need for light. Phyllis shines hers for her own and Sylvan's benefit. Not a sound except their breathing and Teo's soft humming.

A small passageway the size of a manhole opens up to the left. Teo scrambles towards it. The line tightens, a bass twang.

"Easy, Teo." A note of fear in Phyllis's voice. Or excitement. She's tall but limber, and has to straighten out her body and go head first. Sylvan follows, his line chafing between his belly and the earth. The air is heavy and sweet, twice breathed. The silhouette of Phyllis, soles, then calves, then bikini bottoms, shoulders and hair, and Teo's blond corkscrews farther ahead, all caught in the blinks of light, hang on like papercuts in afterimage when Sylvan's eyes close.

Stupid to be doing this in the middle of all those crazy earthquakes. They could die and no one would know. Dumb. Forget that, too late to start worrying now.

At last they emerge from the shaft into an open cavern with a crystal pool. The source of Los Tres Ojos de Agua. Long stalactites hang from the arched ceiling, each paired with a knobby stalagmite. Sylvan flips on his flashlight, dim, but combined with the light of Phyllis's, the beam whitewashes the incandescence from the rock. So he shuts it off. Everything sparkles and glitters, silvery green and pink; columns like upside-down drip candles, lacy helictites, and soda straws. A drip now and then punctuates the silence.

"Like a Gothic cathedral," Phyllis says.

"Earthquake now, we'd be hating life." Sylvan can't keep his fear to himself.

"Like candy," Teo says. He just has to have a flashlight to get a better look. Phyllis gives him hers with a "be careful," and he strokes a fairy-tale stalactite with one hand, keeping a light on it with the other. He cranes his head, squints one eye, then the other, sniffs it, and, inevitably, leans in for a taste. "Salty!"

"Wilcox," Sylvan doesn't say.

"You expected sweet?" Phyllis says.

"Lime or cherry."

Sylvan edges closer to Phyllis. They stand shoulder to shoulder, hip to hip. This cavern used to be who knows how many leagues under the sea. Eerie. He puts his arm around her. She lets him.

"I'm pregnant."

"I am?" Sylvan blusters. "You are?"

"We." She squeezes him close. "I just learned this morning."

"When?"

"Last month. One of the inseminations worked."

He hugs her, then hugs her again. "I'm—"

"Oooops!" Teo shouts. A skew flash followed by a splash.

"—gonna be a father."

Then, darkness. Darker the wider you open your eyes.

"I dropped it," Teo says. Matter-of-fact.

"Were you swinging it back and forth?" Phyllis asks, the maternal hope-you-learn-from-your-mistake competing with the curious in her voice.

"A little."

Sylvan switches on his flashlight. Switches it back. Clicks the button to and fro with his thumb. Shakes it, rattles it, pleads with it. Curses it. "Shit."

"Hmmmm."

Tentatively, testing the silence, Teo says, "I think I'm frighten."

Sylvan gets down on his hands and knees and, making himself into a creature that depends on neither light nor sound to get around, gropes for the flashlight Teo "dropped" in the pool, the fountainhead of the Three Eyes. The water is tepid, body temperature. Crawling in it gives him the uneasy feeling that he is oozing beyond the boundaries of his own skin. He's going to be a father. A different person than he was five minutes ago.

By chance he puts his hand down right on the flashlight, which luckily is the floating kind. He shakes it and flips the switch. Not expecting it to work, he's still surprised when it doesn't.

"Only one thing to do now," Phyllis says.

"Yep," Sylvan agrees.

"What?" Teo asks.

"You tell him," Sylvan says.

"Follow our lifelines out of here."

Since they have two lifelines, they're okay. Sylvan is amused at how big he feels, or small, in this absolute blackness, like a voice in the dark. There's a tug at his line.

"Ouch," Teo says, tripping over it. "Not really. It didn't hurt 'cause it's like we've never been born."

One of those lines, Sylvan thinks, that you'd never believe in a book or movie.

"Teo," Phyllis says. "I want you to crawl out just like you crawled in. You didn't even need the light in the first place. I'll follow you, and Sylvan will follow me."

Teo starts up the tunnel, deft, impatient at the tether keeping him close to Phyllis, who, though she in no way lags, still can't match his preternatural speed. The child, only six, but now the leader of the expedition, proceeds with an ease that instills confidence. Nobody feels compelled to speak.

The cave walls narrow until Sylvan has maybe six inches of headspace. The clay, moist, surprisingly warm (from the bodies that passed before him?), helps him jimmy his way up. He's going pretty fast when he knocks his head on a sharp rock. A warm trickle runs down his forehead and cheek and tastes salty in his throat. Hello again, Mr. Wilcox.

Hell. Oh.

He's always getting himself messed up. It would have to be now. Now that he's going to be a father he may never live to see his son. Or daughter.

Six inches is not enough. What if there's an earthquake now? A shot of panic robs him of his breath, urges him to stretch, thrash, make space, go up for air. To control himself he gathers his breath and pushes his arms and legs against the sides of the cave, expelling. Relax. At least there are no sharks in here.

He pulls his elbows up under his chest and gingerly touches his head wound. It stings, swollen like a chestnut, bleeding profusely. Scalp wounds, he knows from numerous boyhood trips to the emergency room for stitches, bleed profusely. And always look tragic. It's a good thing no one can see the blood.

"Are you okay?" Phyllis asks. From the boxed-in sound of her voice Sylvan estimates she is ten, maybe fifteen feet ahead of him.

"Cut my head on a fucking rock."

"Rub some clay on it."

He does and it soothes, clotting the flow. First the urine, now the clay, she always seems to know what to do.

"The passageway gets pretty narrow there, but it opens up a bit here," she says. Encouraged, Sylvan bellycrawls on. It does get narrow, and it does open up like she said, but only a bit. About a foot and a half of space between his body and the cave wall is all. He reaches out his hand to catch up and is surprised to grab onto Phyllis's hairy ankle.

"Hey there, slowpoke," she says. "Seems we have una problema."

"This tunnel's blocked!" Teo says with perverse enthusiasm.

Sylvan's heart drops. Backtracking feet first down this god-damn passageway?

"We're on the right track," Phyllis says. "But there's a fork, and my cord snapped. Or came loose. Or something. Anyway, here it is, all in my hand."

Sylvan tugs on his lifeline, checking.

"Oooh," Phyllis says as the twine slides under her body.

"Mine's fine."

"Be gentle."

"What now?" Teo wants to know.

"We're going to switch places," Sylvan says, taking control. "Phyllis and me."

He moves forward, feels Phyllis's feet and shins. She's face up. Sylvan grins in the dark. Absurd. He can feel Phyllis beginning to grin, and the goddamn cave. Ha ha ha, Wilcox.

The palms of his hands find her kneecaps and he pulls himself ahead. Her toes tickle his chest, and she wiggles them.

"Here," she says, grabbing his hands. "Teodoro?"

"I'm here." It appears he's ducked into a vug under a drapery and is waiting for Sylvan to take the lead.

"Just checking."

Sylvan lifts himself up and over her legs, his head at her hips, now at her belly. His hands pass over her ribs, breasts, and feel for her shoulders. Can't reach. Holding on to her arms, he inchworms forward, wriggling his, oh no, hips.

"There you go," Phyllis says, and he's sure she can feel his erection pressing against her. Damn. Why do men have to be so obvious about this kind of thing? Why him especially? He creeps onward. There isn't enough room for both of them to take a deep breath at the same time. Flexing his triceps above his head in the most awkward way, Sylvan squirms ahead. But Phyllis suddenly takes a big breath, stopping his progress, pinning him against the clay wall. He can feel her hands working at the buttons of his shorts, and warm lips on his cheek, chin, searching for his lips.

Hands over his head, body flush against body, there's no way he can move, until she opens her legs a few inches, arches her hips, and with her hand, guides him inside her.

Phyllis exhales; Sylvan inhales.

"You guys?" Teo asks, tremulous.

"It's okay, honey," Phyllis says. "Just hard."

"Hurry up," he says.

"Mmm hmm," she says. "I'm coming."

"We're almost there," Sylvan says.

The brilliance of the day—simple green leaves and the blue sky, crisp wind—almost knocks Sylvan over as he comes out of the cave. The light, that physical. How light he feels himself, floating, fantastically clearheaded.

Teo, watching Sylvan emerge, whimpers and steps back, his eyes terror-bright in a black-smudged face, his hair hanging in long dirty strands. Poor kid, looks like an only survivor.

"It's okay, Teo," Sylvan says, realizing he himself must appear just as damaged, worse even, covered as he is with blood. "I may look like a monster, but I'm still Sylvan."

On recognizing his voice, Teo's smile returns.

Next comes Phyllis, the clay graying as it dries in smears all over her body, crusting and caking on her breasts and knees. Fingermarks (his?) run down her sides, and blood (definitely his) streaks her skin. Pregnant, twice over.

"God, you look matted." She grins, eyes on his bloodied and muddied head. "And your face, like an aborigine who's just seen civilization for the first time."

But he feels exactly the opposite.

A NOTE ON THE TYPE

This book is set in a typeface called Méridien, a classic roman designed by Adrian Frutiger for the French type foundry Deberny et Peignot in 1957. Adrian Frutiger was born in Interlaken, Switzerland, in 1928 and studied type design there and at the Kunstgewerbeschule in Zurich. In 1953 he moved to Paris, where he joined Deberny et Peignot as a member of the design staff. Méridien, as well as his other typeface of world renown, Univers, was created for the Lumitype photo-set machine.

Composition by Dix Type Inc., Syracuse, New York.
Printed and bound by Fairfield Graphics, Fairfield, Pennsylvania.